Praise for *Since the*

"Murray's writing is simply gorgeous."
— The Book Commentary

"This was everything my romantic heart needed and then some."
— Reader Review

"This story was heartfelt, hopeful, and so incredibly endearing."
— Reader Review

"An emotional rollercoaster that will make you fall in love with love all over again."
— Reader Review

"A heartwarming story with unforgettable characters who feel like old friends."
— Reader Review

KERK MURRAY
Sun, Sand, and Sweet Romance

BY KERK MURRAY

Pawprints On Our Hearts
Since the Day We Danced
Since the Day We Fell
Since the Day We Kissed
Since the Day We Wished
Since the Day We Left
Since the Day We Promised

Since the Day We Danced

KERK MURRAY

Since the Day We Danced

We Danced

Hadley Cove Sweet Romance: Book 1

Magnolia Press
Savannah

Magnolia Press
785 H King George Blvd
Ste D Box 13 -1016
Savannah, GA 31419

Library of Congress Cataloging-in-Publication Data

Names: Murray, Kerk, author.
Title: Since the Day We Danced/ Kerk Murray.
Description: First edition. | Savannah: Magnolia Press, 2023.
Identifiers: LCCN 2023913679 | ISBN 9798985116137 (paperback) | ISBN 9798985116144 (hardcover)

Printed in the United States of America

To all of my readers who have loved and lost.
May you have the courage to begin again—this one's for
you.

Before You Begin...

You're invited to join my private Facebook Reader Group, where you'll make new book friends, meet other animal lovers, and be the first to know about new releases, book clubs, and special deals.

Join today:
Kerk Murray's private Facebook Reader Group

facebook.com/groups/779562103953550

Since the Day We Danced Playlist

Listen on your favorite music streaming platform.

kerkmurray.com/products/playlist-sincethedaywedanced

Emma's listens:

1. "Lose You to Love Me" — Selena Gomez

2. "Whiskey on You" — Nate Smith

3. "Cruel Summer" — Taylor Swift

4. "Everything Has Changed" — Taylor Swift (Feat. Ed Sheeran)

5. "Can't Stop the Feeling" — Justin Timberlake

6. "Play It Again" — Luke Bryan

7. "I Want Crazy" — Hunter Hayes

8. "Back to December" — Taylor Swift

9. "Far Away" — Nickelback

10. "Moments Like This" — The Afters

Luke's listens:

1. "See You Again" — Carrie Underwood

2. "There You'll Be" — Faith Hill

3. "Springsteen" — Eric Church

4. "You Had Me from Hello" — Kenny Chesney

5. "Waves" — Luke Bryan

6. "Yours" — Russell Dickerson

7. "Love You Like That" — Canaan Smith

8. "Need You Now" — Lady Antebellum

9. "Enough (Reprise)" — Lauren Alaina & Phillip Sweet

10. "Die A Happy Man" — Thomas Rhett

Dear Reader,

As I write this letter, my thoughts wander to the summer of 2019, a season that altered the course of my life in unforeseen ways. It was then that I stumbled upon a homeless puppy on the streets of coastal Georgia, and although I did my best to save him, fate had other plans.

The little pup passed away only days later, and from that moment, I dedicated my life to advocating for animals. And so, I wrote my first book, *Pawprints On Our Hearts*, a tribute to the animals that touch our lives and an ode to the compassion that drives us forward. At this time, I also founded *The Lexi's Legacy Foundation*, a 501(C)(3) nonprofit organization committed to ending animal suffering. A portion of my books' proceeds are donated to the nonprofit and together with the support of my readers, the lives of hundreds of abused animals have been changed forever. For that, I'm eternally grateful.

The purpose of my writing has always been to elevate the stories of animals and to inspire change. With the release of my debut novel, *Since the Day We Danced*, I've never been more excited to carry the mission forward.

Life has been a winding road filled with unexpected twists and turns. If you had told me three years ago I would start a nonprofit, become a vegan, leave my career at Chick-fil-A, and begin writing romance novels, I would've laughed. But as they say, life is full of surprises.

And as I've learned, life is also full of second chances, redemption, and love. In my thirty-six years on this earth, I've endured tremendous heartache, but I've also been blessed with life's most beautiful experiences. It's those defining moments that have compelled me to write this book.

Since the Day We Danced is a tale of love, loss, and the courage to begin again. It's a story of the unexpected connections that can change our lives forever and the hope that lies beyond the pain. When you turn the final page, my wish for you is that you'll have found a piece of yourself in these characters, and through their journey, begin to see the endless possibilities living within you.

Welcome to Hadley Cove. I hope you enjoy reading this story as much as I did writing it. Be sure to check out the extras I've left for you in the back of the book.

With love,
Kerk

"Everything good, everything magical happens between the months of June and August."

—Jenny Han, *The Summer I Turned Pretty*

1

Emma

Hadley Cove, Georgia

EMMA WRIGHT PUSHED HER untouched veggie sandwich away, haunted by the image of Chad, her soon-to-be ex-husband, and his new girlfriend, Ashley, leaving the courtroom arm in arm. A sigh escaped her lips as she reclined in the chair, her fingers sweeping the auburn curls away from her face. She had taken great care in preparing herself for the day's court appearance, aware of the inevitable encounter with the man who had vowed to love her forever and the young woman who had now stepped into the role that was once hers.

Now at forty, Emma's beauty had ripened with time. Her features, though etched with the subtle lines of life's experiences, held an alluring charm. Yet, next to Ashley's youthful glow, she felt the weight of the years she had weathered. Fifteen years younger, Ashley had sun-kissed blonde locks and a vitality that accentuated the striking contrast between her fresh bloom and Emma's seasoned grace—a poignant reminder of the relentless march of time.

"You should try to eat something, Em. We have to head back soon," Lisa said, the contours of her face shaped by worry.

"I know. I just want this all to be over."

"It will be. We just have to hear the judge's ruling. That's it. Soon, today will be a distant memory." Lisa gave Emma's arm a comforting squeeze and rose to her feet, picking up the red plastic basket. "I'll have them wrap this up. You can eat it later."

Emma nodded as Lisa walked away, barely hearing her friend. She sipped the last bit of water from her cup, staring out the deli window. Her brown eyes fixed on a tree, where two birds swooped by. She watched them with a wistful longing as they soared through the air, landing gracefully on the rooftop of the Hadley Cove courthouse. Their effortless flight made her heart's heaviness even more pronounced. Unlike the birds' carefree flight, Emma's life had taken a far rougher path over the past few months.

Sixteen years ago, as she'd said "I do," she couldn't have imagined this day would ever arrive.

"Alright, you ready?" Lisa asked, returning.

Emma stood, clutching her purse. "Let's get this over with."

Back at the courthouse, she took a seat next to her lawyer. He may not have been the most renowned attorney in Coastal Georgia, but he was all she could afford.

Turning to Lisa, seated a row behind, she was met with

a soft smile that felt like silent reassurance. But when Chad strolled in with Ashley hanging from his arm, Emma's heart raced, pounding like a drumbeat through her body.

Every step he took with Ashley felt like a deliberate twist of a knife. She looked on as Ashley reached up to Chad's lapel, picked off a piece of lint, and kissed him on the lips. In return, he gave a light tap on her behind.

The color drained from Emma's face as she swiveled around and drew in a deep, shaky breath, fighting off the tears stinging her eyes. Years that seemed like a lifetime spent beside this man, filled with memories of the relationship she thought she had—and this was how it would all end.

"Don't let him and that homewrecker get to you," Lisa said, placing a hand on her shoulder, gently kneading to ease the built-up tension. "You're worth more than both of them put together."

Emma turned and mouthed, "Thank you," and dabbed her eyes with a tissue from her purse.

Lisa shot daggers at Chad. "That man's audacity never ends. Just say the word, and I'll give them both a piece of my mind."

"Lisa, I love you, but please don't. Remember the last time I confronted him? I can't go through that again. I just want today to be as drama-free as possible."

Lisa's expression softened. "I understand. But if he sends you one more threatening message, we're going to the police. No more excuses. I love you, Em, but you deserve so much more."

Emma's eyes welled up. "I know."

At that moment, the judge walked back in from his chambers. An officer followed him out and stood to the left of the bench. "Court is now back in session with the honorable Judge Hawthorne presiding. All rise."

Emma stood, smoothing out the knee-length black skirt she was wearing, and kept her eyes straight forward. The last thing she wanted was to look at Chad again, knowing she wouldn't be able to control her emotions. It was bad enough her eyes were probably red and puffy. If only she could run to the bathroom to fix her face. But there was no time for that now.

"Please be seated." Emma's heart thudded in her chest as Judge Hawthorne spoke.

"Now that we've had a recess, it's time to finalize the divorce between Chad Alan Jones and Emma Leigh Wright."

The judge shuffled through the papers in his hands, then began to read. "The combined assets of Mr. Jones and Ms. Wright, acquired during the time of their marriage—furniture, jewelry, etcetera—shall be sold, and the profits will be equally divided. Since Ms. Wright has refused alimony from Mr. Jones, she will keep all her personal belongings, as well as full custody of Riley, the rescue dog they adopted together. Next, their place of residence at Fourteen Twenty-Two Muscadine Drive will be sold, with the profits being equally divided between Mr. Jones and Ms. Wright. This will conclude all conjugal property..."

A tear rolled down Emma's cheek at the mention of her house. The mere thought of selling it tugged at her heartstrings, as it had been her grandparents' home before they'd gifted it to her as a wedding present. She had always envisioned it as the place where she would grow old and spend her twilight years sitting on the porch and watching the sunset every evening. Then again, Chad had always been in that picture too. At that point, Judge Hawthorne had finished reading and banged his gavel on the wooden block in front of him, declaring the court session over.

Emma's gaze shifted to Chad. A wry smile stretched across his face as he shook hands with his lawyer. He turned toward Emma with a shrug and flashed her a smirk. A knot tightened in her stomach.

Unable to bear the sight, Emma looked away, closing her eyes. She focused on her breathing, inhaling and exhaling in measured rhythm. Silently, she counted down from ten to recenter herself. Before she could finish, Lisa came to her side.

"You alright?"

"No, not really. I just need to get home. While it's still home, anyway."

───

A few days later, Emma was in her bedroom, packing knick-knacks and books into a box. Her heart sank into a bottom-less pit when she came across the snow globe that Chad had given her on their second date. With trembling fingers, she grazed the smooth surface of the glass dome as if it held all her broken dreams inside.

Lisa entered with an empty box. "How are you holding up?"

"I'm okay. It's the packing." Emma set down the globe

and collapsed onto the bed. "I'm feeling a bit...I don't know. This is all just a lot."

Lisa took a seat beside Emma. "Well, how about a break? I'll make us tea."

"Sure," Emma said, her voice almost too quiet to hear.

"Or we can go out. We could get dressed up and grab some drinks."

"Now that's tempting..." A hint of interest flickered in Emma's eyes as she paused, almost tasting the long-overdue strawberry margarita. "But not tonight. I'd rather stay in. I don't have much time left here."

"How about a movie night, then? We can watch something funny, get our minds off things. I can grab some ice cream—the chocolaty kind with the peanut butter chips that you love."

"I guess. I'm not hungry though."

"You might be in a little while. For starters, let's go downstairs and pick out a movie. We can finish packing tomorrow." Lisa grinned, extending a hand to Emma. "Come on, let's go get our Netflix on!"

Before Emma could stand, all seventy pounds of Riley bounded onto the bed, sending tremors through the mattress. He scrambled onto her lap, his tongue lolling out of his mouth as he whined for attention. It was as if he had forgotten he was no longer the little golden retriever pup she'd adopted five years ago. "Riley, be careful, boy. You're squishing me."

"Ah, canine therapy," Lisa said. "Works every time."

Emma chuckled at Riley's antics and reached down to rub his belly, feeling the soft fur beneath her fingers.

Through every tear, every rage-filled rant, he had been her constant. The judge had been right to give her custody. Chad had never been a fan of animals and had even scolded her when she picked him up from the rescue. But since Riley had kept her occupied and out of Chad's business, he tolerated him.

The divorce proceedings had brought to light the signs that were there all along but were difficult for her to see. Deep down, she had known their marriage was crumbling. Although she'd tried to hold on, to believe that things would get better, they never did. Chad, the man she had once fallen in love with, had changed over time, and the reality of it all was too painful to bear.

Emma eyed the unfinished boxes scattered on the ground.

"So, have you thought about what you're gonna do?" Lisa asked, sinking back on her elbows.

Emma moved up to Riley's ears, scratching behind them, and looked up at the wall. There, above the side of her bed, hung a painting of the ocean that she hardly noticed anymore. But today, her eyes were drawn to its crashing waves, which seemed to mirror her own desire for change. "I think I'm gonna look for a place closer to the water. A small cottage for me and Riley. Don't need a big place...just something cozy and quiet."

"That sounds lovely. Have you started looking yet?"

"No—I should, though. It's a lot to think about right now."

"Don't let this stress you out." Lisa took Emma's hand. "I'll text a few of my realtor friends to see if they have any listings near the water. I'm sure we can find you a place in no time."

"I can't thank you enough." A lump formed in Emma's throat, and her voice quivered. "Seriously, I don't know what I'd do without you."

Lisa leaned in, giving Emma a quick hug. "That's what friends are for. Now let's pick out that movie."

She nodded, then followed Lisa out of the room. As she closed the bedroom door, her thoughts ventured to the prospect of moving into a beachside cottage. The idea filled Emma with hope and excitement, a glimmer of happiness amidst the chaos of her divorce. A small smile tugged at the corners of her mouth as she envisioned herself walking along the shore with a salty breeze in her hair, basking in the serenity of her new coastal sanctuary.

Though as she descended the stairs, a mix of sadness and resolve weighed on Emma. The future loomed, uncertain and intimidating. Yet, she knew she couldn't cling to the past.

Somehow, some way, she would have to learn how to begin again and leave behind the life she thought she'd always have.

2

Luke

Chicago

THE SUN HUNG HIGH, its glare turning the office windows into
mirrors as Luke made his way back from the vibrant pulse of
the city at midday. A morning drowned in conference calls,
client meetings, and a mountain of paperwork had driven
him to seek a rare breath of fresh air—a decision that broke
his usual routine of working through lunch.

Returning to the hushed confines of his workspace, Luke
hung his coat behind the door and sank into his chair,
which felt more like a command center than a simple piece
of office furniture. He powered up his computer, and as the
screen flickered to life, a barrage of new messages flooded
his inbox. One subject line among the rest leaped out: *Urgent.*

Luke,

Upon reviewing the team's performance, I've noticed a concerning trend with your recent work, especially considering you've been our top performer for years. I understand that balancing work and a personal life can be challenging, but clients have started to ask about you, wondering why you haven't been as present. Let's discuss this when I return from New York.

Mark

Luke let out a slow breath, his gaze fixed on the screen. Before he could craft a response, his train of thought was interrupted by Jeannie's voice at his office doorway. "Mr. White's holding again."

Glancing up from the email, Luke sighed. "Thanks, Jeannie. I'll take the call." He reached across his desk and picked up the phone. "Mr. White. I'm sorry I missed your calls earlier. It's been a hectic day. What can I do for you?"

"Ah, Mr. Grayson, yes. I need to talk with you about your son, Jeremiah." Mr. White cleared his throat. "This morning, he was involved in another altercation with a male student, who ended up at the school nurse's office with a bloody nose."

Luke's grip on the phone tightened. He listened while Mr. White detailed his seventeen-year-old son's latest antics: the truancy, the fights, the rebellious angst that had become a shadowy specter since his mother Kate's death almost two years ago. Now, at forty-two, life had brought him through a tapestry of trials, yet the raw, relentless test of guiding his son through this turbulent time was a challenge that left him as uncertain as a ship in a storm.

Mr. White continued after a moment. "I spoke with the young man and a few other witnesses, and it seems Jeremiah was the instigator. He'll be suspended for the rest of the week. We understand things have been difficult for you both, but the discipline policy states that Jeremiah could be expelled, since this isn't the first incident, as you know. There'll be a hearing with the board in a few days to make that decision. We'll call you with further details."

Luke thanked him and ended the call. He let out a long breath, slumping back into his chair. He would need to cancel his afternoon meetings to pick Jeremiah up from school.

As Luke gathered his items to leave, he found himself lost in his thoughts, grappling with a difficult truth. For years, he had tried to justify his absence from Jeremiah's life. Working as a financial consultant at a leading Chicago firm, his job took him far away from home, often traveling to meet clients. Kate learned to live with it, but Jeremiah never did.

After her diagnosis, Luke had made a conscious effort to be a more present husband and father. He cut back on business trips and accompanied her to every doctor's appointment and chemo treatment. Even with the care of the best doctors in the country, the cancer had progressed to stage IV. The harsh reality set in: Kate had a year, at most, to live.

When he took time off from work to care for her, Jeremiah's frustration only grew. They would have frequent shouting matches, with Jeremiah blaming him for not being there during his childhood, which Luke couldn't deny. It was true he had missed many important events—soccer games, family dinners, and birthdays—due to work obligations.

After Kate's death, Luke struggled to bridge the growing divide between himself and Jeremiah. Although they both sought solace with a grief counselor, Jeremiah's animosity toward his father continued to escalate. Kate had always had a way with Jeremiah, and now that she was gone, he thought it would be impossible to connect with his teenage son.

Luke could see it now, clear as day: his absence had left a void in Jeremiah's life. His heart ached with guilt, realizing he had failed his son in a profound way.

He grabbed his coat and headed out the door, passing Jeannie's desk. "Can you cancel all my afternoon appointments? I need to pick my son up from school."

"Consider it done."

For years she'd been a godsend to Luke, always two steps ahead, handling anything at a moment's notice without breaking a sweat. He never quite figured out how she managed to do it all.

"What would I do without you? Thanks, Jeannie."

As Luke approached the school, gray clouds hung low in the sky, threatening a downpour. While he waited for Jeremiah, he recalled advice from a parenting blog he had read earlier in the week: *Breathe. Ask questions. Don't lash out.*

When his son finally emerged, it seemed as if time had unfolded upon itself. Jeremiah's features held an undeniable resemblance to his father's—a strong jawline, dark tousled hair, and piercing blue eyes that seemed to hold a thousand unspoken words. In that moment, Luke saw his own troubled journey through adolescence, a reminder of the grace they both desperately needed.

As Jeremiah slid into the passenger seat, Luke braced himself for a surge of anger and defiance.

But instead, he was met with silence.

During the car ride home, the only sounds between them were the occasional tapping of raindrops on the car roof and the engine's hum. Jeremiah sat with his arms folded, staring out the window. Every now and then, Luke would steal a glance at his son, hoping Jeremiah would meet his eyes, but he never did. As they drove, the wind picked up, bending the smaller trees under its force. The weather reflected the storm brewing inside Luke. He knew he couldn't keep ignoring Jeremiah's behavior, but he also didn't want to make things worse by punishing him.

Later that evening, Luke turned off his phone and cooked dinner. It surprised him when Jeremiah, who had been holed up in his bedroom, joined him at the kitchen table.

This was a rare occurrence.

As they ate, the silence between them was deafening. "Want to talk about what happened today?" Luke asked.

"Not really."

"Well, we've got to change something, Jeremiah. You can't keep getting into fights like this. The principal is talking about expelling you."

"So what? I'll go to another school. Or maybe I won't go anywhere anymore. It doesn't matter to me."

Luke slid his plate aside; any remaining space in his

stomach felt filled with a deep sadness. Remorse lodged itself in his chest as he looked into his son's eyes, seeing the hurt reflected back at him. He hated himself for not knowing how to connect with his own child, for not being there when Jeremiah needed him the most. Pausing, he drew in a deep breath as he searched for the right words.

"I've made big mistakes, Jeremiah. Missing important moments in your life, and I'm sorry I wasn't there for you like I should've been. I let you down, buddy, and I can't change that. But know that I love you more than anything, and—"

"Just stop. It doesn't matter now," Jeremiah said, picking apart a piece of bread on his plate.

"It does matter." Reaching out, Luke's touch on Jeremiah's arm was both an attempt to comfort his son and a silent admission of all the things he had said years too late. "I'll never be able to change the past, but I want to make things right. I know it will take time and—"

"I told you, I don't want to talk about it, okay? Just leave it alone!" Jeremiah yanked his arm away and shot up from his chair, which nearly toppled over.

Luke swallowed the lump in his throat, nodding slightly. "I understand. But please know that I'm here for you whenever you're ready to talk. I love you and I'm sorry."

"Yeah, whatever." Jeremiah avoided eye contact, taking his plate to the sink.

Luke's eyes lingered on the now-empty chair where his son had been moments before. With a deep sigh, he pushed back from the table and followed Jeremiah's path to the kitchen sink.

While rinsing the dishes, his mind replayed the words exchanged during dinner. Once more, Luke's attempts to fix the relationship had fallen flat. As with numerous times in the past, he was left disheartened and unsure of how to bridge the growing gap between him and his son. All the suggestions online and even the advice from the grief counselor weren't working. No matter what he did, Jeremiah had remained distant and unresponsive, shutting Luke out and refusing to communicate or engage in meaningful ways.

After wiping his hands with a kitchen towel, he returned to his office to research more about connecting with his son. For hours, Luke scoured countless articles and forums, yet found no new advice he hadn't already attempted.

Releasing a weary exhale, he eased himself back into the worn comfort of his office chair as his gaze wandered to the laptop's background photo. In the picture, Kate stood in the middle, her arm curled around a much younger Jeremiah. With one hand, she playfully hoisted a sandcastle bucket near the smudge of chocolate ice cream on Jeremiah's cheek. Near the edge of the frame, Luke leaned in toward his family, his arm slung over Kate's shoulder. This treasured snapshot held everything he longed to recapture.

His thoughts drifted to a topic that had often been a source of joy for Kate—the possibility of living on the Georgia coast. A change of scenery from the big city could be exactly what they needed. It was something he hadn't considered before, but the idea starting over in Georgia, all at once, tugged at his heart and filled him with sorrow, knowing that Kate would never get to experience it. Despite the bittersweet emotions, Luke started searching Zillow for properties in the area.

Scrolling through listings, each one painted a picture in his mind of a new beginning in that idyllic place. But none of them felt like the right fit. So, he entered his email and signed up on the site, hoping the perfect place would soon come on the market.

—*ele*—

The next week, at the hearing, the disciplinary board delivered their verdict—Jeremiah would be expelled for the rest of the year. Luke's heart sank as he pleaded with them to give his son another chance, but it didn't sway their decision. Jeremiah hardly spoke a word, as if unfazed by the gravity of the expulsion.

Luke's idea of moving to a new place was now making much more sense. He knew something had to change.

And, as if by fate, change was on the horizon.

One morning, as Luke sat sipping his coffee, his phone buzzed with an email notification from Zillow, showcasing a house that had just become available in Hadley Cove, Georgia. His fingers tapped on the edge of the table as he read the details; the house checked all the boxes for everything they would need. Lost in thought, he barely noticed Jeremiah's heavy footsteps entering the kitchen.

Luke spoke up as Jeremiah poured a bowl of cereal. "Hey Jer, I need to talk to you."

"Okay? I'm here. Talk."

Luke set down his phone and straightened. "Look, we need a change. We've been doing the same thing over and over and it hasn't helped. You're expelled and are going to have to do summer school online so you can go into your senior year. I don't want you to throw your life away. I can't let you do that."

Jeremiah stirred the spoon around the bowl. "Okay...so what changes?"

Luke took a deep breath. "Well, I think moving might be good for us, starting fresh—"

Jeremiah slammed his fist down onto the table. "You're always thinking about what *you* want! What about what I want? I don't want to leave Mom's memory behind. This is the only place where I still feel close to her. And you want to take that away from me too?"

Despite the stifling air that seemed to grow heavier with each passing second, Luke forced himself to breathe evenly. "Son, it's not about leaving her memory behind. You know your mother always wanted to live on the Georgia coast. There's a house I saw that would be perfect for us. She would've loved it. In a way, this would honor her and be a fresh start for us. It'll be a good thing."

Jeremiah folded his arms as tears streamed down his face. "I don't want a new life. I want Mom. I can't believe you would even consider moving away from here."

The depth of Jeremiah's pain struck Luke hard. "Jeremiah, you can hate me, but I'm out of options," he said. "I'm going to call the realtor soon." He glanced back at his phone, letting a momentary silence fill the air. "We're going."

"If you make me leave, I'll never forgive you. Ever."

"If I let you throw your life away, I'll never forgive myself." Luke's voice wavered. "I love you, and I know you can't see that now, but someday you will."

3

Emma

Three Months Later

EMMA WIPED THE SWEAT from her brow, stepping out onto the small front porch to take in the view of the new cottage she now called *home*. The blue exterior with white trim sharply contrasted with her old house's dark-brown façade and forest-green shutters. She only hoped the change of scenery would help her move forward and that the new owners would take good care of her former home.

The sun was setting as she retrieved the last box from the trunk. She sighed feeling a tinge of anxiety, wondering if there would be enough space for all her belongings. Despite giving away several bags of clothes and unneeded items, her thousand-square-foot one-bedroom cottage still felt cluttered.

Upon entering, Riley greeted her, tail wagging, before attempting to dash for the yard, only to be wrangled back in by Emma's quick Dog Mom reflexes. With one arm carrying the box and the other hand holding Riley's collar, she kicked the door behind her and sat down in a nearby armchair, exhausted. She had sent Lisa home an hour ago after getting most of the boxes in, but she didn't realize how much work would be left for her to do on her own.

Emma had moved in just a few days before the much-awaited Fourth of July celebrations in Hadley Cove. The town was known for its grand festivities, which included a bustling street fair, the parade, and a stunning firework display to end the night. Emma and Chad had made it a tradition to attend the festival together, then lay a blanket in their backyard to sip wine and admire the show. The memory of those happy moments made her eyes well up with tears. Blinking them away, she rose from her chair and headed to the kitchen to prepare dinner for Riley.

After placing his dish on the ground, Emma walked toward the window and looked outside, scanning the horizon. The back of the house led to the beach, and the soothing sound of the waves lapping against the shore was a balm to her frayed nerves as she closed her eyes and pictured herself lying on the sand, lost in a captivating novel. But the reality of the week's daunting tasks ahead brought her back from her daydream.

Returning to the living room, Emma surveyed the chaos of boxes and furniture with determination. She paused, envisioning the room with her desk nestled in the corner and a cozy reading nook by the front window, with enough space for a couch and a TV on the opposite wall.

It's all coming together.

She was going to be happy in this cottage. At least, she hoped so.

With each passing day, Emma grew more settled in her new home. Only a few unpacked boxes remained, and she was certain most of what was left would go into the attic. The first box she opened overflowed with Christmas decorations. She closed it and peeked into the next box, which brought a smile to her face. Inside were Riley's adoption papers, tucked away alongside his old collars and some chew toys.

Emma placed his papers on the coffee table, glancing over at him as he snoozed away in his dog bed next to the couch. She let out a gentle sigh, relishing how Riley had been her biggest comfort through it all, especially now after the divorce.

Her thoughts wandered back to the afternoon she found him at Second Chance Rescue, huddled in the corner of his kennel. A volunteer had told her his story: some cruel person had left him in a trashcan at the park with a broken leg where some kids had discovered him. The rescue nursed Riley back to health, and a family had adopted him as a Christmas present for their son. But two months later, they returned him because he kept having accidents in the house. She couldn't believe someone would give up such a sweet dog after all he had been through.

When Emma saw him that day, it was love at first sight. "How could anyone ever hurt this beautiful soul?" she told herself.

She knew the scared little pup was exactly who she needed in her life and adopted him on the spot. There would be no returning Riley, and he would only experience the kind of love that all living beings ought to know, a firm resolve set in her mind. The first few months were challenging as she poured all her effort into training him and helping him overcome his fears. They attended classes together, practiced commands, and took walks on the beach. Before long, Emma's love for Riley had transformed him into a confident and well-behaved dog.

Riley's soft whine pulled Emma from her musings. He sat up and trotted toward her, pawing at her as he rubbed his head against her legs. She smiled, setting down a stack of photos onto the corner of a nearby box, and scratched behind his ears.

"Looks like it's time for your walk. Let me grab your leash."

Riley's bark echoed throughout the cottage as he bolted toward the back door, with Emma closely following behind. His excitement caused him to bump into the box, sending the photos spilling out. She bent over to gather them, and as she did, her heart skipped a beat.

There, amidst the pile of photos, was a snapshot of her and Chad from their carefree college days. Her hand trembled as she shoved it back into the box. The memories flooded her mind with a bittersweet pang. Sealing it shut, she pushed it aside, trying to fight off the rush of emotions.

With a deep breath, Emma attached Riley's leash and opened the back door. As the salty sea breeze brushed against her face, she resolved to let the sound of the waves and the melodious call of distant seagulls soothe her troubled mind.

But as they moved further along the beach, the memory of the photo remained vivid in Emma's thoughts. On the day they met, she had gotten caught in the rain, rushing to class. Chad appeared out of nowhere, heading to the same lecture, and offered to share his umbrella.

From that moment on, they became inseparable.

It hadn't taken long for Chad to ask Emma out before becoming a couple in their freshman year. Their love had blossomed throughout college, and they'd shared countless memories. Late-night study sessions, impromptu road trips, and stolen kisses under the stars had filled their days with happiness and laughter.

Chad proposed to Emma at her graduation party, getting down on one knee and holding out his grandmother's ring. She was standing in the middle of the crowd as she said "yes" with a swift, excited nod of her head that sent her long hair flying around her face. Laughter and cheers pulsated through the air alongside the scent of homemade lemon cake and the faint aroma of the summer blossoms outside. Fairy lights strung across the backyard twinkled like little stars, crowning the evening as the perfect scene of joy and celebration.

As he slid the vintage ring on Emma's finger, her eyes traced the intricate patterns on the band, each delicate swirl a symbol of a story told and retold. It was a treasure from Chad's family, an heirloom that had seen several generations now gracing her hand as a promise of their future.

They had plans to move to Savannah post-wedding, where Chad had landed a job at a prestigious consulting firm. But those plans changed when Emma's grandfather,

Liam, gave them his house in Hadley Cove as a wedding present. Liam had downsized to a smaller place and moved closer to the water after her grandmother, Amelia, passed away a few years earlier. It was the perfect place for the young couple to start their life together, just an hour south of Savannah.

Their early weeks in the new home had been blissful. She and Chad were still in their honeymoon phase, and the house had been the idyllic backdrop for their love story. Thanks to Liam's meticulous care of the house over the years, it was in excellent condition. Only minor updates were needed, like changing a light fixture here or applying a fresh coat of paint there, to truly make it their own.

Even with everything else falling into place for Emma, she struggled to find a job in Hadley Cove. With an art history degree, she settled for a substitute teaching position and became the head of a tutoring program at the local high school. Although things were going well for a while, Chad started coming home late from work, leaving Emma to eat dinner by herself.

As time passed, their once loving relationship turned into a battlefield of passive-aggressive comments and cold shoulders. Chad's criticisms became more pointed, his voice raising just enough to cut through her, reminding her that her job as a substitute teacher wasn't good enough, that she was not the partner he'd envisioned. It wasn't just her career choice that drew his disapproval, Chad had opinions on everything, down to the very clothes she wore. "You're not wearing that, are you?" he'd say as his eyes scanned her head to toe. If the colors were too bright or her heels too tall, he'd make her change into something "more appropriate" or "less attention-seeking."

Emma exhausted herself appeasing Chad, but nothing ever seemed right, and he remained unhappy with her no matter what she did. The more she tried to mold herself into the image he desired, the more she felt herself fading away.

That's when she decided they needed help.

Determined to save their relationship, Emma begged Chad to go to counseling with her. While their situation seemed to improve after they started sessions, she eventually discovered lipstick stains on his shirt collar and the scent of a woman's perfume on his clothes. Despite the tears and heartbreak, Emma held on to the hope that counseling would help him change his ways—but he continued to see other women.

Her very last attempt to salvage their marriage was on their most recent wedding anniversary. She'd taken a day off to whip up a lavish feast for Chad, featuring all his favorites. Emma had spent hours in the kitchen, chopping vegetables and stirring pots, determined to make this day special, to remind him of the love they once shared.

As the day wore on and the clock ticked closer to Chad's expected arrival, Emma stood waiting in her brand-new dress and heels, checking her phone for a call or a text to let her know he was on his way. But as the hours went by, the silence grew louder, suffocating her with each passing minute.

The sudden chime of the doorbell snapped Emma out of her anxiety-fueled stupor. She rushed to answer it, hoping to see Chad's face on the other side. Instead, there was a man wearing a uniform, who handed her an envelope and left without a word.

As Emma read its contents, her chest felt heavy, forcing the air from her lungs. The sudden rush of blood from her head triggered a dizzy spell, blurring her vision. Her legs gave way, and she collapsed onto the couch. Tremors ran through her hands as she fumbled for her phone, dialing Lisa's number.

Lisa dropped everything and drove over right away. Emma sobbed and crumbled into her friend's embrace, letting the envelope and the divorce papers inside fall onto the floor.

Together, they cleaned up the meal that Emma had prepared with such love and care. Every cleaned dish, every wiped counter seemed to erase a piece of the life she thought she had, leaving an emptiness within her, a void where love and trust had once been that now echoed with betrayal.

What made the situation even more devastating was that Chad hadn't been the only man in her life to betray her.

The first had been her own father, Paul.

Emma's thoughts trailed back to her twelve-year-old self, when she was left in her father's care after her mother's passing in a tragic car accident. Paul had begun drinking to cope with the loss, and what had started as an occasional indulgence soon spiraled out of control.

Under alcohol's grip, Paul fell behind on the mortgage payments, eventually losing their home. In a moment of desperation, he dropped Emma off with her grandparents and left town. Many nights she had cried, hoping and praying he'd come back for her, but he never did. The most daunting part for her was grieving someone who was still alive, and in her mind, she had killed him to protect what was left of her shattered heart.

Just then, Riley started barking at a few seagulls up ahead. He yanked on the leash, snapping Emma out of her glum thoughts.

"Riley! Don't scare the birds. They didn't do anything to you."

Riley looked back at Emma and let out another bark, but eventually gave up his quest. Emma turned and headed back down to the beach toward the cottage when her phone began to vibrate. Her face lit up when she saw the caller ID—Kara, the founder of Second Chance Rescue.

"Hey Kara. What's up?"

"Hey Em. It's going well, *especially* for you."

"Is that so? Tell me more."

"Well, we've completely sold out of the dog treats you brought in last week. I'll need more as soon as the Independence Day festival is over. People love your Barking Orders brand. You've even grown a little following at the rescue. I've already had three people ask today when we're gonna be back in stock!"

Her obscure brand of dog treats, which she had launched last year, was finally gaining traction.

Emma felt much better than she had a minute ago. "My goodness, Kara! I had no idea they'd be so popular. And I can have another batch ready for you soon. Thanks again for carrying them. I know it's not like the usual stuff y'all have."

"Oh, it's nothing, girl. It's time for the pet owners around here to try something different. How's everything else going?"

Approaching the cottage's back door, Emma fished out her key. "Oh, it's fine. I'm fine. Just...getting the house together."

"You can tell me anything, Em. No one expects you to be doing okay right now. Listen, I'm gonna come over soon with some ice cream so we can celebrate your housewarming, and the success of your hot new brand. How's that sound?"

Emma let Riley inside the cottage and closed the door behind her. "Sounds like a plan. I could use a girls' night. But I need to know one thing."

"What's that?"

"Is the ice cream vegan?"

"Of course." Kara laughed over the phone. "Do you think I don't know you at all?"

4

Luke

As Luke neared the Georgia state line, a renewed sense of purpose filled him, and he steered his Range Rover toward a rest stop. Hadley Cove wasn't far now, and with it, the hope of a brighter future for him and his son. The long drive had taken its toll on his body, and he couldn't wait to stretch his legs. Pushing open the door, he took in a rush of fresh air as Jeremiah clambered out of the passenger seat.

"Here." Luke pulled out a few dollars and handed them to Jeremiah. "See if the vending machine has anything good."

Jeremiah took the cash without a word and walked away. He had barely spoken to Luke since breakfast, and even then, it was only to ask him to pass the salt. He returned after a short while, giving the cash back to Luke. "The vending machine is broken."

"Maybe we'll have better luck at the next rest stop." He placed a hand on his son's shoulder, but Jeremiah pulled away.

"Are we going?" he asked. "It's so hot out here."

Luke nodded. "You'd better get used to the Georgia heat. I think it'll be cooler on the coast, though. At least, let's hope it will." He climbed back into the driver's seat, eager to hit the road.

The car ride dragged on in silence, broken only by the monotonous hum of the engine and the country songs on the radio. Luke tried to start a conversation but was met with brief and disinterested responses.

Luke understood it would take time for Jeremiah to come around. He promised himself he would be there for him from now on, transitioning from his full-time job and only working part-time remotely so he could focus on repairing their relationship. No more business trips or late nights at the office. Luke was all in for his son, and nothing would stop him from being the father Jeremiah needed.

As they approached the next exit, Luke turned to Jeremiah. "Hungry? We can stop and get something. Or we could wait until we get to the house."

Jeremiah shrugged and continued staring at the window.

"So, is that a yes?"

"No, I'm gonna take a nap."

"Alright then."

Almost two hours later, Luke leaned over and shook Jeremiah awake. He slowed down as they passed a sign:

Welcome to Hadley Cove. Population: 1,883.

Yawning, Jeremiah remarked, "Eighteen eighty-three? There were more people than that at my school."

Luke let out a chuckle. "Things are going to be quite different here than they were in Chicago, but in a good way."

Turning onto Main Street, they passed by a couple of small shops and businesses, including First Coastal Bank, the Hadley Cove post office, and Phil's Diner.

"Look. It's a palm tree." Luke pointed to one next to Gary's Garage. "Did you see it, Jer?"

"Yeah, I saw it. This place is lame. And people are looking at us."

Sure enough, Luke noticed a few people walking down the street in front of Lindsey's Beauty Shop gawking at their jet-black Range Rover.

As they turned down Ocean Drive, they passed All Creatures Animal Hospital and Second Chance Rescue. Luke wondered for a moment if Jeremiah would be interested in adopting an animal; they had never had one in Chicago, since Kate had been allergic to dogs.

"There's sand on the road," Jeremiah said.

"The beach is right over there, so that makes sense. Want to stop and check out the water?"

"No. I just wanna get my stuff unpacked."

"Well, we're almost there."

As they drove down the street, the scene outside their car window transformed into a picturesque vision of Southern charm. The bungalow-style houses lining the street were adorned with intricate details, their porches extending into the front yard. Luke pictured himself sitting on one of those porches, sipping iced tea and taking in the slow pace of life in Hadley Cove.

Trees on the sidewalk had Spanish moss draping from their branches, giving the street an otherworldly feel. The white picket fences separating the front yards from the sidewalk, along with the well-manicured lawns, completed the idyllic scene.

Some of the houses looked older than others, but that only added to their allure. It was as if the town had been frozen in time, preserving its history and old-fashioned way of life.

A few minutes later, Luke turned onto a shady, tree-lined street. The houses were more spacious here, with verdant foliage that lent a touch of privacy and seclusion. As they approached their new home, Luke pulled up next to the moving truck in the driveway.

"We're here. Fourteen twenty-two Muscadine Drive." Luke stepped out and gazed up at the large, two-story cape cod. It was exactly as he remembered it from the pictures on Zillow and the virtual walkthrough with the realtor. The dark-brown color of the house and its forest-green shutters blended in with the surrounding trees.

As Luke walked up the driveway, the sound of someone clearing their throat caught his attention. Turning around, he saw an older woman across the street, watering her plants. Almost immediately, she began looking for a place to set down her hose. Luke, understanding her intentions, smiled and waved in acknowledgment. She took his gesture as an invitation to cross the street, making a beeline toward him.

"Hey y'all! I'm Ada Harrison."

Luke shook her hand. "Nice to meet you, Ms. Harrison. I'm Luke Grayson, and this is my son, Jeremiah—we're new here."

"Oh, call me Ada. I already knew you weren't from around

here."

Luke arched his brow. "You did?"

"Everyone knows everyone here in Hadley Cove. Other than the tourists that come every summer to the beach, we don't get too many new residents around here, especially in this house. Where y'all from?"

"Chicago," Luke said.

Ada eyed their Range Rover. "We don't get many cars like that around here either."

Luke smiled, trying to be polite. "Well, we'd better get inside. It was a long drive down and I know Jeremiah is probably ready for dinner."

"I guess that's my signal to get out of your hair for now. Anyway, I've got to go and remind my husband, Frank, to take his meds. I'll let you boys settle in and rest."

"Thanks, Ada. I'm sure we'll run into each other again."

Jeremiah spoke up as she walked away. "She's so annoying. Why does *she* have to be our neighbor?"

Luke shook his head and laughed. "Jer, be nice."

As Luke walked over to grab their bags out of the trunk, he thanked the movers, who had already finished unloading all the boxes and furniture. He watched the truck roll away before he and Jeremiah made their way to the front door along the paved walkway. Entering the foyer, Luke scanned the surroundings, taking in the details of the almost eighty-year-old house. Despite its age, the interior radiated a warm and inviting atmosphere, without a hint of mustiness.

He looked to his son. "So, what do you think?"

Jeremiah shrugged, sparing only a glance at the house as

he slumped his shoulders and trudged along behind Luke. "It's whatever, I guess."

"I know things haven't been easy lately, but I was hoping this new house would be a fresh start for us. Can't you try to be a little more positive?"

"Why does it even matter? It's not like it would change anything. Can I go to my room and unpack now?"

"Sure, go ahead."

Luke set down his bags, trying to push away his frustration. Releasing a long exhale, he surveyed the area and began exploring the house. He moved through the open space letting his fingers trail along the intricate designs carved into the panels and molding, admiring the craftmanship. In the dining room, he paused to examine the stained-glass window, marveling at how the colors shifted in the sunlight.

As he made his way upstairs, he felt awestruck by the house's beauty. The curved banister and carved newel post were stunning, and the muted floral wallpaper lining the hallway reminded him of his grandmother's home.

A wave of emotions swept over Luke as he entered the master bedroom. Although the movers had dutifully placed his bed, dresser, and nightstand in their respective spots, the room felt both familiar and alien. The weight of grief pressed against his chest as the memories of Kate flooded back. Her absence seemed to echo in the room, and he missed her more than ever. Somehow, some way, he would have to begin life again without her in this new place.

Luke dropped his bags onto the hardwood floor and collapsed onto the sheetless mattress. Staring at the ceiling, he let his mind carry him in a different direction. He wondered why anyone would ever give up such a beautiful home. Still, he was grateful to be the one to carry on its legacy.

Sitting up, he ventured into the hallway, leaving behind the contemplative thoughts in his bedroom. As he approached Jeremiah's room, he noticed the door was cracked. He gently pushed it open and peeked inside. His son was unpacking his belongings.

"I'm going to order a pizza for dinner." He leaned against the doorframe. "Want anything special on it?"

"Mushrooms," Jeremiah called back, without looking up.

Luke bit his bottom lip. He hated mushrooms, and Jeremiah knew it. "Okay, maybe I'll get two then."

He continued down the stairs, taking in the house's details as he went. In the kitchen, he rifled through the packet the realtor had left him, searching for the brochure of local restaurants. The kitchen was spacious and modern, with gleaming stainless-steel appliances and granite countertops. With a wonderful kitchen at his disposal, he promised himself he'd cook another time.

Tonight was meant for pizza and relaxation.

Luke was grateful to find a menu for Gino's Pizza. He dialed the number, placed an order for delivery, and then turned his attention to unpacking the mountain of boxes in the living room.

Rummaging through them, a touch of nostalgia tugged at Luke's heart when he unearthed a framed picture of a beaming five-year-old Jeremiah. As he stood there, cradling the precious memento, he smiled at the memory of the happier times and only hoped they could create more someday.

The fireplace mantel seemed to call out to him as the perfect place to display it.

Walking over with the picture, Luke noticed an etching in the mantel's corner. He leaned in for a closer look and saw the initials "A + L" carved inside a heart.

"Hmm..."

He smiled as he set the picture down next to it. The carving reminded him of Kate, and how he had gotten her name tattooed on his left pec the night of their high school graduation. She had laughed when she first saw it and told him he was ridiculous.

Luke had been in love with her since middle school, but they didn't get together until their junior year. That's when Kate finally broke down and said "yes" to being his date to the homecoming dance. Over the years, they'd weathered many storms together, including a long-distance relationship when he left for Harvard and she was at NYU, or when his father unexpectedly passed before their wedding.

The ache in Luke's heart was a constant reminder of what he had lost in Kate. He longed to feel the warmth of her smile or hear her infectious laughter once again. Sometimes he'd play a particular voicemail she had left for him while he was away on business. Then he'd replay it a few more times, absorbing every word. He knew deep down that he had made mistakes, that he had taken their love for granted. If only he could go back, he told himself, he would do things differently.

A knock at the door interrupted his thoughts.

Luke glanced out the side window, then called up the stairs. "Jeremiah, pizza's here!"

5

Emma

Knock. Knock. Knock.

Emma shifted her gaze from her desk to the front door. She had gotten caught up in doing some bookkeeping for Barking Orders and hadn't been watching the time. She closed her laptop and stood up, doing a quick scan of the room to make sure everything looked tidy. Deeming it presentable, she answered the door to find Kara holding shopping bags and a houseplant.

"Happy housewarming!" Kara said, handing Emma the plant.

"Oh Kara, you didn't have to get me anything! But I appreciate it. This is beautiful."

"It's a succulent. They're easy to care for—minimal water and lots of sun."

"Perfect. This room gets a flood of light during the day." Emma set it by the window, then hugged Kara. "Thanks for coming. I've been looking forward to this night ever since you called."

Kara placed the bags on the coffee table. "Brought ice cream and some vegan treats. Now, get some spoons and we'll find something good to watch."

"Well, I've only got a few more receipts to reconcile. It won't take too long."

Kara waved her hand dismissively. "You deserve a break, Em. It's time to relax!"

Emma chuckled. "I guess it can wait until morning. Let me grab those spoons."

Once she returned, she plopped onto the couch and picked up the remote. Below her, Riley lounged at her feet, eyeing the ice cream on the table.

"You know what's crazy? I haven't watched anything since I moved in. I guess I've been too busy with unpacking. I haven't taken any time to myself."

Kara grabbed a spoon from the table and moved the ice cream tub between them. "Well, keeping busy is good. It can be a distraction from other things."

"Yeah, it can be. So, what are we gonna watch?"

After scrolling through a couple dozen movies, they finally settled on *The Wedding Singer*. Emma had forgotten how funny the movie was, and soon she and Kara were roaring in laughter. As they tore into the ice cream, Emma savored each bite, feeling its creaminess and the crunchiness of the peanut butter chips mingling in her mouth. The sweetness of the chocolate and the saltiness of the chips were perfectly balanced, making it nearly impossible to stop eating.

Realizing he'd get none, Riley gave them a pleading look before retreating to his bed.

Emma reached for another spoonful and heard it hit the bottom with a hollow thunk. "We really ate that whole thing, didn't we?" She looked down at the empty tub.

"It was so good! I'll throw this away so we can start on the other snacks."

"Do you want me to pause it?"

"No, no, that's okay. I'll just be a minute."

As the conversation faded, Emma's attention was drawn back to the screen, where a scene unfolded.

It struck uncomfortably close to home.

Watching Glenn confess his infidelity to Robbie, along with his plans to continue doing so, her thoughts drifted to her painful past with Chad. An icy chill ran through her as memories of the dreadful day she had discovered his betrayal resurfaced. For a moment, the boundaries between the movie and her own reality seemed to blur.

The rustle of snack bags signaled Kara's return. "Sorry Em, I forgot about this part. Let's find a different movie. What do you think?"

Emma nodded, wrestling to keep her emotions in check. "I think that's a good idea."

"No problem." Kara reached for the remote. "Do you like action movies?"

Emma raised a brow. "Do you?"

"Well, possibly, if it has a good storyline." Kara stopped flipping through the endless Netflix suggestions. "Here we go. How about this one?"

Emma looked up, relieved to see a spy thriller devoid of romance. "Sure, that'll be fine."

"Great. I've wanted to watch this one, but Charlotte isn't

interested. Lately, she's more into texting boys than movie nights with her mom."

"You know how we were at her age. Can you blame her?" Emma smirked before stuffing an Oreo in her mouth. "We're not cool anymore."

"Speak for yourself. I'll always be cool."

With a shared laugh, they settled into the movie. As the plot unfolded, Emma's mind wandered, and she found herself grateful for Kara's friendship that had blossomed after she adopted Riley from her rescue. Since then, they had bonded over their shared passion for animals, spending countless hours together helping strays in the community.

As the credits rolled after the movie, Kara stretched her arms over her head, letting out a yawn. "It's getting late. We should do it again soon."

"This was a lot of fun...I didn't know how much I needed it."

Kara threw her arms around Emma, pulling her into a hug. "I'm here for you anytime. You know that, right?"

"I know. You never let me forget."

Kara let go of her and stood up. "I'm leaving the rest of the goodies for you."

Emma walked her over to the door, opening it for her. "Next time we'll do it at your place, and I'll bring the snacks."

"Sounds like a plan."

"Goodnight, Kara. Get home safe."

As Kara waved and climbed into her car, Emma stepped onto the porch to watch her drive off. In the stillness, her gaze drifted upward to the moon and the shimmering stars, the humidity of a South Georgia summer night tingling on her skin, while the distant chorus of cicadas serenaded the twilight.

Things are gonna work out.

Once back inside, Emma started clearing the mess they had made on the table and took out the trash. After tidying up, she noticed the time, surprised at how quickly the hours had slipped by. As she prepared to turn in for the night, she glanced over at the dog bed, finding it empty.

"Riley?"

Emma searched the cottage's living area before heading to the bedroom. As she moved from corner to corner, her search grew increasingly frantic. A faint whimper drew her attention to the bed.

When she knelt to look underneath, her shoulders relaxed and her lips curved into a soft smile. "There you are. Come on boy, it's night-night time."

As she changed into her pajamas, Riley hopped onto the bed, finding his favorite spot near the pillows. She turned off the lights, and the two of them lay down together, with the sound of gentle waves outside her bedroom window lulling her to sleep.

—— *ell* ——

The next morning, Emma woke to Riley's wet tongue sliding across her cheek. She giggled and reached up to scratch behind his ears. "Well, good morning to you too!"

He let out a whine and wagged his tail.

"Alright, alright. I'm up," she said, stretching.

After feeding Riley, Emma took a quick shower. Once dressed, she headed to the small office nook in her living room, flipping open her laptop. An unread email caught her eye—it was from a supermarket in the nearby town of Bridwell Bay. As the words registered, her eyes widened. Bayview Foods had placed the largest order she had ever received for her homemade dog treat business.

A thrill coursed through her veins, and she let out a gasp. "Well, today just got interesting."

Riley ambled into the living room and put his head on Emma's lap, signaling he was ready for his morning walk. "Okay boy. It's gonna have to be a short one. Momma's gotta run to the store."

After sending a quick thank-you reply and closing her laptop, she made her way toward the backdoor. Riley jumped and pawed at her legs. "Hold on, mister!" she laughed, fumbling for his leash. "Let me get this on you first."

The moment the door opened, Riley dashed out, dragging Emma behind him.

When they returned, her breath came in quick, shallow bursts. "Where'd all this energy come from?" she asked Riley, more a statement than a question, as he darted through the cottage.

In the kitchen, as she poured herself a glass of water, Riley trotted in, tongue lolling. "Wore yourself out, huh? I bet you're thirsty too, after all those zoomies," she said, pouring fresh water into his bowl.

Guilt gnawed within Emma at the thought of leaving him alone, especially with the Fourth of July approaching and the possibility of early firework displays. She knew he hated the loud noises.

"I need to head out for a bit, buddy." She bent down, ruffling Riley's fur and gave him a gentle kiss. "You be a good boy, okay?"

With a final affectionate glance, she grabbed her purse and walked out the front door.

6

Luke

July 3

LUKE APPROACHED THE WINDOW and peeled back the curtains, revealing the soft, warm sunlight of a new dawn. He stood motionless, enchanted by the morning songs of the birds and the glimmering reflections in a pond nearby. Slowly, he turned to his king-size bed, making it with deliberate care—each fold a step toward a new chapter in his life.

Before the move, Luke had bought new furniture, deciding to part with the bed he and Kate once shared. Letting go of the tangible reminders of their love was gut-wrenching, but trying to hold onto them had proved just as painful. Although guilt tugged at him for doing so, he believed Kate would have wanted him to find happiness and move forward, especially for their son's sake.

Glancing over at his nightstand, he was surprised to see it was only seven. Jeremiah wouldn't be up for a while, probably hours, especially since school hadn't started yet. Kate would always cook a big breakfast for their son whenever he was down in the dumps, and it seemed to work most of the time. He recalled watching Jeremiah devour nine pancakes in one go. That fond memory sparked an idea: he would surprise Jeremiah and pick up one of those breakfasts with pancakes, hash browns, and freshly squeezed orange juice.

After slipping into a wrinkled shirt and worn jeans, he went downstairs into the kitchen and opened the fridge. The only thing in it was a box of leftover pizza from the night before. Kate would have never let the fridge get this empty.

He'd have to pick up some groceries.

Grabbing his keys, Luke headed out the door and drove to the nearest store he remembered seeing when they first arrived in town. This was a familiar errand. But today it felt different, tinged with the sadness of being in a new place and facing life's daily routines without his beloved Kate.

The golden glow of the morning sun had touched everything in its path when he pulled up in front of the local supermarket. A couple of people on ladders were tying patriotic streamers to the lampposts as a gentle breeze blew, making them flutter in the wind. Luke smiled at the festive atmosphere, his heart light and mind at ease, knowing in some inexplicable way he was exactly where he needed to be.

After parking, he stepped out and the breeze caught his hair, bringing with it a profound realization: he had arrived at a new phase of life, one small task at a time, each one drawing him away from the past and toward a future where he might find peace.

As he made his way through the parking lot to the doors, he saw a note taped to the glass:

Closed for the holiday weekend.

If only he had thought about going to the store last night. They'd have to make do with the pizza leftovers.

As he returned to his car, the sign for Phil's Diner across the street caught his eye. Through the window, he saw a bustling crowd of locals chatting and laughing over plates piled high. Maybe this place would have what he was looking for, and the groceries could wait until tomorrow.

Crossing the street, he smiled at a few people passing by with curious glances. Their knowing looks seemed to suggest that, like Ada, they were aware he had just moved to town. It was a change that would take some getting used to. In the fifteen years they'd owned their condo in Chicago, he could count on one hand the number of times he'd talked to their neighbors. The contrast from big-city life was striking, and he felt a mixture of apprehension and excitement about becoming part of this tightly knit town.

Pushing open the diner's door, the tantalizing scent of pancakes wrapped around Luke like a warm embrace. As he went over to the counter, an older woman in a light-blue waitress uniform zoomed past him with a large plate of steaming hash browns in her hand. Luke slid into one of the red booths, eyes roaming over the fifties-themed décor. The counter stretched down the room; little jukeboxes adorned the white tabletops and oldies songs pumped from a speaker.

Luke grabbed a laminated menu and read through the breakfast options.

Just as he was losing himself in the choices, the waitress popped up on the other side of the counter. "Alright, honey, what can I get ya?"

Luke ordered two Phil's platters to go.

As she scribbled down his order and darted toward the kitchen, a voice addressed him from the side. "Ain't you the new guy in town?" To his right, a man with dark hair, dressed in coveralls, stared back at him.

"Yeah, I guess that's me. Luke Grayson." He held out his hand.

The man smiled and shook it. "I'm Gary Harmon. I own the car shop down the road. That's the Range Rover SV, ain't it? I didn't know they released the new one yet."

Luke chuckled. "You know your cars. I bought it last week before my son and I drove down here from Chicago."

"Chicago? That's quite a drive. I've never traveled north beyond Charleston myself. Anyway, this is my son, Tate. He works at the garage with me." Gary gestured to the teenage boy seated on the next stool down, who looked like a younger version of him.

"Nice to meet you all." Luke wasn't used to all this friendliness, but Gary seemed nice enough.

As they waited, Gary introduced him to a few other members of the town sitting nearby. Among them was a large red-faced man who came bounding out of the kitchen, his apron smeared with grease.

"Hey there! I'm Phil. Heard you put in an order, so I thought I'd come out and say, hey."

Looks like I'll meet the whole town before my food's ready, Luke mused. Then, addressing Phil, he said, "Nice to meet you and everyone else here."

"Newcomers always stick out like sore thumbs in Hadley Cove." Phil clapped his hands down on the bar counter. "But don't you worry, we take good care of folks around here."

"Good to know."

Phil nodded. "Well, I gotta check the food. Be right back with your platters."

As Phil disappeared into the kitchen, Luke struck up a conversation with Gary and his son, making the wait fly by. Before he knew it, Phil returned with a large bag full of Styrofoam containers in hand.

"Here you go, Luke. Two Phil's platters and some extras for ya. Don't be a stranger."

Luke looked at the bags, confusion written across his face. "I think you might have put someone else's order in there, too."

Phil laughed, shaking his head. "No, this is all for you. Enjoy your breakfast and come back soon."

Grinning, Luke took the bags from him. "Thanks, Phil. I'm sure I'll be back again."

As he headed outside and over to the Range Rover, he noticed more decorations had gone up around town. The colorful banners swayed in the wind, making the shops even more inviting. Luke considered returning later to join the festivities, if not for the unpacking awaiting him at home.

After the short drive back, he pulled into the driveway and was surprised to see a lady standing on the front porch talking to Jeremiah. He grabbed the takeout bags and walked over.

"Good morning!" Ada turned around and smiled at Luke as he approached.

"Morning, Ada. How are you today?"

"I'm fine, darling. I was just bringing over some banana bread. Wanted to make sure you boys had something to eat." She smiled, showing off the dish.

"Thank you. You didn't have to."

"Oh, it's nothing really. I love to bake. There's no dairy or nuts in case y'all are allergic. Jeremiah was telling me you still have lots of unpacking to do. I'm good at organizing if you need some help."

Jeremiah caught Luke's eye and shook his head subtly, out of Ada's view.

"That's kind of you to offer, really," Luke said. "But I think we can manage."

"Well, if you change your mind, you know where to find me. You boys should come over for dinner sometime soon. Frank and I would love to have y'all."

"Maybe we will," Luke said, though he had no intention of doing so.

Ada took a few steps forward, cornering Luke. "I'll whip up something special for y'all. How about next week? Monday's out since Frank has poker night." Before Luke could respond, Ada walked off the porch. "So, I'll see y'all Tuesday evening at my place. I'll let Frank know as soon as I get back. Ta-ta!"

Luke laughed. "Looks like we're booked for Tuesday dinner." He handed the bags to Jeremiah. "Got us breakfast.

Probably enough for tomorrow too."

Jeremiah lifted a brow, and the corners of his mouth turned upward. "Pancakes?"

"Of course."

As Jeremiah went into the kitchen, Luke sat down on the porch steps, leaning against a post. He had met so many friendly people in the town so far. Though usually a private person, he appreciated Ada's generosity. Something like that would never happen in Chicago, where small talk and neighborly gestures were a rarity.

Closing his eyes, Luke took in a deep breath of the crisp morning air, letting it clear his mind. For a moment, he forgot about all the unpacking he still had to do. He simply enjoyed being present, soaking up all the small-town vibes of Hadley Cove.

7

Emma

WHEN EMMA LEFT THE store, a sudden burst of crackles and bangs caught her off guard.

Fireworks? Now?

Clearly, someone was ringing in the Fourth of July a day early.

Then it hit her.

Riley.

The loud explosions spurred Emma to floor it, pressing the gas pedal down as images of Riley's anxious face filled her mind.

Upon reaching her driveway, she hurried, grabbing the bags from the back seat and hauling them to the front door. As she walked inside, she let out a long, slow exhale at the sight of Riley snoozing away in his dog bed. She dropped the bags on the floor, and he awoke and trotted over to inspect them, wagging his tail.

"Hey buddy. These aren't for you." Emma leaned down

to scratch behind his ears, then picked up the bags and carried them to the kitchen. Riley stuck close to her heels, ever watchful for anything that might fall.

"Riley, you already had lunch." She turned and looked down at him. "Don't act like I don't feed you."

A whine rolled through the air, and Riley retreated to the living room as Emma busied herself in the kitchen. She pulled out all the ingredients to make her special blend of dog treats, filling mixing bowls on the countertops with pumpkin purée and coconut flour. Hours slipped away as she baked and packaged the treats, her mind occasionally drifting to memories of past Independence Day celebrations with Chad.

Back then, on the Fourth of July, they would cuddle on a blanket, sipping champagne and watching the sky light up. But since their divorce and her growing awareness of the impact fireworks had on wildlife and other animals, especially dogs like Riley, those memories had soured. The discomforting reality that more pets are reported lost on the Fourth of July than any other day weighed heavily on her mind. The fireworks that once represented happiness now only brought distress.

As evening settled in, she pulled out the sixth batch from the oven and was startled by a loud popping sound outside. Emma peeked through the window, her face tightening at the sight of red sparks bursting through the sky. With a wearied exhale, she cleaned up the countertops and put everything away, her movements more deliberate as thoughts of Chad played in her mind.

The echo of fireworks followed her as she left the kitchen

and checked that the front and back doors were locked before heading to the bedroom. There, she found Riley whimpering, hiding under the bed. Emma dropped to her knees and coaxed him out with gentle words and encouragement. When he finally emerged, she cradled him in her arms, placing him on the bed and stroking his soft fur.

"You're safe here with me, boy," she whispered, holding him close. "I'm never gonna let anything hurt you."

As she looked into Riley's eyes, she realized their love for one other was pure—an uncomplicated affection, free from the deceptions that had marred her marriage.

"You and I, we've got each other." She kissed him on his head. "And that's all that matters."

Emma settled into bed, snuggling Riley as his trembling slowly ceased. The persistent sound of fireworks, the booms and whistles, filled the air. Her eyes focused on the window, where occasional flashes of light appeared.

Why do we cling to things that we know cause harm?

The question wasn't just about the fireworks. It was also a reflection of her relationship with Chad. How many times had she tolerated his harsh words and dismissive behavior? Why had she let him intimidate her, time and time again?

With the sound of the last fireworks dwindling into the night, Emma's thoughts grew quiet, and she drifted into a peaceful sleep.

———ℓℓ———

The following morning, Emma slept in, waking up later than usual, around eleven. As she rose from the bed, she noticed Riley hadn't been there to greet her with his usual face licks. She stretched her arms, welcoming the salty scent of the ocean that had entered through the partially opened window. Gazing out at the sparkling sandy beach, a feeling of contentment washed over her as she prepared to start her day.

"Riley? Where are you, boy?" she called out in a singsong voice.

As she made her way through the cottage, the sound of water droplets drew Emma to the bathroom, where she found Riley lapping up water from the faucet.

"Silly boy." She giggled as she crouched to pet him. "You're such a goofball."

After feeding Riley and starting the coffee maker, Emma showered and dressed in a patriotic ensemble of blue shorts and a red-and-white striped top. She pulled her hair up into a neat bun, then went to the back door, ready to walk Riley. Just as she clipped on his leash, her phone buzzed in her back pocket—it was Lisa calling.

"Hey girl!" Emma chirped.

"Hey! Happy Fourth."

"Same to you. How are you doing?"

"I'm good. Just calling to see if you're going to Phil's before heading down to the beach?"

"Of course I'm going. How could I miss that?"

"Well, I wanted to make sure. I'm gonna be there soon. Maybe we'll get lucky and meet a couple of hot guys at the beach later."

"Maybe," Emma said, letting out a nervous laugh.

Lisa's tone turned serious. "Really though, I just want to

see you happy again. I figured if you met someone new, it would help."

"I appreciate you looking out for me, but I don't think I'm ready for all of that." Emma's voice carried traces of past heartache as she shook her head. "It's too soon. I've only been divorced for three months."

Riley trailed Emma as she stepped outside with her phone and leash in hand. As the stubborn door handle closed behind her, she made a mental note to fix it later.

"Take all the time you need, Em. You're an amazing, intelligent, beautiful woman. And anyone would be lucky to have you."

Emma sighed, her eyes falling upon a flock of seagulls taking flight near the shoreline. Lisa could be right about finding someone new. Still, the idea of opening her heart again was daunting. She could only hope that, eventually, she'd find the courage to take that leap of faith.

"Thanks, Lisa. You always know what to say." Emma walked into the kitchen, grabbing Riley's water dish from the floor.

"I'll see you at Phil's in a bit, okay?"

"Sure thing. See ya then." Emma hung up and filled the dish to the brim.

With a busy day ahead, the decision to leave Riley at home alone stirred guilt within her. But really, what other choice did she have? He never did well in large crowds, like last year's town Christmas parade, when he snatched a pretzel from a kid's hand, bolted off, and narrowly escaped being caught under the wheels of the truck pulling Santa's sleigh.

As Emma crouched to say goodbye to Riley, she reached for his collar and noticed the absence of the familiar jingle. The tags were gone. Her heart skipped a beat as she inspected the collar, noticing the ring that held the tags was twisted open.

Then it struck her—the bushes.

Yesterday, during their walk, Riley chased a squirrel into a thicket of bushes, where she had carefully untangled him. The tags must've snagged on a branch, coming loose as he backed away. She hadn't thought to check the tags afterward.

I'll swing by on the way to Phil's. They have to be there.

Before Emma could merge onto the main road leading into town, she veered onto the winding path trailing back to the patch of bushes from yesterday's walk. She parked her car in the nearest spot and stepped out, her eyes sweeping the area where she and Riley had played.

Her heart thrummed as she drew closer, memories of yesterday's laughter and barks echoing in her mind. She knelt, hands combing through the foliage, hoping for a glimpse of the shiny metal. Moments later, her fingers brushed against something cool and metallic, catching the sunlight.

A sigh escaped her lips as she picked it up, wiping off the dirt. The tag was slightly scratched, but the important details—her name and phone number—were still legible.

With no time to spare, Emma hurried back to her car,

tucking the tag into her purse. She drove the short distance to town and parked on a side street, a couple blocks from Phil's Diner, where the usual spots were already taken.

The sun beat down on her shoulders as she passed the stop sign, making her way onto Main Street. Digging into her purse, a sudden realization caused her fingers to pause.

Of course. Forgot the sunscreen.

Emma hoped Lisa had brought some; otherwise, her fair skin would soon turn a painful shade of red. The thought quickened her steps along the cobblestone pathway, and she momentarily set aside her guilt about leaving Riley behind.

The diner was packed.

She took a seat at the counter and waved at Margie, the seasoned waitress, and Phil, who had popped out of the kitchen. "Hey, Em! Good to see ya."

"You too, Phil," she said, nodding to a few familiar faces before Lisa slid onto the stool next to her, coffee in hand.

Lisa gave her a playful nudge. "Looking festive today."

Emma stuck a pose with her hands under her chin, batting her eyelashes. "I try, sometimes."

Margie approached with her notepad ready. "So, what'll it be, honey?"

"I'll have a large veggie wrap—with fries this time," Emma said, surprising even herself.

"You got it." Margie winked, tearing off the order and heading to the kitchen.

Lisa's eyes widened. "Fries? That's a first."

"Yeah. I figured I'd treat myself, for the holiday and all."

Usually, Emma would settle for a small salad. But today

felt different. For years, Chad would scold her whenever she dared to stray from the safe, low-calorie options on the menu. His critical glances and sharp comments always made her feel insecure about her figure. Chad's obsession with her maintaining a size six had been a constant pressure in their marriage, and though she'd dieted diligently, the struggle to meet his exacting standards had worn on her.

While waiting for her meal, Emma was greeted by her old neighbor, Ada Harrison. "Hey stranger! I haven't seen you in ages. How are things at the new house?"

"Hey you!" Emma pulled her into a hug. "Things are going well. The new cottage is coming together finally. It's smaller than what I'm used to, but it's perfect for me and Riley."

"I'm glad to hear that." Ada's mischievous grin lit up her eyes. "You wouldn't believe who moved into your old place. He's from Chicago, and what a dreamboat! His son is as handsome as he is. And no wife, either. Boy...if I was about ten years younger, I'd think about leaving Frank for him."

Several people chuckled at the story, while others leaned in, intrigued by the town's latest gossip. A couple near the window exchanged amused glances, while a woman at the counter sipped her soda with a knowing smile.

"He stopped by this morning," Phil said. "A nice guy. Very nice guy."

"Ada certainly thinks so!" someone called out from one of the booths.

The walls of the diner shook with laughter, bouncing sound waves through the crowded space, drowning out the clinking of dishes and the hum of conversation. Emma was caught mid-laugh as the door chime drew her attention.

Every face turned toward the door, and in an instant their raucousness faded to a hush. Silence gripped the diner like a vise.

Her eyes darted to see who had entered, a smile still on her lips...until she saw the man she hadn't seen since their divorce.

Chad waved to the diner patrons, including her, then led Ashley to a booth.

Turning away, Emma fought to compose herself as her breath hitched. *How could he move on so easily?*

Phil leaned in. "Want me to kick him out? I don't have to serve someone like him, not after what he did."

"I don't want you to lose business on my account, Phil. Let them stay."

Phil's eyes narrowed as he reached across the counter and squeezed Emma's hand. "Okay, sweetie. But if you change your mind, let me know."

"Thanks, Phil." Emma lowered her gaze as Phil walked away.

"Are you alright?" Lisa whispered.

"Not really." Emma knew this day would come. She had imagined this moment countless times in her mind, preparing herself for the encounter, but now that it was happening, she still wasn't ready for it.

Just then, Margie set down a veggie wrap and fries in front of Emma, who felt a sudden certainty that she wouldn't be able to eat a single bite.

"I need to go," Emma murmured to Lisa as Margie walked

away.

"I'll go with you. You still need to eat. Do you wanna take this over to the beach?"

"I can't, Lisa. Not now. I'm sorry, but I need to go." Emma's hands trembled as she reached for her wallet, pulling out a couple of bills and placing them on the table.

"Is everything okay? Is something wrong with the wrap?" Margie asked.

Emma shook her head and stood. "No, it looks great. I'm just not hungry anymore."

"Okay, dear, I'll get this boxed up for you."

After Margie had returned with a plastic bag, Lisa walked Emma to the door. "Want me to go with you? We can just do margaritas at your place."

"No, you stay, have fun. I'll call you later."

Emma scrambled to her car, hoping no one would try to make her stay. The thought of trying to have fun with Chad and his girlfriend nearby made her stomach turn.

Once inside the car and away from prying eyes, she shifted it into drive. As she did so, the tension within her began to unravel. With every mile she put between herself and Chad, she could feel her racing heartbeat returning to its normal rhythm.

———

Arriving home, she grabbed her bag and walked inside, eager to spend the afternoon watching movies and cuddling with Riley rather than pretending to be in a good mood. She looked over at his dog bed in the corner, hoping to see him snoozing, but it was empty.

"Riley? Where are you?" Emma walked into the kitchen, putting her wrap in the fridge.

She searched the bathroom, then the bedroom, checking in the closet and under the bed.

"Where are you hiding, boy?"

A sinking feeling clawed at her chest, and a bead of cold sweat trickled down her neck. The house was unusually quiet. As she stepped back into the living room, her gaze was drawn to a sliver of sunlight sneaking in from the open back door.

How in the world...

Her mind raced back to earlier that day: the phone call with Lisa, the slightly stubborn door handle, her distraction. She remembered thinking she'd fix it later.

Every second felt heavier as the realization crashed over her.

The previous summer, she'd read an article about a dog that had bolted from his home, frightened by fireworks, and had been lost for weeks. The image of the distressed dog, ribs showing, with once bright eyes now dull and fearful, was seared into her memory.

Tears sprang to her eyes as she thought of Riley, her sweet, lovable boy, alone and terrified, lost among the deafening blasts of fireworks.

No. No. This can't be happening.

She called out for him while running onto the porch, hoping he hadn't strayed too far. "Riley! Here, boy! Come here!"

She scanned the beach for any trace of him, even asking the beachgoers if they'd seen a loose golden retriever. But no one had.

With a lump in her throat, she reached for her phone and dialed Kara's number.

Kara answered on the second ring. "Hey Emma. Charlotte and I just made it to the beach. Are you here somewhere?"

"No, I'm not at the beach." Emma's voice shook. "It's Riley. He got out. I can't find him anywhere."

"Okay, he couldn't have gone far. I'll start walking toward your cottage and ask anyone if they've seen him."

"Thanks, Kara. I'm heading out to look around the neighborhood."

Emma grabbed her keys and sprinted out the door. She drove through the familiar streets of town, down winding roads and narrow lanes, stopping everywhere, asking anyone and everyone if they'd seen Riley. She covered the outskirts too, calling out his name into the nearby woods and fields. But it was hopeless.

No one had seen him.

As the sun dipped below the horizon, casting long shadows across the road, her phone rang. It was Kara. Emma pulled over as her heart raced in tandem with the fading light. "Did you find him? Please say you found him."

"Sorry, Em. No luck on our end, but it's not over. Our volunteer team is gonna search around town early in the a.m. I texted our coordinator, and she's arranging it as we speak."

Emma broke down in tears, regretting she hadn't been more careful. "Kara, how could I let this happen? I should've shut the back door. He doesn't have his tag on; it fell off yesterday. And I...I never got him chipped."

"Don't be so hard on yourself. Accidents happen. Go home and get some sleep. I'll text you in a bit to let you know when we're meeting."

There was something reassuring in Kara's voice that allowed Emma to regain her composure. At least somewhat. "Okay, sounds like a plan. And I should've said this earlier, but thanks for today. You and Charlotte didn't have to spend your day doing this."

"Emma, we'd do anything for you. You know that."

After they hung up, Emma leaned back into the seat, massaging her temples to ease the tension behind her eyes. She sat for a moment longer before pulling back onto the road.

On the drive home, the surrounding world blurred past her car windows as she clung to hope, praying for a miracle to find Riley soon.

8

Luke

THE FAINT ECHOES OF last night's fireworks seemed to linger as Luke awoke. While most of Hadley Cove had been reveling in the Fourth of July celebrations, he had been knee-deep in unpacking. Stretching away the fatigue, he sat up, eager to get an early start on settling into their new home. Though he had made progress yesterday, a mountain of boxes still awaited him. After getting dressed, he headed down to the kitchen to make breakfast.

He noticed the empty banana bread dish by the sink.

All gone—Jeremiah must've enjoyed it.

He washed the dish and put on his shoes, deciding to return it to Ada's house across the street. As he approached front door, a strange noise caught his attention.

What's that?

The scratching sound continued, growing louder and more insistent. When Luke opened the door, his eyes widened.

There, sitting on the welcome mat, was a golden retriever.

"Hey, buddy." The dog barked and wagged his tail. Kneeling, Luke scratched behind the dog's ears and took a moment to inspect the collar. "Where's your tag, boy?"

Before he could investigate any further, the dog shot past him into the house, padding into the kitchen with an air of familiarity. Luke chuckled, following him, wondering if he had been there before or had strayed from a nearby home.

"You must be hungry. Let's see what we've got for you." Luke prepared a makeshift meal from leftovers and filled a bowl with water. He set them down, and the dog devoured the offering.

After eating, the dog settled down on a quilt near the fireplace and dozed off. Luke gazed at him for a moment longer and smiled, struck by nostalgia over Moose, his childhood dog.

"Where'd he come from?" Jeremiah's voice cut through Luke's thoughts.

"I'm not sure. Found him on the porch this morning. Seemed friendly, so I let him in. Sort of."

Jeremiah nodded, heading into the kitchen with Luke trailing behind.

"Are you hungry? We could grab a bite in town."

Jeremiah reached into the fridge and pulled out a half-empty bottle of water. "Not really."

"Well, could you maybe pick up some groceries? I've got a list. You can use my card."

"Do I have to?" Jeremiah looked up from his phone. "I've got better things to do."

"Son, can you help me out here, please? I need to find this dog's owner."

Jeremiah hesitated, then snatched the list and card from Luke's hand, leaving without a word.

Luke sighed, rubbing his forehead.

With the dog now awake, he decided to make a trip to the local vet clinic. The tech took the retriever into a back room to check for a chip. After a few minutes, she returned with the news that he wasn't chipped. Luke frowned; finding the dog's owner had just become even harder.

"Thanks for checking," Luke said, taking the leash from the vet tech.

Arriving home, he mulled over what to do with the dog. He certainly wasn't going to surrender him to the shelter. So, he pulled out his phone and made a post about the dog on the Hadley Cove Facebook page. He'd care for him until the owner was found. After all, the four-legged company was a refreshing change, Luke thought.

Refocusing on the task at hand, he delved back into unpacking. As he sifted through the boxes, one in particular caught his attention, causing him to pause in reverence. Inside was an old photo album, capturing moments with Kate from their high school days.

As he opened it, a wave of joy and melancholy swept over him. It was a treasure trove of memories, a window into a time long gone, but still so vivid in his mind. His fingers traced the edges of the pages, and he could almost hear

Kate's laughter echoing in his ears.

With a smile, Luke stared at the photo from their first date at the bowling alley, where he had let Kate win. He still remembered the mischievous glint in her eyes when they reviewed the final score, and how she had doubled over when he spilled ketchup-soaked fries on his jeans. Over twenty years had passed since those days.

Then, as he turned the page, a well-worn piece of paper slipped out. It was a letter Kate had written. Her last words to him. Though he had read it a thousand times, each felt like the first.

My Dearest Luke,

I know that by the time you read this, I'll no longer be with you.

I want you to know that I'm at peace, and I have no regrets. I have lived a life full of love, and that's because of you. You've brought so much light into my life, and for that, I'll always be grateful.

As for Jeremiah, I left you a few letters to give to him at a later time: one for after I pass, one after his graduation, and one on his wedding day. Encourage our son to pursue his dreams, whatever they may be. He'll do great things. I just know it.

And lastly, I want you to find love again. You deserve it, and I want nothing more than for you to be happy. Whoever she is, tell her that I'm thankful for her.

I know losing me will be hard, but please don't let it consume you.

Remember, my love will always be with you. Keep it close to your heart and know that I'll be watching over you and our son.

Until I see you again,
   Kate

The world blurred as Luke held the paper delicately between his fingers, fearful that his touch might smudge the ink. The room seemed to recede, leaving just him and the letter. With each line, he felt Kate's presence—she was everywhere, yet nowhere.

A bittersweet longing swelled in him, tightening his chest. *She always knew what to say, even now.*

Brushing away the tears, he closed the album and set it on the shelf. Luke then redirected his focus to unpacking, methodically sorting through the remaining clutter. Once he reached a natural stopping point, he paused, taking a final, contemplative look around the living room before heading to his office for a handful of Zoom meetings with clients.

While booting up the computer, a soft patter of paws on the hardwood floor echoed through the room. The dog sauntered in, letting out a high-pitched bark that drew Luke's attention.

"Want to go out? Come on, boy. Let's go."

The fenced-in backyard was a perfect space for the dog to roam free and play. Luke watched for a few moments as he ran off to sniff at a bush. The dog seemed at home, so he left the door cracked and headed back inside.

As Luke settled in for his meetings, his focus was divided. Thoughts of the lost dog weighed on his mind. He kept refreshing the community Facebook page, hoping for a response from the dog's owner. But so far, no news.

During a break, he stepped outside and found the dog lying in the sun, chewing on a stick. His tail wagged as Luke approached.

"Bet you're missing home." Luke squatted down, ruffling the dog's ears. "We'll find your family soon, but until then, consider this place yours."

The serene moment, however, was cut short when Luke's phone buzzed. The caller ID flashed: *Hadley Cove Police Department.* Panic spiked through him as he answered.

"Hello?"

A gruff voice spoke from the other end. "Mr. Grayson?"

"Yes, this is him."

"This is Sheriff Daniels. Are you the father of Jeremiah Grayson?"

A knot formed in Luke's stomach. "I am. Has something happened?"

"Yes. I'm afraid your son has been involved in an assault, with him being the aggressor. The other boy who was involved is at the doctor right now, getting stitches."

Luke bit his lip. They hadn't even been in Hadley Cove for two days and Jeremiah was already in trouble. Real trouble. "I'll be right there."

His grip tightened around the phone as he hung up.

This was *not* the new beginning he'd pictured.

He brought the dog back inside, grabbed the keys from the counter, and slammed the door behind him with a muttered curse.

Upon arriving at the station, Luke stormed over to Jeremiah, who was slumped in a chair next to the sheriff's desk.

"I told you to get groceries, and you ended up in a fight. What were you thinking?"

"Dad, it's not what you—"

Before Jeremiah could respond, a man holding a few papers approached. "Mr. Grayson, I assume?" Luke turned around. "I'm Sheriff Daniels. We spoke on the phone earlier."

"Yes. Can you tell me what happened?"

Jeremiah raised his voice. "Dad, just hear me out. It wasn't—"

"Jeremiah, just give me a minute."

With an impartial tone, Sheriff Daniels delivered the news. "Jeremiah and the boy got into a scuffle outside the supermarket. The boy's hand was sliced open on a broken beer bottle. His parents are pressing charges."

Luke gritted his teeth.

"Dad, you've got to listen to me—"

"I don't want to hear it, Jeremiah. Not now."

Jeremiah lowered his head into his hands.

As Luke continued to scold his son, the office door flew open. A distressed teenage girl, followed by a woman, made a beeline for Sheriff Daniels.

"Sheriff, you've got the story all wrong...he was trying to protect me!" The teenage girl bent over, gasping to catch her breath. "Please, just let me tell you what happened."

The woman smiled politely and extended her hand to Luke. "Hey, we haven't met yet. I'm Kara, and this is Charlotte, my daughter. I think she might add a little more color to what happened this morning."

Sheriff Daniels motioned Charlotte to explain. "Go on."

Charlotte's eyes darted between Luke and the Sheriff as she cleared her throat. "I was going into the store when I heard Tony call out to me. I had ended things with him at the start of summer, but he acts like we're still together. I dumped him because he's a complete jerk. He thinks he's funny, but he's just a bully."

Luke listened attentively as Charlotte recounted the incident, sensing the anxiety in her voice.

"I tried to ignore him, and that's when he ran in front of me. He wanted us to get in his car and talk, but I didn't want to. I was afraid he would drive off somewhere. So I told him I wasn't getting in, and he grabbed my arm and started pulling me. And out of nowhere, this guy here stepped in and pushed him off me. Tony punched him and he fought back. That's when Tony tripped and fell onto the broken glass."

Charlotte pointed to a bruise forming under Jeremiah's eye that Luke hadn't noticed before. "See? That's where Tony hit him."

Luke turned to Jeremiah. He searched his son's face, seeking a hint of forgiveness, but only found the telltale signs of hurt.

Why hadn't I listened? Luke added that thought to his growing list of failures as a father.

Following Charlotte's account and the ensuing formalities, the Graysons' drive home was marked by a stifling silence.

—ell—

Over the next week, a quiet stillness hung in the air between them, the tension thickening until it became almost suffocating as they prepared for Jeremiah's hearing in juvenile court.

On the day of the hearing, the court ordered Jeremiah two hundred hours of community service, with the choice between roadside cleanup or volunteering at an animal rescue. To Luke's surprise, his son chose the animal rescue and would start the following week. He considered joining Jeremiah, wondering if it would help mend their strained relationship or just make things worse.

Probably worse, he thought, running a tired hand through his hair.

Why can't I fix things with my son?

9

Emma

THE MIDSUMMER SUN FILTERED through the windows of Phil's Diner, brightening the lively scene: a waitress, her apron stained with the day's work, laughed with a regular at the counter, while a family in a booth celebrated a birthday. From the corner jukebox, Taylor Swift's latest song played, drawing a few patrons into a silent sing-along. Everything seemed right in the world.

All except one thing.

For Emma, each second felt like an eternity as she stared at the flyer with Riley's face taped to the diner's door. She glanced at the wall clock, each tick seeming to amplify the void left by his absence. Taking a deep breath, she let the aroma of roasted coffee beans offer a fleeting distraction from her thoughts. As the comforting scent faded, Emma slid into an empty booth and pulled out her phone, hopeful for an update on Riley's whereabouts. But there were no texts or notifications.

Nothing.

Over the past week, the community had rallied around her: neighbors formed search parties, the local radio station and TV channel broadcasted Riley's story, and several businesses contributed whatever resources they could. Everywhere she went, she was met with sympathetic eyes and gentle reassurances. Though they hadn't found him, every pat on her back and word of encouragement gave her hope that Riley was still out there, somewhere, waiting to be found.

"How are you holding up, honey?"

Emma looked up at Margie, who had walked over with her notepad. "I've had better days. I just wish I could find him."

Margie reached out and squeezed her hand. "I know, Emma. Try not to worry. I'm sure he'll turn up when you least expect it."

Her shoulders slumped as she nodded. "I hope you're right."

"In the meantime, you've got to eat. What can I get you?"

Emma skimmed the menu, even though she knew the vegan options by heart. "I'll take the black bean burger."

"Good choice. Phil made a fresh batch this morning. What do you want for your side?"

She hesitated, her eyes darting between the virtuous side salad and something more exciting that could induce a carb coma. "Some of that vegan mac and cheese would be great."

"Coming right up."

Margie headed toward the kitchen, leaving Emma to her thoughts. As she grabbed her phone to check her Facebook posts, Ada Harrison approached her table.

"Hello dear, how are you doing?"

Emma forced a smile. "I'm alright. How are you?"

Before Ada could respond, the bell above the door chimed, drawing Emma's attention to a stranger approaching the counter with a bag of Barking Orders treats in his hand.

"Can I get two turkey wraps to go?" he asked Margie.

"Sure thing, Luke." She smiled at him as she rang up his order.

Ada followed Emma's gaze and waved. "Luke! Over here. I want you to meet someone."

As he drew closer, Emma's eyes landed on the approaching figure. Her gaze drifted upward, tracing the lines of a sculpted jaw and full lips. She found herself momentarily caught in a pair of blue eyes that held the depth of the ocean meeting the horizon on a clear day. Their intensity, accentuated by his dark-brown hair, was almost mesmerizing. She blinked, pulled back to the moment when Ada's voice cut through her trance.

"Emma, this is the new neighbor I've been going on and on about." Ada paused, giving her a playful wink. "Luke Grayson, meet Emma Wright. She was the former owner of your new home."

Luke smiled, revealing a dazzling set of perfect white teeth. "It's nice to meet you."

"Nice to meet you too." Emma held out her hand and shook his, smiling back.

"He came all the way down from Chicago," Margie said, refilling coffee mugs without missing a beat. Her eyes sparkled as she turned to Luke. "I hope Hadley Cove offers enough to keep your handsome self here."

Luke chuckled. "Well, I think the big city was what I was trying to get away from. Hadley Cove has been very welcoming so far."

As the conversation meandered, the murmurs and glances from the local women didn't go unnoticed, adding a layer of intrigue to their meeting. Occasionally, Emma's eyes wandered, observing the subtle dance of his eyebrows, lifting in bemusement as he gracefully navigated Ada's relentless questioning.

While voices rose and fell in playful banter, Margie returned to the table, placing Emma's black bean burger in front of her.

There's something different about him. Emma couldn't quite put her finger on it.

Sensing his discomfort from all the flirting, Emma decided to save him and pointed at the bag of treats in his hand. "I hear dogs love those. What's your dog's name?"

Luke glanced at the bag, then gave her an appreciative nod as he looked back up. "Oh, these? Yeah, I picked them up at the pet store in Bridwell Bay—kind of surprised we don't have one in town. But I don't actually have a dog of my own. They're for a stray I found curled up on my porch."

"Oh?" Emma's interest piqued, both at the mention of the stray and the treats. "I know those treats well. I started making them a couple of years ago to help our local animal rescue."

"Really?" A look of surprise flickered across Luke's face. "That's incredible. He loves them. Been caring for him for about a week now."

A spark of excitement edged into Emma's voice. "Happy to hear they're being put to good use. So, about this stray—does he happen to be a golden retriever?"

"Yeah. Sandy-colored male. He had a collar, but no tag. I made a post on the community Facebook page, but an admin hasn't approved it yet."

No way.

Emma pulled off the flyer she had taped on the window and passed it to Luke. "Is this him?"

He looked down at the paper, just as surprised. "Yeah! I'm pretty sure that's him."

Emma gasped. "Really? You have Riley?"

Luke nodded as he handed back the flyer. "Only one way to find out. When can you swing by to pick him up?"

"Do you think I can come over now? Are you busy?"

"No, not at all. I stopped by to grab some lunch for me and my son, and I'm heading home after that. You're welcome to come and take him if you'd like."

Her voice brightened. "That would be amazing!"

Emma felt a surge of excitement. Yet, she tried not to let her hopes soar too high, knowing the disappointments of the past week had taken a toll on her. Regardless, the possibility of reuniting with her beloved Riley filled her with quiet optimism.

The conversation reached a natural lull as Margie arrived, perfectly timed, with Luke's wraps in hand. Emma gave her an apologetic smile. "If it's not too much trouble, could I get this to go? Luke might have found Riley. We're about to leave."

"That's wonderful! See, I told you not to worry, Em. Sometimes things just have a way of working themselves out." Margie gave her a hug. "Just give me a minute to throw this into a box for you."

"Thanks Margie. You're the best." Emma looked toward Luke. "Are you parked close by?"

"Yeah, that's me right across the street." He pointed out the window to a large black Range Rover.

"Nice car." She imagined it cost much more than her little Honda Civic.

"Thanks. I bought it before we moved down here. Thought I'd get something durable."

Just then, Margie arrived with her to-go bag. "Congrats on finding Riley. It's good to see a smile on your face again."

"Well, let's hope it's him." Emma grinned and turned to Luke. "Shall we?"

After exchanging final goodbyes with Margie, he held the door open as they stepped outside the diner. "Do you want to follow me?"

"I think I remember how to get there." Emma chuckled. "I'll see you at the house."

—⁓—

Emma pulled into the driveway behind Luke and got out. With restrained eagerness, she stood back, allowing him to unlock the door as her anticipation grew.

When he opened it, Emma was enveloped by the rich smell of the old wooden floor and the subdued sunlight streaming through the curtains. Though the furniture bore the personal stamp of someone else's life, the essence of the home—her home—still lingered.

"Ah, there he is," Luke said as they stepped into the living room.

Emma looked over; Riley was gnawing at the rug in front of the fireplace. "Riley! That's a no-no."

At the sound of her voice, he bounded over and jumped up on his hind legs, nuzzling her with his wet nose. She laughed and sank to her knees, burying her face in his fur. "Oh, Riley. You scared me."

Luke smiled. "When I first found him, I didn't see a tag. Even took him to the vet to see if he was chipped."

She nodded, feeling a bit embarrassed. "It fell off in some bushes. Long story. But I've been meaning to get him chipped. Just never got around to it, I guess," Emma said, looking up to meet Luke's eyes. "But it looks like he was well taken care of."

Luke rubbed the back of his neck. "Well, about that—I don't actually have any dog food for him at the moment. But I have some leftover treats."

A light laugh escaped her. "Do you have a bowl?"

"Sure do." Luke gestured for her to follow.

Together, they moved into the kitchen, with Riley at their heels. Luke carefully opened the bag and put half the treats into a bowl, then placed it on the ground. Riley dove straight in, gobbling up the treats as his tail whipped back and forth like a pendulum in overdrive.

Emma leaned against the counter, allowing her gaze to wander around the familiar space.

"Can I get you a cup of coffee?" Luke asked.

"Only if you're having one too."

"Great." Luke walked over to the cupboard and pulled out two mugs. "So, you used to live here?"

Emma nodded. "With my husband. It's a wonderful house."

"Why'd you sell it? If you don't mind me asking." He filled up one mug and handed it to her.

"That's alright. I got divorced a couple months ago, and our lawyers decided it was in our best interest."

Luke stopped what he was doing and looked up at her. "I'm sorry. I never would've asked if—"

"No, it's okay, really," she assured him. "It's nice to have someone in town who doesn't know all my business."

Luke continued topping off his mug. "Milk or sugar?"

"I'm good. Thanks, though." Emma took a small sip of the piping-hot coffee. "I see you haven't changed much of anything in the house yet."

Luke looked around and shrugged. "I'm not sure what I'd change. Maybe a coat of paint in the dining room, but other than that, I'm not really sure."

Emma's lips curved into a knowing smile. "Yeah. The dining room could definitely use it. It looks exactly how my grandpa left it."

"Your grandpa?"

"Yeah. It was my grandparents' house. He gave it to us as a wedding present. After my grandma passed, he wanted to move into something smaller."

"I'm sorry about your grandma." Luke's eyes met hers. "I know losing someone isn't ever easy."

Emma took a moment to soak in his kind words. "Thanks

for that. It was years ago though, and we knew it was coming. I'm alright now."

Luke gave a small nod, as if acknowledging the gravity of her loss, before breaking into a grin. "Maybe you can solve a mystery for me," he said, motioning for her. "Come check this out."

Emma followed him into the living room and over to the mantel. He pointed to the *A + L* carving.

"A and L. Who were they?"

"Amelia and Liam," she answered. "My grandparents. They were married fifty years before she passed. They met when they were kids."

"Wow! Fifty years. They sound like me and my wife. We were high school sweethearts."

"And where's your wife now?"

"Well..." Luke paused, steadying his breath. "She passed a little over two years ago. It was cancer. She always wanted to live on the Georgia coast. That's one of the reasons we moved down here."

Emma's eyes softened. "Luke, I'm so sorry."

At that moment, a teenage boy bearing a striking resemblance to Luke descended the stairs.

Emma turned to him and smiled. "Hey, I'm Emma."

Her greeting was ignored as the boy fixed an icy stare at Luke. He spun on his heels and stormed upstairs. The unmistakable sound of a door slamming echoed back to her.

"Excuse me. I'll be right back." Luke took on a serious tone and walked up the steps.

Emma nodded and took a seat in an armchair, glancing toward the staircase where Luke had disappeared. She tried to make sense of the muffled voices filtering down. The words were indistinct, but the tone was unmistakable: frustration, hurt, anger.

Luke's trying, she thought, clasping her hands in her lap. *That's all any parent can do, right? Try, fail, apologize, and try again.* She felt a strange ache for both of them, a knot of empathy and sadness.

Suddenly, a clear voice cut through the muffled argument: "...another woman home. Have you forgotten about her completely?"

"Of course I haven't! And lower your voice. Come down here and meet—"

"No! You think some stranger can just waltz in and take her place? She was better than you...I wish it was you who died."

The door upstairs slammed with a force that reverberated throughout the house, shaking the windowpanes. *Time to go.* Emma looked at Riley, who had trotted back in after finishing his treats, and sat next to her. He seemed as unsettled as she felt, as if sensing that the moment for a graceful exit had arrived.

Luke reappeared, his face taut but controlled. "I'm sorry you had to hear that."

"Oh, it's alright," Emma said. "I was just leaving anyway. I have to get home."

"I'll walk you out." Luke followed her to her car.

Emma whistled softly to Riley. His ears perked, then he dashed over. She guided him to the backseat, then turned toward Luke. "He didn't mean it, you know."

Luke shifted his gaze to the ground. "I wish I could believe that."

"Being a substitute teacher at the high school, I see teens act out all the time. It's often just misplaced emotion."

Letting out a heavy sigh, Luke ran his fingers through his hair. "I'm struggling, Emma. I've tried every expert tip I could find, read books, consulted therapists. I still go to therapy, but Jeremiah refuses to join me. We moved here thinking it would be a new beginning. Now I'm wondering if it was just a huge mistake..." His eyes drifted to some distant point. "Sorry if that was too much."

"It's not too much, Luke. And don't be so hard on yourself." Emma reached over, placing her hand on his arm. "I think the best thing you can do right now is to be patient with him. He'll come around."

"I hope so. It's nice to hear there's light at the end of the tunnel."

"There usually is," Emma said, opening the driver's-side door. "Thanks again for looking out for my sweet boy. I'll see you around."

"Anytime. See you later."

Emma climbed into her car and pulled away from the home she once knew so well. She caught a last glimpse of him in her rearview as he went inside. A bittersweet blend of sadness and relief tugged at her heart. Although she missed that house, she found comfort in knowing someone like Luke had moved into it—someone she believed would take good care of it. After all, he had cared for Riley when he didn't have to.

As she drove through the winding roads that led her back

to her own life, her thoughts were a swirl of past and future, of what-ifs and maybes.

I wonder when I'll run into him again.

The thought stirred a sense of guilt within her, although Chad was the one who had betrayed their vows. She reminded herself that it was perfectly acceptable to entertain such musings now that she was divorced. And so, with a tender smile, she dismissed it as nothing more than a gentle crush.

After pulling into her driveway, she took a deep, steadying breath, releasing the accumulated tension of the day. She shifted into park and turned toward her beloved companion, their eyes meeting in a moment of silent understanding. "Riley, you gave your momma a big scare. I'm never letting you out of my sight again. We're getting your tags on before you get a snack. And you're getting chipped next week."

He tilted his head, as if contemplating her words, then let out a bark.

"Okay, boy, we can go inside."

10

Luke

AFTER WAVING GOODBYE, LUKE felt the noticeable quiet without Riley's lively bark. He smiled knowing Riley was back with Emma, a woman who radiated love and kindness. She also was easy on the eyes.

When Emma's car disappeared around the bend, Luke walked back inside a house that seemed to hold its breath, mirroring the tension hanging in the air.

Things are worse than I thought.

While Luke unpacked several untouched boxes, Jeremiah stayed put in his room. Even as he emerged briefly for bathroom breaks, the distance between father and son felt as if it stretched wider and wider, with no end in sight.

As evening settled and the house grew quieter, Luke prepared dinner. The soft clatter of cutlery echoed through stillness as he set a tray with food outside Jeremiah's door. Standing there, he hesitated, his hand hovering over the doorknob. He felt the cool metal under his fingertips along-

side the weight of words left unsaid, of apologies and conversations that had happened years too late.

With a heavy heart, Luke let his hands fall to his sides,
then retreated to his room. He grabbed his battered copy of
Meditations by Marcus Aurelius from the nightstand before
collapsing onto the bed. Tonight, the normally grounding
words swam hazily before his eyes. Despite his fight against
sleep's pull, he drifted off with the book resting on his chest.

The following day, Luke woke up early to prepare breakfast, hoping the aroma of freshly cooked pancakes would
entice his son downstairs. To his delight, it worked, but only
long enough for Jeremiah to fix himself a plate, pour a cup
of juice, and walk back toward his room. Still, Luke thought
it was progress as he trailed him out of the kitchen.

"Hey, I'm heading out for a haircut. Want to tag along?"

Jeremiah shook his head. "No. I don't need a haircut."

"Need anything while I'm out? I can swing by the market.
Or the diner?"

Jeremiah ignored him and continued up the stairs without looking back.

"Okay then. Text me if you need anything."

Luke looked toward the staircase, only hearing the latch
of the door click shut. Letting out a deep sigh, his mind
filled with thoughts of what could go wrong before he came
back home. He downed his coffee in one desperate gulp,
hoping the caffeine would calm his nerves, but the knot in
his stomach remained.

As Luke drove away, his grip on the wheel tightened.
Visions of Jeremiah plagued his thoughts.

What if he gets into something he can't get out of this time?

A wave of guilt crashed over him; his career had always come first, and now he was scrambling to be the father he should have been years ago. Luke wondered if he had already failed Jeremiah beyond repair.

Turning onto Main Street, his attention was drawn to the bustling townspeople, moving in an almost constant stream. After circling around the block a few times, he finally found a parking space in front of the salon. He waited almost an hour for a trim that took mere minutes. But the hairdresser did a good job, and under her careful, practiced hand, his shaggy hair fell away from his face. Now with a fresh cut, he started to feel human again.

After leaving the salon, Luke looked up and down the street, catching sight of the ocean at the far end. Although he had lived in Hadley Cove for over a week now, he still hadn't set foot on the beach. Curiosity nudged him, and he slipped his car keys back in his pocket and headed toward the stretch of water, crossing the road on the way.

At the entrance, he removed his shoes, feeling the warm sand beneath his feet, and fixed his gaze on the ocean waves lapping against the shore. Listening to the rustle of the palm fronds in the breeze, he soaked up this moment with no hurry—a luxury he hadn't often had back in Chicago.

Despite the number of people out and about in town, there was hardly anyone at the beach, except for a young family playing in the water nearby. Memories swept Luke away as he watched them, remembering how summer lake trips used to be a family ritual. Jeremiah would rush into the water, kicking up sprays of laughter, while Luke tried to keep up. Kate would be on the dock, camera in hand, capturing each precious second. Her voice, cheering them on, now played like a distant melody in his mind. He made a mental note to look for those photos, thinking it would be a good idea to frame some and put them around the house. Maybe, just maybe, they'd remind Jeremiah of happier times, of a family that once was.

Luke was yanked out of his daydream by a familiar bark to his left. Startled, he turned and his smile broadened upon the appearance of the figures approaching him along the beach.

"Hey, stranger!" Emma called out as she waved.

Grinning, Luke waved back. "Hey there!"

Riley pounced onto Luke's leg, wagging his tail and licking his hand.

Emma tugged on his leash. "Sorry about that. I've never seen him take to someone so quickly."

Luke shrugged and squatted to Riley's level before reaching out to give him a scratch behind the ears. "No need to be sorry. He's a good boy."

"Most of the time he is," Emma said, her eyes scanning the horizon before settling back on Luke. "How's Jeremiah doing?"

Luke stood, brushing sand off his pants. "Oh, he's fine. He's said a total of eight words to me since the big fight yesterday, so I think we're making progress."

"Baby steps. He'll come around." Emma offered an encouraging smile that seemed to say she had faith in the situation. "Listen, I was headed to grab lunch. If you're not too busy, you should join us."

"Sure. That sounds nice."

At Phil's Diner, Riley received a celebrity-like welcome from several customers, clearly enjoying his small-town fame. Carried along by the warm welcome, Emma spotted an empty booth and took a seat while Luke slid into the spot across from her.

Phil appeared with a plate of scrambled eggs. "For the honored guest," he said, placing the plate on the ground for Riley. "How are you folks today?"

"Pretty good," Emma said. "We ran into Luke on the beach and invited him to grab some lunch."

"Well, you've come to the right place." Phil wiped his hands on his apron. "I'll give y'all some time to decide what you want."

As Phil walked away, Luke skimmed the menu, even though he was already familiar with it from his recent visits. Lifting his eyes, he caught Emma staring at him. "What is it? Do I have something on my face?"

She shook her head. "Did you get a haircut?"

"Got it this morning. Didn't expect the salon to be packed."

Emma chuckled. "Never go on Tuesdays. She books all her long-term clients then. You'll eventually get in, but it'll be a while."

Luke ran a hand over his newly shorn hair. "I'll have to remember that. Kate used to cut it at home for me and Jeremiah. Even after two years, I'm still getting used to going out to get it cut."

Emma gave him a pitying look. "Oh, I'm sorry."

"No worries. It's okay." Luke appreciated her words but wasn't looking for sympathy.

"It must have been really hard for Jeremiah to lose his mom at such a young age..."

"Yeah. They were like best friends. I worked a lot, and Kate stayed home with him. I know Jeremiah resents me for not always being there. And I've been trying to make it up to him, but most of the time I just feel like a terrible father."

"I don't think you're a terrible father," Emma said softly. "I mean, you're acknowledging the fact that you and Jeremiah could be closer, and you're actively trying to make that happen. To me, that's what makes you a wonderful father."

"Thank you, Emma," he said, choked with emotion. "That means a lot to me."

She reached across the table and squeezed his hand. "I want you to know that you're not alone in this. And if you ever need any help or support, let me know."

As her fingers tightened around his, the warmth of her grip seemed to fill a space in his soul that had been empty since Kate's passing. He nodded. "I appreciate it, truly."

Emma's expression grew solemn. "When my mother died, my father became depressed and completely neglected me. There were so many times when I wanted him to ask me how my day was, or even yell at me when I didn't clean my room. I just wanted some sort of reaction from him, but I never got it. He was too sad to even care and eventually left town without me. That's why my grandparents raised me."

Luke listened intently as Emma's words echoed in his

heart. Her story struck a deep chord within him, stirring up emotions over how he had failed Jeremiah through the years.

"That sounds terrible, Emma. How old were you when she died?"

"Twelve. So, a few years younger than Jeremiah. I'm sure some of his behavior is just normal teenage angst. He'll eventually grow out of it, trust me."

Luke hoped she was right. "You don't have any kids, do you?"

Emma's lips pressed into a thin line as she glanced away. "Chad and I argued about it a million times, but he didn't want any. He said it was a career-killer. So, I rescued this fur baby instead."

They both looked down at Riley, who had lain down for a nap.

Luke found himself enjoying Emma's company more than he had expected. They had only just met, but there was a natural ease to their conversation, like they had known each other for years. From across the table, he admired how her auburn ringlets cascaded down around her shoulders into perfect curls, framing her face and highlighting her delicate features. He felt a magnetic pull toward the kindness in her warm, chocolate-brown eyes, almost getting lost in their depth.

With a resounding *clap* of his hands, Phil approached the table. "So, what'll it be?"

Luke's eyes darted down to the menu. "Uh, ham and Swiss. With potato salad if you have it."

"We sure do," Phil said. "And for you, madame?"

"I'll take a veggie wrap. Do you still have some of that vegan mac and cheese?"

Phil smiled, then nodded. "We do. And even if we didn't, I'd make it happen for ya. I'll go ahead and put your orders in."

As Phil walked away, Luke turned to Emma with a raised brow. "Are you vegetarian?"

"Actually, I'm vegan. It's been about ten years now."

Luke's eyes widened. "Oh, geez. I should've ordered something less meaty. Let me see if I can change that—"

Emma reached out and grabbed his arm. "No, it's fine. I lived with Chad for years, and he was the biggest carnivore I knew. Trust me, I'm used to it."

Luke relaxed his shoulders. "Okay, I'll take your word for it. So, I hope this isn't too intrusive, but what made you go vegan?"

She leaned toward him, her eyes brightening with passion. "Well, I think people are vegan for different reasons. Some for health, some for the planet. But for me, it was for the animals. Years ago, I was having dinner with friends and as I looked down at the veal on my plate, it just hit me. I thought to myself that this represents what is most awful in this world: fear, suffering, and death. Right then, I realized all animals are *someone*, not something."

Luke tilted his head.

She inhaled deeply, continuing her story.

"Eating some animals while loving others never felt right to me. When it comes down to it, ultimately, being vegan is the belief that an animal's life is worth more than a sandwich. I'd like to think most people believe that."

Luke's jaw dropped a fraction and his eyebrows rose. "I'd never thought of it that way before. It makes sense, though. I love how you acted on your convictions. You're inspiring."

Emma smirked at his compliment. "Thanks for that. I know I'm pretty awesome."

Luke chuckled, the sound rumbling deep in his chest as he leaned against the plush cushion of the booth. Her eyes sparkled as they met his, and the sunlight through the diner's window illuminated the subtle shade of pink on her lips. He was entirely lost in the moment.

Emma broke the silence with a playful grin. "But enough about me. Now it's your turn. Tell me something I don't know about you."

As they awaited their meals, Luke shared anecdotes of his life in Chicago, while Emma recounted tales of her upbringing in Hadley Cove. He hung on to her every word, admiring how her love for life came alive through her animated gestures. With Emma, conversation was refreshingly simple, and her sharp sense of humor brought out fits of laughter he hadn't experienced in ages.

After they ate, Emma stood up and grabbed Riley's leash. "I think it's time for us to head back home. It was fun hanging out, Luke."

"I had a lot of fun too. Thanks for the invite. And all your help with Jeremiah." His heart sank at the thought of her leaving.

Emma shot him a reassuring smile. "Don't even mention it."

As Luke watched her walk out of the diner, he felt a pang of longing in his chest. Her presence had left behind an invisible force he couldn't quite rationalize, yet it was undeniably felt. His mind rushed with thoughts of Kate, her memory the yardstick by which he measured all things.

Is it too soon to feel this for another woman?

11

Emma

Knock. Knock. Knock.

Emma shifted beneath her blankets, uncertain whether she had really heard that sound at her door or if she had dreamt it.

Knock. Knock. Knock.

No—she definitely wasn't dreaming.

She swung her feet out of bed and into her slippers, then moved through the hallway, grabbing her robe as she went. Riley, ears perked, was already alert and sniffing at the front door.

"Open up! It's me," called a female voice from the other side.

When Emma unlatched the door and pulled it open, Riley's tail kicked into overdrive, wagging frantically as if he sensed a familiar presence.

Emma stretched and yawned. "Lisa? You're up early."

With one hand holding Tupperware, Lisa reached down

to give Riley a scratch behind the ears. "You always know how to make someone feel welcome, don't you boy?" Straightening up, she looked at Emma. "You're gonna love what I brought."

"What'd you bring?" Emma followed Lisa as she breezed by into the kitchen, with Riley trailing behind.

Lisa set the container on the table and lifted the lid. "Your favorite—blueberry pancakes!"

Emma's mind flooded with the nostalgia of childhood mornings at her grandma's house. Even as an adult, blueberry pancakes always brought her back to those cherished times. "You didn't!" Her mouth dropped. "So, to what do I owe this early morning pancake delivery?" she asked, still marveling at the surprise as she moved to grab plates and utensils.

Lisa shrugged, taking a seat at the kitchen table. "I just thought it would be a nice way to start the day. Besides, it's been a while since we caught up."

"That it has," Emma said, setting a plate in front of Lisa and another for herself. Riley watched intently as she began serving the pancakes, perhaps hopeful one would fall his way.

As the aroma of fresh blueberry pancakes filled the air, Emma felt grateful for the simple joys that made life sweeter—even if it meant starting her day a bit earlier than planned.

After grabbing the syrup, Emma took to the coffeemaker, preparing a brew, then fetched two mugs from the shelf above the sink. Turning, she noticed Lisa's fingers tapping against the smooth surface of the table.

"So, anything new happening lately?" Lisa asked.

Emma sat down and picked up her fork. "Not really. Business is good, and my summer tutoring sessions are starting back up soon."

"Is that *really* it?"

Emma took a bite of her pancake, shaking her head. "I don't know what I'm supposed to tell you."

"Are you telling me you don't know what everyone's saying?"

"No, I don't." Emma scrunched her forehead.

"The word around town is that you're seeing Hadley Cove's most eligible bachelor. I can't believe you didn't tell me first!"

Emma's fork danced around her plate, picking up another piece of pancake. Before responding, she enjoyed another mouthful, savoring its warmth and syrupy goodness. "I'm not following."

"Tall, dark, and handsome. A butt that looks great in jeans...new in town? I'm quoting your old neighbor," Lisa said, wiping her face with a napkin. "She told me you went over to his house."

Emma paused. A faint blush crept up her cheeks when she realized whom Lisa was referring to. "Yeah, I went to Luke's to pick up Riley."

"Well, apparently everyone in town is talking about the date y'all had at Phil's."

Emma rolled her eyes and leaned back. "Date? It was just lunch. And everyone in town? Really?"

"Mm-hmm." A devilish grin spread across Lisa's face as she rose to pour the coffee. "So, I'm gonna ask you again, why didn't you tell me first?"

Emma turned back to her pancakes, shaking her head and chuckling. The Hadley Cove grapevine was nothing short of astounding. The speed and scale at which misinformation could be circulated was mind-boggling.

"Are you denying it?" Lisa teased. "Because I can always tell when you're lying."

"There's nothing to tell." Emma set down her utensils and made eye contact with Lisa. "And no, I'm not lying. Do you really think I'd keep something like that from you?"

"Maybe. But only to make me suffer." Lisa pouted with a playful frown.

While Lisa's words were lighthearted, a deeper urgency pulsed beneath Emma's need to set things straight. "I went over to his house and picked up Riley. He asked me a few things about the house, and I left. Then I saw him the next day on the beach, and we had lunch together...as friends. That's all that happened."

"So, you think you'll run into him again anytime soon?"

Emma raised her shoulders in a slight shrug. "Probably. Easy to do that here. But just because we may bump into each other occasionally doesn't mean I'm seeing him. We just met."

"He'll at least be a good rebound. I can see it now," Lisa said, with a mischievous glimmer in her eyes. "Y'all would have the cutest couple's name: 'Lemma.' I'm Team Lemma already."

Emma's gaze shifted to the old photograph on the wall, taken at the town fair last year. It reminded her of simpler times. "I'm happy on my own. I have Riley and my business, and that's all I need right now." Her voice carried the weight of her past and the strength of her present. "I'm not looking for anything serious after what Chad did to me."

Lisa recoiled at the mention of Chad's name. "I get it. But someone like him shouldn't prevent you from finding love again with someone special. You're amazing, funny, smart. And not to mention, drop dead gorgeous. I hate that loser ever made you think otherwise. Anyone in their right mind would be more than lucky to be with you."

Memories of broken promises surged through Emma. The hurt, the deceit—she closed her eyes briefly and folded her arms. "It's not that simple—"

"For sure. I get it. We all know I've had my fair share of disaster relationships." Lisa leaned forward. "Chad was terrible to you, and you didn't deserve that. I just don't want you missing out on something real, whether that's with Luke or someone else. That's all."

A silent understanding passed between them as Emma recognized the sincerity and love behind her friend's words. But as much as she understood where Lisa was coming from, she wanted lighter conversation.

Looking down at her half-eaten pancakes, she slid the plate aside and reached for her coffee. "Looks like it's going to be a nice one out there today." She squinted into the sunlight gleaming through the window. "I should probably take Riley out soon. You can join us if you have time."

"Yeah, let's go! Want any more pancakes before we head out?"

"No more pancakes." Emma patted her stomach. "I'm stuffed. But thank you."

Lisa smirked. "Glad you liked them. Making them this morning gave me a break from everything going on. Speaking of which, having some downtime from my mom's bed-and-breakfast has really helped. It's allowed me to focus on launching my new products."

Emma's eyes lit up as she smiled at Lisa. "That's right! How's that coming along?"

"Well, you know those t-shirts I started off with, the ones with Hadley Cove Beach printed on them? Now I'm selling monogrammed mugs, tote bags, and hats too. I've even got a display at the surf shop. So I'd say it's going pretty well."

"From t-shirts to a display at the surf shop? That's big! How'd you pull that off?"

Lisa sipped her coffee. "Let's just say it helps to have friends in the right places."

Emma was thrilled to see Lisa thriving, especially after all she had been through years ago with her ex. "That's fantastic news! You should've told me earlier. I'll definitely check it out. It seems like your business is taking off."

"Yeah, it is! Of course, I know it's mainly because of the tourist season, but I hope I can keep the momentum going even after summer ends."

Emma nodded thoughtfully. "You've always had that entrepreneurial spirit, Lisa. It's amazing to see it in full swing. Just remember, you can hook me up with that 'best friend' discount whenever I come shopping," she added with a wink.

The two shared a laugh and stood, clearing the breakfast table and rinsing the dishes. Afterward, they took Riley out for a leisurely stroll on the soft, sandy beach. They reminisced about old times and caught up on each other's lives with the sun's warmth on their faces.

Eventually, they circled back to Emma's cottage and stepped inside, hugging goodbye before Lisa went home. Pulling back the curtain, she watched Lisa's car grow smaller in the distance, her mind lingering on their earlier conversation.

Was everyone really saying they were together?

She sighed deeply, a mixture of exasperation and amusement. The peaceful sound of birds chirping in the background and the sight of Riley tracking a squirrel from behind the slightly opened window made her momentarily forget the town's whispers.

Glancing at the clock, Emma realized that time had slipped away. She had to get ready.

After taking a quick shower and drying off, she rummaged through her closet, opting for a simple T-shirt and shorts combo. Emma had anticipated this day all week, and now it had arrived.

It was Saturday.

Saturdays were reserved for volunteering at Second Chance Rescue with her grandfather, who shared the same passion for supporting animals. It had become a weekend ritual for them since she had adopted Riley from there. For Emma, it was her way of giving back to a place that had changed her life, and an opportunity to spend time with her aging grandfather.

Before leaving to pick him up, she took one last look around the house.

Phone? Check.

Riley's food and water bowls filled? Check.

Back door properly secured? Check.

With everything in order, she grabbed her keys and headed out.

When Emma pulled into her grandfather's driveway, she spotted him waiting on the porch, nestled in his rocking chair. As she parked, Liam stood up and made his way to the car.

"Good morning, Em." Liam leaned over and planted a gentle kiss on her cheek after getting into the passenger seat. "You're looking lovely today."

"Grandpa, you say that every time," she said, flipping her hair dramatically with a hand.

"Well, it's true every time." Liam chuckled, giving her arm a playful pinch as she started the car and headed toward town.

"So, how was your week?" Emma asked.

"Pretty good. Although I did hear a few tidbits about you."

She groaned, bracing herself for whatever teasing he had in store for her. "I don't know what you're talking about, Grandpa."

"Whatever you say, my dear." Liam flashed a grin and steered the conversation in a new direction. "Want to grab some ice cream after we're done?"

"Sure, that sounds great."

Liam nodded. "But nothing will ever top that ice cream you made with Grandma. That was the best I've ever had. It was her recipe."

Emma glanced at him with a softened gaze, then refocused on the road. Growing up without her father, Liam had been her rock, and over the years he had taught her life lessons that she carried into adulthood. He'd shown her the intricacies of maintaining a home, the compassion to care for animals, and the strength to stand up for herself. She was grateful for him beyond words.

"So, Grandpa, how do you even have time to keep up with all this gossip?"

"Oh, I make time. Especially for something involving *you*," he said with a wink.

Emma shook her head as she turned onto Main Street. "Well, whatever you think you've heard, you probably got it all wrong. You should get your hearing checked soon."

Liam laughed softly. "My ears are as sharp as Riley's. So, tell me about this newcomer in town? I hear he's quite the sought-after gentleman."

"He's no one, Grandpa. I only met Luke because he was the one who found Riley. And then we had lunch together—as friends. It was nothing, really."

"Ah, I see," Liam mused.

Emma tightened her grip on the steering wheel. "I'm being serious. It was nothing and won't ever be anything. Not anymore."

Liam placed a hand on her arm. "Em, it's perfectly okay to take a breather, to allow your heart to mend. But from what I know about life, it has a mysterious way of bringing people together when we least expect it."

The weight of his words echoed in her mind, gently nudging her guarded heart. She knew his advice came from a place of love, but the memories of her failed marriage were still vivid. It was a pain she didn't want to revisit.

When they arrived at Second Chance Rescue, Charlotte ran over and went straight for Liam, hugging him like she hadn't seen him in years.

"Hello, sweetheart," Liam said. "How have you been? How's school?"

Charlotte bubbled over with excitement as she spoke. "Well, I was voted president of the history club. And I think we have a real chance of bringing home the state championship in the History Bee this year."

"That's great news!" Liam raised his hand for a high-five. "I guess I'll have to keep telling you my old stories so you can win."

Emma watched with a smile, taking in Liam and Charlotte's lively exchange. After retrieving bags of dog food and other supplies from the trunk, she made her way into the rescue center. As she walked in, the familiar chorus of barks and meows greeted her, guiding her to the volunteer room.

The moment she laid the bags on the table, Kara's voice rang out. "There you are!" She approached Emma with a smile and gave her a hug.

"Hey, you!" She squeezed Kara tightly, then pulled back and scanned the room. "Looks like there's been a lot of new arrivals since last weekend."

Kara sighed. "It's been a busy week. But every bit of help counts. Oh, and before I forget, this is for you." She handed Emma a volunteer shirt. "What do you think? Lisa designed them for us."

"Love these! They're cute. Yeah, I just saw her an hour ago." Emma slipped into the shirt.

"Oh, yeah? We all need a girls' night soon."

"Yes! We totally should."

As the conversation wrapped up, Emma joined the others in cleaning the kennels and feeding the animals. It was always a humbling experience for her to see the resilience of these animals who had been abandoned or abused. They still had so much love to give, and she felt privileged to be a part of their journey in finding a forever home.

After a few hours of hard work, it was time for a break. Emma grabbed a bottle of water and sat in the courtyard, where Liam and Charlotte were walking some of the dogs.

While she sipped her water, Liam's words from the car ride replayed in her mind: *Life has a mysterious way of bringing people together when we least expect it.*

She thought back to her lunch with Luke and how the honest sparkle in his eyes and the softness in his voice made her momentarily forget the outside world. Their conversation had, at times, drifted beyond mere small talk, making her wonder about life's what-ifs.

Emma closed her eyes, letting the sun kiss her face as those what-ifs swirled like falling leaves. She felt an unsettling mix of nostalgia, longing, and caution course through her—remnants of her history with Chad. Yet her heart whispered truths her mind dared not voice: she couldn't ignore the undeniable connection between her and Luke.

She shook her head, clearing away the thoughts. It was simpler to label what they had as just two lives intersecting briefly in a small town. Friends, nothing more.

But as the sunlight played with the shadows, in the quiet corners of her heart, perhaps there was a wish for something more.

12

Luke

CHECKING HIS WATCH, LUKE called up the stairs. "Jer, come on—we've got to go!"

"Be right there!" Jeremiah's voice resonated through the house as he descended the staircase.

"Didn't mean to yell," Luke explained, opening and shutting the front door. "Just want you to be on time for your first day at the rescue. That's all."

On the drive over, Jeremiah didn't speak a word. Luke suspected he wasn't excited about doing community service but hoped this experience might change his mind.

As they pulled up to the animal rescue, they were greeted by a chorus of eager barks and the chirping of birds in a nearby tree. Luke's eyes traced the charming outlines of the building: the bold red door and the pristine white trim framing the stories of many rescued souls. The architecture was reminiscent of a small cottage, with a pitched roof and small windows accented with flower boxes. A polished brass sign hanging above the entrance featured a silhouette of a cat and a dog—it had been engraved with *Second Chance Animal Rescue.*

When Luke got out of the car, he saw the girl from the sheriff's station standing a couple of yards away. He glanced over at Jeremiah, thinking he would be thrilled to work with her, especially after he had protected her from her ex-boyfriend. Instead, Jeremiah's face turned red and he lowered his head, walking over to Luke.

"I changed my mind. I'd rather do the roadside cleanup," Jeremiah whispered.

Luke raised a brow. "What? Why?"

Jeremiah shrugged, avoiding eye contact. "It's no big deal. I think it might be better for me."

"You're *here* now. Give it a shot, son," Luke urged gently.

Jeremiah stormed off, brushing past him.

Luke shook his head as he grabbed the community service form from the center console and went inside.

"Here," Luke said, holding out the form to Jeremiah. "Don't forget you need them to sign it after you're finished."

Jeremiah snatched it from his hand and handed it to the woman behind the desk.

She looked surprised to see him. "Hey, I think I remember you. From the sheriff's office, right?" the woman said, looking at Jeremiah.

"Yeah, that was me," Jeremiah murmured.

"Thanks again for what you did for my daughter. I'm Kara, by the way. I'll give you a tour of the rescue, and then we'll get you started," she said, leading the way to the kennels.

Luke flashed a smile at Kara and then directed his attention to Jeremiah. "I'll pick you up in a few hours, okay?"

Jeremiah didn't reply, ignoring him completely.

Luke let out a sigh then made his way back to the parking lot. As he swung the door open, a sudden rush of warmth and the soft scent of a familiar perfume hit him before he realized he'd knocked into Emma and an older man entering from the opposite direction.

Emma staggered back. "Oh, Luke," she said, a ripple of surprise spreading across her face. "I'm sorry. I didn't mean to run right into you."

He shrugged off the impact. "No, no, it's on me. I should've been paying more attention."

"Well, it doesn't matter now. What are you doing here?" Emma asked.

"Dropping off Jeremiah. He's volunteering today."

"It's good to have new blood around here," the older man added.

Emma stepped forward, gesturing between the two. "Luke, this is my grandfather, Liam. Grandpa, this is Luke."

"Nice to meet you, young man," Liam said, adjusting his glasses.

"It's nice to meet you too, sir." Luke extended his hand, which Liam grasped firmly. "And hopefully my son doesn't give you any trouble. We're both going through a bit of a rough patch at the moment."

"I'll look out for him today, don't you worry."

Luke offered a grateful nod. "I appreciate that."

"Sure thing, Luke. And I'll see you later, kiddo." Liam kissed Emma on the top of her head, then went inside.

With Liam gone, leaving only Emma beside him, the air seemed to thicken. As their eyes met, Luke exchanged a polite smile with her, searching for the right words. He shifted his weight, his fingers drumming softly against his thigh.

Nothing came to him.

She must think I'm awkward.

After what felt like an eternity, Emma broke the silence. "It's funny."

"What is?" Luke asked, raising his hand to shield his eyes from a sudden ray of sunlight.

"How we literally and figuratively keep bumping into each other," she said, tucking a loose curl behind her ear.

"Guess that's small-town living, right? So, are you volunteering today?"

A seagull cried out in the distance, its sound mingling with the chatter of other volunteers.

"True. And yeah, I already did, but only for a couple of hours. I'm heading out now. I still need to replace the knob on the back door. Don't want Riley getting out again."

"How's he doing? Is he getting used to his new home?"

"I think so." She tapped a finger to her chin. "He hasn't destroyed anything yet...I left him behind today, and he didn't seem to mind."

"That's good to hear. It was nice having him around, though," Luke said. "Reminds me a lot of my childhood dog."

"Was he a Golden Retriever too?"

Luke shook his head. "A husky. His name was Moose."

"Moose?" Emma's brows lifted as her lips curled into a smile. "Is there a story behind the name?"

Luke's gaze went distant, his eyes clouding with memories from a time that seemed both a moment and a lifetime ago. "Yeah, Moose. I was five years old when I named him, and I like to think I was pretty creative back then. Moose and I used to do everything together. There was a park across the street from my dad's apartment, and I'd walk him around it every day before school. And then again when I'd get home later in the day. He slept at the foot of my bed every night, and always woke me up in the morning by licking my face."

Emma leaned in. "Aww. Riley does the same thing."

"I noticed." Luke chuckled, rubbing the back of his neck. "Riley's a special dog. Just like Moose was."

"I'm glad you think so." Emma glanced at the ground then back at Luke. "Now I'm a little bummed I didn't bring him with me."

"Well, that's okay. Other than fixing your doorknob, do you have any plans for the day?"

Emma shifted the car keys in her hand. "Just picking up my grandfather later."

Luke glanced toward the horizon, where the cerulean blue of the sea met the sky. A gentle breeze ruffled his hair, carrying the scent of salt and freedom. "Well, how about going for a walk?" He pointed vaguely in the direction of the ocean. "I haven't seen much of the beach yet. Maybe we can grab a bite afterward?"

"I'm down for that. There's a secret spot that the tourists don't know about—I could show you," Emma responded, a playful glint in her eyes.

A grin unfolded on Luke's face. "Let's do it. Lead the way."

13

Emma

With Luke by her side, Emma felt her heart race as they stepped onto the street. The sound of the waves crashing on the shore accompanied them as their footsteps echoed on the pavement on the way down to the beach.

As they walked together, she found herself drawn to his easygoing nature, his thoughtfulness, and his genuine kindness. He was a breath of fresh air, and she felt comfortable around him in a way she hadn't with Chad.

Continuing down the boardwalk, Emma confided in Luke, giving him advice about Jeremiah, and he listened attentively, showing a level of care and understanding that touched her heart.

Although Luke's warmth and sincerity were disarming, memories of her failed marriage still lingered, reminding her of the façade that some men put on in the early stages of a relationship, only to reveal their true colors later. Emma was no stranger to ignoring red flags in the past. She had hoped Chad would change, so she'd turned a blind eye to the warning signs, only to end up where she was now.

Was she setting herself up for heartbreak again?

Lost in her thoughts, she was pulled back to reality by the familiar scent of the sea and the sounds of the lively beachfront.

As they neared the beach entrance, Emma's nose twitched at the tantalizing aroma wafting from a nearby food truck. Without realizing it, they found themselves drawn toward the source of the inviting smells.

"Is there anything vegan here for you?" Luke asked, his eyes scanning the menu displayed on the side of the truck.

Emma smiled, touched by his consideration. "I usually go for the boardwalk fries. I haven't had them in almost a year."

Luke turned to the cashier. "Can we get your largest size of boardwalk fries?"

"Coming right up!" The man behind the window smiled as he took Luke's payment.

Emma let out an amused chuckle that hung in the air. It was the sound of someone who had been through this before and knew what to expect.

Luke looked at her, his brows knit together. "What?"

"That's what." Emma raised her arm, pointing ahead.

Luke's eyes widened as he turned back to the vendor. He had accidentally ordered the jumbo size, which was enormous—roughly equivalent to a quart of fries doused in vinegar and salt.

"Well, I hope you're hungry," Luke said.

Emma picked up a piping-hot fry and examined it before

taking a cautious bite. "These are *perfect*."

As they stepped onto the sandy shore, Emma took the lead, moving in the opposite direction of the beachgoers frolicking in the water and lounging under the sun.

She noticed the curiosity in Luke's eyes.

"Where are we going?" he asked.

Emma flashed a mischievous grin. "Just keep following me. I promise it'll be worth your while." Leading him to a stone wall, she slipped behind one of the larger rocks.

Luke trailed behind her, peering over her shoulder. "Wow! This is incredible."

"Wait until you see where it leads," Emma teased with a smile. "Come on."

She led him along the hidden path until a towering lighthouse emerged in the distance.

Emma's eyes scanned the surroundings until she spotted a picnic table nestled at the base of the lighthouse. "Let's sit there," she said, nodding in its direction.

As they strolled toward it, the ocean came into view, stretching as far as Emma could see. A small sloop bobbed on the waves, leaving a trail of white foam in its wake. Nearby, palm trees lining the beach rustled and swayed with the gentle ocean breeze.

They settled down at the picnic table, diving into the fries and deeper conversation. As they exchanged stories about their lives, hopes, and dreams, time seemed to slip away. Before they realized it, not only was the jumbo bucket of fries empty, two hours had also passed.

Emma's eyes darted down to her watch. "Is that really the time?"

Luke chuckled. "I guess it is. We should probably head back now, don't you think?"

Emma nodded, and as she rose from the bench, her foot caught on a large rock. She stumbled.

Luke reached for her, his arms wrapping around her waist in one swift movement. "Steady."

"Th-thank you," Emma stammered, her pulse quickening as she met his gaze. "For catching me."

Luke smiled. "Anytime."

Emma turned away, heat flooding her cheeks. Her thoughts swirled, trying to make sense of the sudden pull she felt.

She took a deep breath to compose herself and decided it was best to focus on the path ahead.

As they walked back, Emma replayed the moment in her head, reliving the sensation of being held in his arms. A mix of emotions tugged at her, blending attraction with the haunting fear of past mistakes. In the silent spaces between each heartbeat, she grappled with these conflicting truths.

When they arrived back at the rescue parking lot, Emma turned and faced Luke. "Thanks for the walk. And the fries. And for making sure I didn't face-plant," she said with a smile.

"Well, I wasn't just going to watch you fall." Luke laughed. "Next time, I'll think twice about ordering the jumbo size. I probably won't have to eat lunch now. We should do it again sometime."

Emma's heart fluttered at the thought of spending more time with him, but she tried to play it cool. "Yeah, that would be fun."

With a pause that felt a touch too long, charged with unspoken words and possibilities, they finally said their goodbyes.

Afterward, Emma walked toward the rescue building, replaying the day's events. As she neared the entrance, the doors flew open.

"Ugh!" Charlotte groaned, storming out. Her toffee-toned hair swayed behind her as her tall, slender frame moved quickly. Just as she was about to run into Emma, a gust of wind blew, causing some strands to whip forward.

Emma reached out, grabbing Charlotte's arm. "Hey, hey, hey, wait a minute. What's going on?"

Charlotte shook her head, and as she did, her hair fell onto her face. She irritably brushed it away. "Oh, nothing. And everything." She sighed, her shoulders slumping. "Why do guys have to be so frustrating sometimes? Or all the time?"

"You'll have to give me a little more than that," Emma said.

"Jeremiah told me I look prettier when I smile, but I'm not his type because I'm way 'too bossy' for him," Charlotte said, holding up air quotes. "He's just mad because I had to babysit him today when we had to walk the dogs. He couldn't even put on their leash harnesses without my help!"

Emma observed Charlotte's uncharacteristic irritation and anger. She had never seen her so affected by anyone before, except when she argued with her mother, which was always infused with humor. She almost wanted to laugh but knew it wouldn't help the situation.

From her vantage point, Emma noticed Jeremiah emerge from the rescue, his gaze darting toward Charlotte. In response, Charlotte stiffened, crossing her arms and tilting her chin up, pointedly ignoring his presence. Amused by the scene, Emma couldn't help but let a smile slip, quickly masking it as she turned to look at Luke's car.

After Jeremiah settled into the passenger seat and Luke began to pull out of the parking lot, he raised his hand in a farewell gesture to Emma. She waved back.

"Don't wave at him." Charlotte grabbed her hand and forced it down. "He doesn't deserve it."

Emma turned back to the sulking teenage girl. "Who? Luke?"

She shook her head. "Ew, gross! I meant Jeremiah," she said. "He's such a baby. Like, go back to pre-K and learn some manners."

Emma wanted to tell Charlotte to give him a break but decided against it. She was already mad enough, and Emma didn't want to make it worse.

"There's my best girls." Liam walked up and put a hand on each of their shoulders. "Don't worry about that boy, sweetheart."

Charlotte sighed. "I'm going back inside."

Liam and Emma watched as Charlotte hurried back through the main doors.

"Well, shall we go and get some ice cream?" Liam asked.

"Oh..." Emma put a hand on her full stomach. "Can I take a raincheck on that ice cream?"

Liam smiled. "Of course. It's about time for my afternoon nap anyway."

"Let's head back to your house then."

—⁓⁓—

A few minutes later, Emma pulled onto the road and started off in the direction of Liam's house. The road ahead meandered along the coastline, with sparkling blue waves on one side and quaint beach cottages on the other.

"Hey, Grandpa, how was Jeremiah today?"

Liam turned to her. "He was fine. Quiet, that one. Although he did say something to Charlotte that got under her skin."

"Jeremiah's mother, Luke's wife, passed away two years ago," Emma explained, her eyes on the road. "Ever since then, he's had difficulty expressing his emotions, especially around his father. I'm sure you noticed how they don't talk much."

Liam pursed his lips, nodding slowly. "Yes, I saw. He's a good kid deep down. I just wish he didn't upset poor Charlotte."

Emma chuckled. "Poor Charlotte indeed."

"So, why do you care so much about Luke and his son?" Liam teased. "Are you trying to tell me something?"

"Grandpa, come on."

"Where did you two run off to? Don't think I didn't notice."

Emma blushed and looked out her window as they pulled into Liam's driveway. "We just took a walk. It was nothing."

Liam grinned. "Okay, Em. If you say so."

Emma chuckled at her grandfather's playful teasing and

they said their goodbyes. As she left his house and arrived home, an energetic Riley greeted her at the door. After tending to Riley's needs, she yawned and settled into a well-deserved nap on the couch.

A few hours later, refreshed, Emma tidied up the house before making dinner. She pulled out a bag of frozen vegetables and tofu to stir-fry. When she had thrown everything into the wok, her phone started buzzing. She rushed to grab it from the counter; it was a text from an unknown number.

Unknown: *Hey, it's Luke. I hope it's alright if I text you.*

The grin on Emma's face spread from ear to ear as she added him to her phone contacts.

Emma: *Of course, it's alright. But how'd you get my number? And why didn't you ask for it earlier? :)*

Luke: *I got it from Ada, who insisted I reach out to you, even though I told her I just saw you this afternoon. And I didn't ask for it today because I didn't want to seem too forward.*

Emma: *It's not too forward. Text me anytime. :)*

Luke: *Okay, I will.*

Sitting back, Emma clutched the phone close to her chest and read the message not once, but twice more. She wasn't sure why she had done that, but it was clear Luke had sparked something in her that she hadn't felt in a long time.

14

Luke

THE GENTLE CHIRPING OF crickets filled the evening air, and Luke, standing on the porch, took a deep breath, letting the soothing sounds calm his restless mind. Glancing at his phone, he realized he had texted Emma impulsively. Although he had used his nosy neighbor as an excuse to start a conversation, the truth was that he wanted to talk to her.

Deciding to head back in, Luke stepped through the door and entered the kitchen, surveying the aftermath of their dinner—scattered dishes, crumpled napkins, and open drawers.

How could two people create such a mess?

Despite the usual silence between them, tonight had marked a small change. To his surprise, Jeremiah had joined him at the table for dinner. Granted, they ate without conversation, and as soon as Jeremiah finished his plate, he retreated to his room, leaving Luke to clean up the mess alone. Even so, to Luke, it was progress.

After tidying up the kitchen, wiping down the counters, and rinsing the dishes, he moved to the living room, switching on the TV. He flipped through the channels until he found a baseball game he was somewhat interested in watching. During the commercials, he scrolled through the messages between him and Emma, rereading each word.

Luke felt an irresistible force pulling him toward Emma—one he found both comforting and unsettling. Although her eyes held a guarded caution, he understood, for he too was nursing his own heartache. In his world, the memory of Kate still lingered. Though two years had drifted by, the pain was as raw as it was precious.

Would the pain ever go away?

Could he dare to open his heart to the possibility of love once more?

He wasn't certain.

But as he reflected more on his emotions toward Emma, he convinced himself it was just his body's response to being around a beautiful woman after such a long time. He didn't want to risk losing their friendship by acting on his attraction. And the last thing he wanted to do was lead her on, especially considering what he had heard about her ex-husband; she had endured enough heartbreak for one lifetime.

Luke switched off the TV and rose from the couch, making his way around the house to turn off the lights and secure the doors for the night. After climbing up the creaky stairs toward his bedroom, he paused briefly outside Jeremiah's room and smiled.

More than anything, he wanted to be a stable presence for his son. He knew it would be best to avoid any potential romantic feelings for Emma, despite the undeniable connection he felt.

⁓ele⁓

Several days passed before Luke and Jeremiah stood in the principal's office at Hadley Cove High School. The walls of the room were lined with rich mahogany bookshelves and a large oak desk at the center. Principal Kennedy sat behind the desk, framed by a large window that offered a view of the tranquil courtyard.

After Jeremiah's transcripts arrived from Chicago, Principal Kennedy requested a meeting with the father-son duo to discuss Jeremiah's academic standing and plans for the upcoming fall semester. Despite the impressive surroundings, Luke couldn't shake his apprehension regarding Jeremiah's behavior. He hoped his son would cooperate this time; another expulsion was simply not an option.

They took their seats as Principal Kennedy cleared his throat. "Let's get straight to the point, Jeremiah," he said in a stern voice. "Your grades from last year are concerning, and I have reservations about admitting you as a senior. We take academics seriously here."

Jeremiah looked at the ground, his arms crossed tightly over his chest.

Leaning slightly forward in his seat, Luke addressed Principal Kennedy. "If I may, sir, Jeremiah was an honor roll student all throughout middle school and his freshman year," he said. "The reason his grades suffered afterward was because of the passing of my wife, his mother. It was cancer."

"I see," the principal said. "I'm very sorry for your loss."

Luke nodded. "Thank you, Mr. Kennedy. It hasn't been easy. Jeremiah and his mother were close. But this year I've reduced my work hours and plan to be more involved in Jeremiah's education."

Jeremiah glanced at his father before looking back down at the floor.

"Looks like we might need to take some time with this," Principal Kennedy said. As he shuffled through Jeremiah's transcripts, the intercom on his phone buzzed, and he pressed the blinking button. "Yes?"

"Sir, the staff supervisor of the history club is here," the secretary said. "He has some forms for you to fill out to participate in the National History Bee this year."

The principal paused, glancing up from his desk. "Can it wait? I'm in a meeting right now."

"The deadline for the forms is tomorrow, sir."

Principal Kennedy sighed and pushed his chair back. "My apologies. I'll be right back."

Luke nodded as the principal left the room and closed the door. As they waited, Luke turned to his son. "Jeremiah, can you try to show a little interest?"

Jeremiah began examining his fingernails. "Maybe I'll just drop out."

Luke paused, gathering his thoughts. "Drop out? And do what?"

Jeremiah threw his hands up. "Whatever, I don't know. You never cared before. Why do you care so much now?"

Luke felt a pain in his chest at Jeremiah's words, but he didn't let it show. "Think about what your mother would've wanted for you. Do you think she would've wanted you to drop out and not finish high school? She had high hopes for you to go to a good college. What do you think she'd say now?"

Jeremiah shot Luke a glare, then looked back down at the floor. The uncomfortable silence hung in the room until Principal Kennedy returned to his desk.

"A thousand apologies for the interruption," he said. "We're preparing to enter the National History Bee for the upcoming year. Last year and the year before, two of our students placed in the spring competition. We're hoping this year we can finally bring home the championship."

Luke smiled while Jeremiah continued to stare at the floor.

Principal Kennedy picked up the transcripts and began flipping through them again. "Now hold on here. It says in your freshman and sophomores year you took part in the History Bee championship. You were the Illinois State History Bee champion, and the second runner-up at the National History Bee two years ago. Why didn't you say so?"

State champ? National runner-up? Faintly, Luke recalled receiving texts from Kate about Jeremiah's competitions while on business trips, but he had never followed up for one reason or another.

Jeremiah looked away and shrugged nonchalantly.

Luke reached over, placing a hand on his wrist. "Principal Kennedy is asking you a question."

Jeremiah snatched his wrist away. "I guess it slipped my

mind."

Luke gave him a stern look as Principal Kennedy chimed in. "You shouldn't be so modest, Jeremiah," he said. "A streak like yours is unheard of. Better than anything we've seen from any of our students over the years."

Luke sat frozen.

How could he have missed so much of his son's life? And for what? Spreadsheets? Meetings? Needy clients?

He didn't think he had been *that* terrible of a father, but now more than ever, he realized his shortcomings.

Looking at his son, he longed to wash away all his mistakes, to tell him sorry for everything. But right now, all he could do was hope the principal would allow Jeremiah to start his senior year.

Principal Kennedy began typing at his computer. "I'm finding all the competitions you've participated in over the years. Quite remarkable, Jeremiah."

Pride swelled within Luke as he looked at his son. "He is, isn't he?"

The principal leaned back in his chair. "I'll tell you what, Jeremiah and Mr. Grayson. I'm impressed. Now, I understand the impact a death can have on a student's coursework, so here's what I propose: I'll pass you to your senior year with the condition that for the first semester you'll be on probation to see how things go. It would also be nice for you to join the school's history club. They sure could use your help."

Luke's heart leaped. "Thank you, sir. We really appreciate it."

Jeremiah, however, remained quiet and looked down at

his hands. Luke knew his son was still upset with him, and he couldn't blame him.

Principal Kennedy stood up and extended his hand to Luke, who shook it firmly. Then he turned to Jeremiah.

Luke gave Jeremiah a gentle nudge, prompting him to shake the principal's hand. When Jeremiah finally reciprocated the gesture, Luke's shoulders relaxed. "We look forward to registering for classes later in the week," Luke commented, making his way to the door.

Jeremiah was the first out of the office. Luke hurried to catch up, struggling to match his son's quick pace.

"Son, I'm so proud of you and I'm so sorry for missing all your competitions," Luke said.

Jeremiah sighed, dismissing him with a cold shoulder as they reached the main entry doors. Luke wanted to keep praising him but sensed now was not the time.

When they arrived home, Jeremiah headed upstairs and slamming his bedroom door.

After a moment's pause and a deep breath, Luke stepped into his office. Sitting down, he opened his laptop and logged in to his wife's digital scrapbook, labeled *Kate's Mementos and Memories*, which she had put together before falling sick.

A bittersweet smile tugged at the corners of his lips when he saw a picture of himself, Kate, and a five-year-old Jeremiah, happily together. The files were organized by year, and he clicked through the folders of Jeremiah's freshman and sophomore years. Within those folders, he found photos of Jeremiah holding the trophies and medals he had earned from competitions, videos of him practicing with

Kate, and recordings of the competitions themselves.

Letting out a heavy sigh, Luke shut his laptop and slumped back in his chair. Tears welled in his eyes as he reflected on the growing distance between him and Jeremiah, each memory like a needle pricking his heart. He made a silent pledge to himself: he would do whatever it took to fix things with his son.

As the weight of the day pressed down on him, the comfort of Emma's presence lingered in his mind. There was something about her he couldn't quite put into words. Maybe it was the way she listened or how she seemed to always know exactly what to say. Whatever it was, Luke felt an undeniable pull toward her he hadn't expected.

He reached for his phone and began to type:

Hey Emma, how are things going?

He paused, rereading the message. Erasing it, he tried again:

Emma, hope you're doing well tonight.

But that didn't sound right either. Deleting the words again, he typed a third time:

Was thinking about our last chat. How are you?

Staring at the screen, his fingers hovered over the send button a second too long. With a sigh, he deleted the message not wanting to seem too eager or desperate. He placed the phone facedown, telling himself that next week would be a better time.

15

Emma

FOUR DAYS HAD PASSED since Luke had last texted her.

Four.

Emma glanced at the clock, half-expecting to hear from Luke. *Why am I even waiting for a text?*

While his image occasionally drifted into her mind, she quickly reminded herself it was just a fleeting crush. She reasoned that his outreach had only been out of concern for his son.

Pushing the thought aside, she resolved to move on, dismissing the short-lived infatuation.

Fortunately, the timing couldn't have been better for Emma. She had just begun teaching summer classes at Hadley Cove High and had also been occupied with her tutoring sessions, leaving her little spare time to dwell on her thoughts.

One day after locking up her classroom, she was surprised to see Luke and Jeremiah exiting the front office.

Luke, with a hefty stack of papers in hand, seemed to be discussing something with Jeremiah, who looked disinterested.

Emma had no choice but to head in their direction.

Approaching Luke, she straightened her posture and consciously relaxed her muscles. But as she drew nearer, her cheeks flushed. "Well, hello," she said, maintaining her best poker face. "Fancy meeting you here."

Luke smiled. "Hey there. What are you doing here?"

Emma's heart fluttered at the sound of his voice. "Summer school." She held up her ID badge. "I teach a couple of courses. And run tutoring sessions as well."

"Ah, that's right." Recognition seemed to flicker in Luke's eyes. "I think I remember you mentioning that," he said. "Sorry I forgot."

A rush of warmth coursed through Emma. "No worries," she said, wiping her sweaty palms on her pants. "How about you two? What brings you here today?"

Jeremiah rolled his eyes. "Registering for the fall semester."

Luke interjected, "Yeah, we picked up the syllabi for his classes so he can start preparing."

Jeremiah let out an exasperated sigh. "Keys?"

Luke retrieved a set of car keys from his pocket. "Take these with you as well." He handed the stack of papers to Jeremiah, who snatched them and walked off.

Emma watched their exchange, then turned back to Luke.

"We met with Principal Kennedy yesterday," he explained. "As long as he stays out of trouble, he'll be able to start his senior year. I really hope it works out this time."

As Luke spoke, Emma found herself getting lost in his ocean-blue eyes. She had told Lisa and her grandfather that there was nothing between her and Luke, but being in his presence made it difficult to remember that.

Emma nodded. "I promise I'll pay extra attention to him. If he needs it, I can help with tutoring or extra credit too."

"I'd appreciate that. I better go before Jeremiah takes off to Mexico," Luke said with a laugh. "See you around."

"Sure. Yeah. See you later," Emma said, releasing a deep breath she hadn't realized she'd been holding.

After her conversation with Luke, Emma continued down the hallway and saw Kara and Charlotte walking through the main doors. Charlotte appeared somewhat glum.

"Hey, y'all. What's up?"

Charlotte sighed. "Lame summer school. That's what."

"She needs to bring her math grade up a bit," Kara said. "So, she has to take some classes for extra credit before the fall semester starts."

Emma offered Charlotte a reassuring smile. "Hey, at least you're stuck here with me."

"I guess." Charlotte gave her a half-smile, then walked away.

Kara shook her head. "I love her, but she is such a handful sometimes."

Emma raised a brow. "Really? I thought Charlotte was one of those self-sufficient kids."

Kara leaned in, lowering her voice. "She used to be such a breeze, but now? Every little thing is an episode."

Emma smiled. "There's never a dull moment with you two."

Kara rolled her eyes with a playful smirk. "Add the attention from boys into the mix, and it's a whole new level of drama."

"Boys, right? You remember how we were when we were her age."

"That I do. Speaking of boys, will you be seeing Luke anytime soon?" Kara teased.

Emma's cheeks turned tomato-red. She looked down and cleared her throat. "I should get to class."

Kara grinned. "Alright, I won't pry. But keep me updated. See you later."

"Take care," Emma said as she hugged Kara.

She watched Kara walk down the hall, then turned on her heel and headed in the opposite direction.

As she passed by the front office, Principal Kennedy called out to her. "Oh, Ms. Wright! Ms. Wright! You're just the person I was looking for."

Emma turned in his direction. "Yes, what can I do for you?"

"Well, it's what you can do for *us*, actually," he said. "Do you remember Mrs. Anderson?"

Emma paused, narrowing her eyes. "She teaches calculus, right?"

"You've got a good memory. Well, she was expecting at the end of the spring semester, and she's due any day now. The sub we'd lined up resigned. Would you be willing to cover her class full-time during her maternity leave, through the end of October?"

Emma nodded. "Of course, I'll step in."

"You're a lifesaver, Ms. Wright. Here's Mrs. Anderson's classroom roster and the keys," the principal said, handing them to her. "In case you want to check her lesson plans, she mentioned having them in a filing cabinet behind her desk."

She took the items from him. "It looks like I have my work cut out for me."

Emma chuckled to herself as she made her way to Mrs. Anderson's classroom. She had never held a full-time substitute position for that long before.

Glancing down at the roster, Emma read through the names. *Charlotte Walker, Jeremiah Grayson*...both in the same class. *This should be fun*, she thought with a wry smile.

16

Luke

One month later

THE WARM AUGUST SUN hung brightly overhead as Luke eagerly finished his afternoon conference call. He looked up at the clock—it was almost time to pick up Jeremiah from his first day of school. He hadn't received any frantic phone calls from the principal yet, which he considered a positive sign.

On the drive over, Luke rolled down the windows of his Range Rover, putting on an upbeat country song to set the mood. As he cruised down the coastal highway, he realized this small town's charm was growing on him.

At the school, Luke spotted Jeremiah bursting through the main doors, making a beeline for the SUV. Once his son was settled inside, Luke rolled the window up and switched off the music.

"So, how was it?" Luke asked, turning out of the parking

lot. "Make any new friends?"

Jeremiah turned away and stared out the window.

"Well, how about lunch? Was the food alright? We can pick something up later if you want to bring it in tomorrow."

"Don't act like you care," Jeremiah said.

Luke's body tensed, coiled like a tightly wound spring, as he pulled the car over to the side of the road.

Jeremiah whipped his head around. "What are you doing? I can't be late to the rescue. Right?"

Luke centered himself with a measured breath to steady his nerves. "Look, son. I'm not perfect. And I know I've failed you in every possible way. But since Mom passed, I've been trying to make things right between us. I'm trying—I really am." He hesitated, his voice cracking slightly. "You know, I lost her too."

Jeremiah kept his eyes fixed out the window and didn't respond.

Embracing the silence, Luke dropped the subject, hopeful that some of his words had struck a chord with his son.

As they arrived at Second Chance Rescue, Luke spotted a group of playful puppies tumbling around in the outdoor enclosure. "I'll be back here in three hours. We can pick up some pizza for dinner—your choice."

Jeremiah gave a faint nod and quickly stepped out and went inside.

With a few hours to spare, Luke wasn't quite ready to head straight home. The nearby beach seemed inviting, especially with such great weather. He decided to drive over and parked right by the entrance.

After locking the car, he fell into step with the other beachgoers. The scents of saltwater taffy and popcorn drifted from the nearby vendors as seagulls circled overhead, their calls mingling with the murmur of the waves.

Venturing farther down the shoreline, he passed dunes covered in tall grass swaying in the gentle breeze. Beyond them, the water sparkled in the sunlight, reflecting the azure sky above. The sand was cool under his bare feet, and the water just as refreshing as it lapped at his toes. With each step, memories of Kate, Jeremiah, and the move to this small town surfaced in his mind.

Had it been the right decision?

Kate always seemed to think it would be. She didn't mind the big city, but he knew she only lived there for him. She belonged in a place like this near the water, and strangely enough, now so did he.

Luke's heart skipped a beat at the sight of a familiar face bounding toward him. "Riley!" he called out with a smile, kneeling to pet the dog he had come to know during his week-long stay. Riley wagged his tail, clearly happy to see Luke, as though they were old friends. "What are you doing out here, boy?"

Luke's eyes swept the area, looking for Emma, hoping he'd see her again.

"Riley! Riley, where'd you go?" a woman called out.

Luke turned around to see a blonde woman he hadn't met before. Her smile hinted at a curious sense of recognition, as if she already knew him.

"Luke, right?"

"That's right," he said, tilting his head. "But I'm sorry, I have no idea who you are."

The woman burst into laughter. "I'm Lisa," she said with a smile. "Emma asked me to bring Riley down here for a walk since she got stuck at school."

He held out his hand. "It's nice to meet you, Lisa."

"Likewise. And she'll be here any minute now, in case you were wondering," she said with a wink.

How'd she know?

Luke's lips curved into a smile as he scanned the beach for any signs of Emma.

Lisa's voice interrupted his search: "Oh, there she is."

As Emma ran across the sand toward them, the breeze coming off the water made her auburn curls loosen and break free from her bun. Loose strands of hair bounced against her cheeks and neck, chasing each other across the canyon of her collarbones and chest. He had never seen her look more beautiful than she did at that moment.

"Hey!" Emma called out, pushing her hair from her face. "I didn't expect to see you here."

"I didn't either," he said. "Well, I thought maybe after seeing Riley I might."

She smiled. "Out for a stroll?"

Luke nodded. "It's the perfect weather for it."

"I agree," she said, still standing a couple of feet from him.

"Oh! Lisa." Emma turned to her friend as if she had forgotten she was there. "Thanks for taking Riley for me."

"No problem." Lisa handed over the leash.

"Have you two met?" Emma asked.

"Just now." Luke reached down to scratch Riley behind the ears. "Well, this sweet boy came up to me first, and then

I bumped into Lisa."

"I can hold on to him for a little while longer," Lisa said. "He's good at snagging hunks that are walking along the beach."

A crimson blush crept up Luke's cheeks as he chuckled. He noticed Emma smile as she gave Lisa a slight elbow. Her smile held a mesmerizing power over him that soothed his soul and reminded him of all the wonderful things in life.

As Luke stared into Emma's eyes, he recalled a card he had received from an old friend after Kate's funeral. Written on it was a C. S. Lewis quote, originally penned in a letter to Mary Willis Shelburne in 1963:

There are better things ahead than any we leave behind.

Ever since he first read it, he had wanted to believe those words—not to replace his love for Kate, but to find happiness again.

Maybe it is true, he thought.

At least he hoped it was.

Just then, the sounds of laughter and splashing caught Luke's attention. A group of teenagers shrieked as a wave caught them off guard, sending them tumbling into the surf.

Weeks had slipped by since he last saw Emma, and now they stood together at the shoreline. The beach was a place of endless possibilities and seeing her again felt like a breath of fresh air. Being apart from her had made him realize how much he enjoyed her company, and he couldn't wait to find out what else the day would bring.

17

Emma

The beach, a familiar sight, always had a way of speaking to Emma's soul. Its timeless beauty had been the backdrop of many memories. But today, the unexpected presence of the one man she couldn't forget took her breath away.

There, against the amber glow of the endless horizon, stood Luke. His white shirt, ruffled by the wind, seemed to merge with the foamy waves behind him, creating a vision that was as much a part of the beach as the sand beneath her feet. But it was his eyes, those deep pools of sapphire, that truly captivated her.

"I'm gonna take Riley further down." Lisa grabbed the leash back from Emma. "Y'all should hang out."

"Thanks for taking Riley. I'll text you when I'm on my way back."

"Take your time." Lisa flashed a hashtag sign with her fingers and mouthed "Lemma" as Luke looked away.

Emma rolled her eyes and turned toward Luke as they

began to walk down the beach.

"Had a good day back in the classroom?" he asked.

"It was so busy I hardly had a moment to think, but I loved every bit. Teaching just feels right for me."

Just then, Chad's biting comments about her teaching job seeped into her thoughts. *Just a teacher,* his voice echoed, as if she had settled for less. The weight of past criticisms tried to pull her into a spiral of insecurity, but she shook it off, focusing on Luke.

"What about you? Tell me about your work," she asked.

He began sharing details about his career as a financial consultant and his travels. Each word Luke spoke, filled with confidence and stories of faraway places, drew her in, making her wish the day would never end.

Rounding a bend, they spotted a beachfront bistro with a blinking neon sign: *The Point.*

"That place any good?" Luke asked.

Emma nodded, a grin spreading across her face. "The food is to die for. I haven't been here in forever," she said, her eyes brightening.

"Well, I'm hungry," Luke said. "How about you?"

She laughed as her stomach growled. "Famished."

Luke held out his arm with a devilish smile on his lips. "Shall we?"

As Emma hooked her arm around his, a surge of excitement coursed through her. The sensation of his muscular arm linked with hers triggered memories of the moment he had caught her. Together, they walked toward the entrance of the restaurant.

Emma's eyes darted to the people entering the foyer. She

gripped Luke's arm tighter. A shiver raced down her spine. *Why here? Why now?*

Luke raised an eyebrow. "You okay?"

Emma felt an invisible weight pressing down on her chest, squeezing the air from her lungs. "Chad and Ashley are here," she said, turning away, hoping they hadn't spotted her.

Luke followed her gaze, then turned back to her. "Well, I'll be by your side the whole time. But it's up to you if you want to go in or not. We can always find someplace else."

Emma tried to take a deep breath, but it was like inhaling through a narrow straw. Gathering her courage, she responded, "Let's just go in. It'll be fine," more to reassure herself than anyone else.

When Luke took her hand, a warm, electric sensation pulsed through her veins. Each step they took together felt significant, like the chapters of a story she had never dared to imagine.

Her chest tightened—not from anxiety this time, but from an overwhelming sense of security she felt with Luke, unlike with anyone else before.

With Luke by her side, she felt as if nothing and no one could hurt her.

By the time they reached the top, a gentle gust of wind reminded her to inhale deeply, to absorb not just the air, but the magic of the moment.

As they neared the entrance, Emma summoned the strength to glance toward where Chad and Ashley sat. Their eyes locked and she could see a hint of surprise, and maybe even a twinge of jealousy on Chad's face. It was a look that, in the past, would have unraveled her, a look that would have had her second-guessing her every move.

But the fear and trepidation that had once dominated her life was no longer there.

The satisfaction of that moment, of standing tall with Luke, was sweeter than she had imagined.

They had reached the hostess stand when the sudden clearing of a throat interrupted her thoughts. The soft glow of lights and the aroma of delicious food greeted them, alongside the distant hum of dinner music.

The owner, Luis, with his receding hairline and a thick black mustache, approached with a smile. "Emma! You're back."

"It's good to see you too," she said.

"And you've brought a friend with you?" Luis raised his eyebrows suggestively.

Emma giggled. "Luis, this is Luke." She gestured toward him. "Luke, meet Luis, the owner and a good friend of mine."

Luke extended a hand with a friendly nod, and Luis grasped it in a welcoming handshake. Luke looked down at Emma and chuckled. "So, I guess you come here pretty often."

"Well, I used to." She paused, taking a moment. "With Chad."

Luke squeezed her hand. "Well, you're here with me now. So, here's to new memories."

A smile danced on Emma's lips, her eyes meeting his. "To new memories," she whispered.

"I have to run and grab Carmen. She'll be dying to see

you," Luis said as he scurried off to the back.

As Luis disappeared, Emma turned to Luke. "Carmen is Luis's sister. They own this place together. They're really nice people."

Luke surveyed the inviting restaurant. "I love the vibes here."

Not long after, the gentle sound of quick footsteps approached. Carmen, with her graying-black hair pulled into a tight bun, rushed up to the hostess stand. Her eyes lit up as they landed on Emma.

"Emma!" Carmen bounced on her toes. "Oh, my goodness, it's been ages!"

"I know. Right?" Emma flashed her a dazzling smile and leaned in for a hug.

Carmen pulled back, her gaze sweeping over Emma. "You're glowing!" She shot a glance at Luke, raising an eyebrow. "I can see why."

"Aww. Thank you," Emma said. "This is Luke. He's new to Hadley Cove."

Carmen reached her hand out to him. "What a catch." She leaned closer to Emma and whispered, "I call dibs on this one if you decide you don't want him anymore."

Emma laughed, giving Carmen's arm a light swat. "Oh, I'll be sure to let him know."

"You're in for a treat tonight. The chef's specials are amazing. I'll get someone to seat you shortly."

"Is your terrace open?" Emma asked.

"It is, but no one's sitting out there yet. It's still early."

"We'd like to, if that's alright."

"For you, anything! Come with me."

Emma exchanged a glance with Luke as they followed Carmen, their fingers interlaced. Excitement and uncertainty surged through her, being here with someone who made her feel so alive.

Soon, they settled on the terrace, the ocean stretching out before them. The golden light of the afternoon sun created a shimmering path on the water's surface as waves rose and fell, their white crests crashing against the shore in a spray of foam. Seagulls soared overhead, their calls blending with the distant sound of boats and jet skis.

As Emma took in the scene, Luke gave her hand a reassuring squeeze. She daydreamed about a future with him—walks on the beach, lazy Sundays curled up together.

But as quickly as her thoughts wandered into this fantasy, in the quiet corner of her mind, Emma felt a flicker of doubt.

18

Luke

LUKE SETTLED AT THE table, a smile tugging at the corners of his mouth; he'd thoroughly enjoyed the lively banter between Carmen and Emma. Carmen's humor was contagious, and the sound of Emma's laughter was music to his ears.

"Does your nephew still perform here?" Emma asked Carmen, taking a sip of her water.

"Oh, yes! Antonio's here. They haven't started yet, but they'll go live soon. So if you have any requests, better get them in now."

Emma chuckled. "I'm sure he'll play all of my old favorites."

"If he knows you're here, then definitely. Let me get drinks for you both—on the house. Be right back."

"Thanks, Carmen. You're the best," Emma remarked as she picked up the menu and began scanning the options.

"So, what do you recommend?" Luke asked.

"Everything vegan," she said, with a smirk.

Luke tilted his head and smiled. He paused, rubbing his chin. "Where are they on here?"

Emma leaned forward, lowering her menu. "Well, there's spaghetti marinara, butternut squash ravioli, and sweet potato gnocchi. That's one of my faves. I'll probably get that. The pasta here is made without eggs, so it's all vegan. They even have vegan meatballs if you're feeling brave."

Luke tapped his finger on the table. "It all sounds good. I guess I'll try the gnocchi."

A grin crossed Emma's face. "You can have some of mine if you want to try something else."

"Then vegan meatballs it is!" Luke closed his menu and took a gulp of his water.

"Look at you, trying something new," Emma giggled. "But I guess there's a first time for everything."

As Carmen returned with two margaritas and took their orders, Luke glanced at his watch, mindful of his commitment to Jeremiah. He had promised to pick him up from the animal rescue and order pizza for dinner. Luckily, he still had two hours to spare.

Twenty minutes later, their meals arrived. Emma picked up her fork and took a small bite, her eyes closing. "This gnocchi is *everything*."

Luke watched her for a moment, savoring not only his meal, but the way the sun traced each freckle on her face. "What's the most adventurous thing you've eaten?"

She paused, her fingers twirling the edge of her napkin. "In my pre-vegan days, I ate fried crickets at a restaurant in Florida," she admitted, her eyes meeting his with a mix of mischief and mild embarrassment. As she spoke, her nose crinkled, a gesture Luke had come to find endearing. "Not recommended," she added with a playful grimace.

Luke chuckled, leaning in closer. "I can't imagine you crunching on crickets."

She laughed, pushing a stray hair behind her ear. "It was a dare. And I never back down from a dare."

Luke raised an eyebrow. "Oh, really?"

"Of course." Emma tilted her head. "And what about you?"

He paused, bringing a hand to his chin. "Once, during a business trip to Japan, my buddy dared me to try fugu—the pufferfish. It's poisonous if not prepared right."

Emma's eyes widened. "That sounds...terrifying. Did you?"

Luke nodded. "I did. And here I am, alive and well."

They both laughed and continued their light-hearted banter, discussing travel, favorite books, and their most memorable childhood memories. As they delved deeper into conversation, Luke found himself captivated by Emma's stories, learning about her love for astronomy and her dream to visit Greece.

After his second glass of wine and half a plate of sweet potato gnocchi and vegan meatballs, Luke was stuffed. "Those meatballs might be better than the real thing," he said, wiping his face.

Emma chuckled, spearing one off his plate. "It's a bit odd to call them 'meatballs,' don't you think?"

Luke watched as she cut one in half with her fork and knife. "What about neatballs?"

A light blush crept up his neck, realizing how that might've sounded.

Emma bit her lip before bursting into laughter. "That's pretty dumb, but I like it."

Luke took a long drink of water. "Maybe I should lay off the tequila after that one."

"Ah, you're fine," Emma said, cheeks flushed from laughter. "I'm just messing with you."

"Actually, I'm going to use the restroom, if you'll excuse me."

"Sure, I'll be here, picking food off of your plate."

The men's restroom was empty. After finishing his business, he walked over to the sink to wash his hands. As he reached for the soap, he sensed a presence behind him. Instinctively, he turned.

There, standing in front of him, was a man whose face seemed strangely familiar. Their eyes met, and a smug grin spread across the man's face.

Luke's jaw tensed as he turned on the water, finally recognizing the man. "Sorry," he said, the realization sinking in. "Didn't see you there."

"Well, I did see you," Chad said. "Listen, buddy, can I give you a word of advice?"

Luke glanced up at him in the mirror. "What might that be?"

"If I were you, I'd end things with her. It'll only get more complicated. Take it from me," Chad drawled, combing his hair back in the mirror. He didn't wait for Luke to reply before he left.

Luke let those words hang in the air as he dried his hands

with a paper towel.

Leaving the restroom, Luke exchanged its cold tiles for the warmth of the bistro. But an internal chill remained. That smug grin, the underlying warning in Chad's voice—it all was disconcerting.

The band started to play as he came back out and made his way to their table. He sat back down, and found himself watching Emma more intently. She was even more charming than she had been a few minutes ago. Her eyes, like distant stars, shone with each musical note, and her smile, as bright as a coastal sunrise, graced her face as she swayed in tune with the melody.

Her smile grew as he continued to stare at her. "What is it?" she asked. "Do I have something in my teeth?"

Luke shook his head. "No, just looking at you."

Emma's cheeks deepened to a dark shade of scarlet. She took a sip of her water and fanned herself with a napkin. "Does it feel hot in here? Or out here, rather?" she asked, gesturing to the terrace.

"Feels a tad warm." Luke nodded toward the beach. "We could go for a swim."

Emma laughed, shaking her head. "Not *that* warm."

Luke's eyes danced over her figure for a moment, a hungry glance that ended with a playful smile. "Just trying to help."

He noticed a subtle mixture of surprise, intrigue, and perhaps a hint of something more in her gaze. The exchange between them lingered in the air, a spark of connection that neither could deny.

The band had finished playing an upbeat Italian tune

and, as the last notes of music faded away, a slower, sweeter song took its place.

Emma gasped. "I love this song! Antonio sings it with so much emotion." She closed her eyes, as if absorbing the lyrics:

"With every ending, there's a new beginning, a heart once lost always finds its way again..."

Emboldened by the moment, Luke stood up and walked to her side of the table.

She blinked open her eyes, smiling. "What are you doing?"

He reached down, offering his hand. "First time for everything, right? How about a dance?"

"Oh, Luke," she said as her eyes darted around the now crowded terrace. "I don't know. I'm not really a good dancer. And—"

"Well, we don't have to." His voice was gentle and understanding. "But it'd be a lot of fun," he added with a cheeky grin.

Emma chuckled. Despite her initial hesitation, she put her hand in his, allowing him to lead her to the center of the terrace.

As Luke wrapped his arm around her waist, Emma seemed to unwind. "I haven't danced like this since my wedding," she admitted.

"Well, you should do it more often," Luke said with a smirk.

As they swayed to the music, Luke's gaze locked onto Emma's warm, velvet-brown eyes, and his heart raced. The sounds around them faded into the background, and he felt himself being drawn closer and closer to her. He could almost taste the sweetness of her lips, which were only inches from his.

All it would take was one daring move—a gentle lean forward...

19

Emma

Luke pulled back, clearing his throat.

The lingering touch of Luke's fingers left an impression even as he drew away, and the song dwindled to a close, drowned out by the soft applause of the gathered crowd.

"That was...um...Thanks for the dance," Emma said, catching her breath as she sat.

He returned her smile. "Anytime."

The soft chime of his phone alarm broke the spell they were under. "That's my cue to get Jeremiah," Luke said, looking at his phone. "Want to walk back with me?"

The intensity of their moment left Emma flustered. Despite her desire to leave with him, she found herself rooted to the spot, feeling like her knees might buckle if she tried to stand. "I think I'll hang out a bit longer and wait for Lisa. I'm sure she'll want to grab something to eat. It's the least I could do after she watched Riley for me."

Luke smiled. "Alright. I'll take care of the bill." He reached into his wallet and pulled out some cash to leave on the table. "I'll call you soon." He leaned over, giving her a quick hug, then stepped off the terrace and onto the beach.

Pulling out her phone, she quickly texted Lisa. *I'm done. Can you meet me at The Point?*

Emma set her phone down and looked back into the restaurant, observing the other couples eating, drinking, and laughing. She was relieved she hadn't seen Chad and Ashley again; their table had been cleared and seated with another couple.

The evening air began to cool, carrying with it the refreshing hint of salt from the nearby sea. Distant murmurs of crashing waves harmonized with the soft buzz of conversations from neighboring tables.

Though the band played on, the music faded into the background of her thoughts, which were consumed by the spicy, warm scent of Luke's cologne.

Why didn't he kiss me? Emma sighed and discreetly tested her breath with a quick exhale onto her hand. *Well, it wasn't that.*

While a part of her wished Luke had kissed her in that perfect moment, she also understood the need to tread carefully.

A soft touch on her shoulder brought Emma back to the present. "Why'd your man pay and leave you here?" Carmen asked.

Emma smiled, a touch of sadness in her eyes. "He had to pick up his son."

Carmen slid into the seat Luke had vacated moments ago. "You looked happy with him."

"Well, he's a great guy," Emma said, blushing.

The sound of Riley's bark announced Lisa's arrival on the terrace. Emma greeted him with a pat as she took his leash. "Hey, boy."

Lisa dragged a chair over, wedging herself between Emma and Carmen. "Looks like I'm late to the party. What did I miss?"

"I'll tell you about it on our walk home. I need a few minutes," Emma said, massaging her knees.

Lisa batted her eyelashes with a knowing look. "Don't make me wait. Can we stay for one drink? Please? Pretty please? I did watch your dog while you went on a date with Mr. Dreamboat."

"It wasn't a date," Emma said. "It was two friends grabbing food. And yes, one more drink—my treat."

"Sounds like a plan." Lisa turned to Carmen. "Can I get a large piña colada?"

"And I'll take another margarita," Emma added.

When Carmen stood up to fetch their drinks, she winked at a couple entering the bistro, signaling them to a particularly cozy corner table. Emma watched as Carmen exchanged a few brief words with the bartender, pointing toward their table.

She smiled and reached down to give Riley a head scratch. "Did you have fun with Aunt Lisa?"

Riley put his nose up to her hands.

"You're probably hungry. Don't worry, I'll feed you when we get back home."

"Hey, I've got a little something for Riley." Lisa dug into her beach bag, retrieving a small container of dog treats and handing one to him. He gobbled it up before lounging comfortably at their feet.

A few moments later Carmen returned, skillfully balancing a tray with their drinks. "I hope I didn't keep you ladies waiting too long." She placed the drinks on the table. "Things are picking up inside. I'll catch you both later."

Emma lifted her margarita, offering a small toast. "To Carmen."

Lisa grinned, raising her glass as well. "Best service in town. Cheers!"

With Carmen's nod of acknowledgment, Lisa turned back to Emma. "Alright, you have to tell me what happened. Every detail."

Emma sighed, taking a deep breath. "Okay. So, we were walking down the beach toward The Point..."

Nearly an hour passed before Emma finished telling the entire story. The sun had descended toward the horizon, painting the sky a warm palette of oranges, pinks, and purples.

Lisa's mouth dropped open as she leaned back. "I'm all in for Team Lemma!" She reached up, forcing Emma to give her a high-five. "So, how did you two leave it? When are you going to see him again?"

"He said he'd call," Emma said wistfully.

"What's wrong?" Lisa asked.

"I'm a little worried that it's too soon after the divorce to have feelings for another man," Emma confessed, her gaze dropping to the table, fingers tracing the rim of her glass.

"Em, he makes you happy. That's what matters." Lisa reached over to grab her hand. "The heart wants what it wants, and it doesn't always have to make sense."

"I just wonder—what if I'm using Luke as a rebound? I don't want to hurt him like that," Emma said, taking a sip of her margarita.

Lisa tilted her head. "You're overthinking things again, Em," she said softly. "Love has no timeline. You deserve to be happy. And if Luke is the one providing that, then so be it. Don't be too hard on yourself."

"You might be right," Emma admitted.

Lisa swirled the straw in her empty glass. "Another round?"

"No way," Emma told her. "I'm already gonna have a headache tomorrow with a classroom full of kids. I think it's time for us to go."

Lisa sighed, nodding as she began collecting her belongings.

Just then, Emma's phone buzzed with an incoming call, drawing both their attention to the caller ID.

"I can't answer it." Emma pushed the phone away. "I have too much on my mind about all this."

"Stop stalling," Lisa teased, picking up the phone and answering it.

She handed it to Emma.

20

Luke

As THE FOURTH RING filled the night, Emma's voice finally broke through. Luke could almost feel her presence beside him, even from a distance. His shoulders relaxed and he took a deep breath, soaking in the gentle chirping of crickets and the distant hoot of an owl.

"Hey, Luke. Did you forget something?"

"No, I said I'd call you. Remember?"

"Didn't expect you to call this soon," Emma said with a light laugh.

"Oh." The faint strains of music reached Luke's ears. "Are you still at the bistro?"

"Um, guilty," Emma said. "Lisa wanted to grab a drink, so I indulged her."

"That was nice of you."

She sighed. "Yeah. But I think we're heading home now—or back to my place."

Luke hesitated, adjusting his grip on the phone. The

background music from Emma's location seemed distant, overshadowed by the pounding in his ears. His thoughts swirled, battling between doubt and the desire to be transparent. Taking another steadying breath, he prepped himself for a conversation he'd been pondering since their time at the beach.

"You know, Emma," he began slowly, "there's something I've been wanting to tell you."

"Really? What's up?"

He inhaled deeply, weighing his words. "After everything with Kate, it's been tough to be open about my feelings. But I find myself drawn to you in a way I haven't felt in a very long time."

She remained silent.

"Look, I've been trying to rebuild bridges, especially with Jeremiah. And that journey has taught me the importance of seizing the moment," Luke continued. "I sense there's something between us, something worth exploring. And I could be wrong, but maybe you feel it too?"

There was a pause, and Luke's heart rate ratcheted up a notch. An eternity passed.

Emma finally spoke. "Luke, I like you a lot too. It's just—it's scary, you know?"

"I get it," Luke responded, looking out into the distance. "I don't want to push you into anything you're not ready for. We can take things at your pace."

Emma let out a soft sigh. "Thanks. I'd like that."

"Of course. I just want us to be on the same page," Luke said. He took a deep breath before asking the question that had been lingering in his mind. "So, would you like to get together again?"

He shifted his weight from foot to foot as he waited for her response.

"Yes, I would," Emma said.

A rush of warmth tingled through him as he leaned against a tree, feeling the rough bark press into his back.

"But it'll have to be next week," she said. "I've got class and tutoring every day this week, along with baking at night for the dog treat orders coming in. Is that okay?"

"Yeah, of course. I'm just glad you want to see me again."

"I thought that was pretty obvious," she giggled, making Luke's heart skip a beat. "I can't wait to hang out again."

"Me too. There's just one thing." Luke paused, biting his bottom lip. He looked down at his feet as he began pacing. "I really want to share this with Jeremiah, but I'm not sure when or how to do that yet. So is it alright if we just keep this between us for now? I'd hate for him to find out through the grapevine."

Emma groaned. "Oh no. You've heard of the grapevine?"

"Hard not to," Luke admitted with a chuckle. "The most eligible bachelor in Hadley Cove? Yeah, I know about the grapevine."

"Well, at least everything they're saying about you is positive," she teased, and a burst of laughter followed.

"Hopefully it stays that way," he said. "Or if they didn't include me at all in the Hadley Cove gossip, that'd be fine too."

"I definitely can't promise that. But we can keep our date on the down-low," Emma said, her voice reassuring. "And don't worry too much about Jeremiah. You'll know exactly what to say when it's time to talk to him."

Luke let out a sigh. "Thanks. That makes me feel better." He glanced up at the illuminated house, grateful that Jeremiah's bedroom didn't overlook the backyard.

"How did it go with Jeremiah when you picked him up?" Emma asked.

"Really well, actually. We stopped and grabbed a pizza, and he told me about his day without me prompting him every five seconds. Felt like a breakthrough."

"That's awesome! I'm so happy for you. It's all about those baby steps and little victories."

Luke smiled. "It's nice to hear that someone's on my side."

"I'll always be on your side," Emma said. "So, what are you thinking?"

Luke stopped pacing. "About what?"

"For our date next week."

"Oh. Well, maybe dinner again?"

"Eating is one of my specialties," Emma said. "How about Sea Breeze Tavern? It's a bit off the beaten path. Not many town folks visit."

"Perfect. How's next Tuesday?"

"I think I can make that work," Emma said. "Seven?"

"That sounds great to me. I suppose I'd better let you go now. Have fun with Lisa."

"Good night, Luke."

"Night, Emma."

The gentle glow from the house guided Luke's steps as he headed toward the patio. But just as he reached for the door, he was startled by a presence in the kitchen. Jeremiah.

"Who was that?"

Luke had to come up with something quickly. "Just a client I had to call back from earlier."

"Oh." Jeremiah didn't ask any follow-up questions and headed out of the kitchen toward the stairwell. He stopped short of it and turned to face Luke. "Thanks for the pizza night, Dad."

"Anytime, son," he said, relishing the sound of the word *Dad*. "We'll do it again soon."

Luke's heart swelled as he watched Jeremiah walk away. It had been a challenging journey, fraught with ups and downs, but moments like this made it all worthwhile.

The word *Dad* held a depth that Luke had missed hearing for years. It was a reminder of what he was fighting for.

Yet, his footsteps felt heavy as he went upstairs. A weight of guilt pressed down on him for lying to Jeremiah. It was inevitable that he would have to come clean, one day, about him and Emma.

But not tonight.

Luke found himself at a crossroads, torn between his son's trust and the newfound happiness he'd discovered with Emma. To him, love and honesty were important, and he wanted to find a way to honor both without sacrificing either.

21

Emma

EMMA'S HEELS CLICKED ON the wooden floor as she burst into her bedroom. Hangers clinked and clothes flew in every direction as she rummaged through her closet. Dresses, skirts, and blouses swayed with each tug and pull, but none seemed right for her night out with Luke. There was the purple dress, but she'd need to pair it with a sweater, and it was too warm for that. There was also the green skirt and white blouse, but it was a little too casual. Each ensemble she imagined fell short in one way or another.

Browsing through rack after rack, she had almost lost hope when she pushed the last one over and saw it: a forgotten dress she bought last summer. A light sea-foam color with white lace along the bodice and the hem. Slipping into it, she caught her reflection in the mirror.

It fit like a glove.

She matched it with tan strappy heels and let her hair fall to her shoulders. Closing her eyes, she remembered the way

Luke's fingers, warm and gentle, had brushed a stray curl behind her ear. But her daydream was interrupted when a chill shot up her spine. The last time she'd worn this dress was the night Chad served her divorce papers.

She exhaled, pushing that thought aside as she stepped out of her bedroom and walked over to Riley's dog bed.

"How do I look?" she asked, turning in a circle. "Think he'll like it?"

Riley let out a whine and put his head down.

"Well, thanks for the encouragement, buddy."

She walked into the kitchen, making sure his food and water bowls were full, then checked if the back door was locked. Afterward, she took a final look in the mirror and released a deep, steadying breath. The corners of her lips twitched into a smile as she made her way to the door and headed to Sea Breeze Tavern.

Emma arrived about fifteen minutes early, but decided to go in and get a table anyway. As she walked through the entryway, she came face-to-face with Charlotte and Jeremiah.

Masking her surprise, she smiled at them. "Hey guys! Small world, isn't it?"

"Hey, Ms. Wright!" Charlotte said, while Jeremiah offered a more reserved nod. "So what brings you here?"

Emma laughed nervously. "Just picking up a takeout order."

Charlotte looked Emma up and down. "You look awfully dressed up just to be picking up some food."

Emma gave a lighthearted wave of her hand. "Oh, you know me—any excuse to put on a nice outfit." Out of the corner of her eye, she noticed Jeremiah observing her.

Did he know about her planned evening with Luke?

Emma forced a smile just as the hostess walked over to seat Jeremiah and Charlotte.

Charlotte nodded then waved. "Enjoy your dinner, Ms. Wright."

"Will do, thanks!" Emma said, as she watched them vanish around a corner.

Turning on her heel, she quick-stepped to the parking lot and dialed Luke's number.

"Hey, I'm almost there—"

"Luke. We need to go somewhere else." Emma started pacing.

There was a pause. "Why? What do you mean?"

"Uh, your son is here with Charlotte. They already saw me all dressed up and started asking questions."

"You're all dressed up?"

Emma laughed. "Yes, but that's not the point."

"Sorry. So, what's the new plan? I'm all ears."

"Have you ever been to the Treehouse Café?"

"Nope. Never heard of it."

"It's just outside the city limits. The only time people go there is for a wedding anniversary or some other big occasion, and I doubt anyone in Hadley Cove is celebrating theirs on a Tuesday night."

"Okay, let me pull over and put that into my GPS." She waited a minute until he came back on the line. "This is on the other side of Hadley Cove, heading toward Bridwell Bay, right?"

She winced. "Yeah, it's a bit of a drive, but they're open late. I promise it'll be worth it. Heading there now."

"Okay. See you soon."

—ll—

Forty minutes later, Emma pulled up to the Treehouse Café, adjusted her dress, and made her way to the entrance. She went inside, her eyes darting around as she tried to find Luke, hoping she wouldn't bump into anyone she knew.

A familiar voice rang out from behind her. "Hey there."

Emma turned, finding Luke grinning at her.

"You did get dressed up," he said, stepping back to look at her.

Shrugging, she scanned his suit and tie. "You did too."

"You look beautiful, by the way," he added with a playful wink.

"Thank you, sir. And you look rather dashing yourself."

Luke grinned. "Thanks. Now, shall we sit down?"

"Did you already get a table?"

Luke gestured toward the seating area. "Right this way, ma'am."

As they stepped into the grand atrium, Emma admired the stunning view of the high ceilings and tall glass windows, complemented by thick wood-paneled walls covered in heirloom paintings and hanging lanterns.

Luke's head swiveled as he surveyed the surroundings. "Now I see why they call it the Treehouse Café."

"It's stunning," she remarked as they settled at a table by the window, which held a spectacular view of the woods under the twinkling stars.

As Emma picked up the menu, her stomach rumbled and

they both laughed.

"Sounds like someone's ready to order," Luke said.

Emma chuckled, her cheeks warming. "Seems like it."

As they settled on their orders, the server brought over two glasses of wine and a basket of rolls. Emma took a sip, letting the wine's rich taste calm her nerves. Luke plucked a roll from the basket, broke it in half, and buttered it. "Try one," he said, holding out the basket to Emma.

She paused for a split second. Normally, she'd avoid bread before a meal, but she hadn't eaten since lunchtime and couldn't resist tearing one open and taking a bite.

As they shared the rolls, Luke's eyes drifted to the window. "That's the Bridwell Lighthouse, right?"

Emma nodded. "It's a short walk from the beach, but by car, you'd need to loop around the cove to get there."

Luke seemed lost in its beauty.

Emma smiled. "Did you know it's the tallest lighthouse in the country? It dates back to the American Revolution."

He raised his eyebrows at her. "Really? You're like a walking history book."

"Blame it on my grandpa and his endless stories," Emma said, chuckling. "We should walk up there after dinner."

"At this time of night? I don't know. Isn't that something teenagers would do?"

She gave a playful shrug. "Maybe, but why let them have all the fun?"

He chuckled. "You've got me there. Let's do it."

Emma grinned, raising her wineglass. "Here's to us living in the moment."

When the plates arrived, they dug in, savoring every bite.

Even in silence, Emma was comfortable in Luke's presence. She didn't need to fill the air with small talk to feel connected with him.

As she twirled a forkful of butternut squash ravioli into her mouth, she noticed how each ingredient had been perfectly crafted to create a symphony of flavors and textures on her taste buds. She closed her eyes and allowed herself to be fully immersed in its artistry.

When Emma opened them, she saw that Luke seemed to be enjoying every bite of the meal as much as she was. She marveled at how someone like him existed, and her heart overflowed with gratitude for this unexpected gift, as if destiny had orchestrated this very moment.

After finishing their meals, Luke reached for the bill, insisting on paying for dinner, while she protested for a split check. They finally reached a compromise, agreeing that Emma would pay for the next date as they left the restaurant.

Stepping out into the warm Georgia night, the sight of fireflies greeted them. The tiny insects bobbed up and down, illuminating their bodies like miniature spotlights.

Feeling the soft earth beneath her, Emma paused and slipped off her heels, opting to carry them instead. She shot a glance at Luke. "Not the best choice for a little hike, right?"

Luke chuckled, looking down at the heels and then back at her. "Good call."

Emma's gaze settled on a worn wooden sign near a tree-lined path. It had an illustration of the lighthouse. "It's just up that way." She pointed.

Luke extended his hand toward Emma. "Shall we?"

Grinning, Emma slid her hand into his. "Let's go."

The instant warmth and solid feel of his hand sent a gentle, tingling sensation up her arm.

They followed the winding path through the trees, which dipped and rose with the contours of the woods. The fireflies Emma had spotted earlier seemed even more abundant here, flickering their lights in the darkness, allowing them to catch glimpses of the lighthouse through the trees.

They emerged from the woods, and the towering structure came into view, casting its shadow on the water.

A moment of quiet passed between them before Luke broke the silence. "Do they still have lighthouse keepers?"

Emma shook her head. "No, lighthouses are automated nowadays. This one's still maintained, but only comes on for certain occasions, so there's no one inside."

Luke sighed. "It's a shame. I always imagined some quirky old guy living at the top of one."

"Well, there's only one way to find out."

Luke looked down at her. "What do you mean?"

Without answering, Emma led him toward a seemingly forgotten door at the base of the lighthouse. Pushing it gently, she whispered, "It's never locked. Come on."

She opened the door and pulled him inside, lighting their path with the flashlight on her phone.

"Isn't this illegal?" Luke asked, his flashlight beam darting around the room. "Maybe we shouldn't be here."

"It'll be fine. We'll just go up the steps and come back down," Emma said. "I want you to see the view up top."

Sighing, Luke took out his phone and turned on the flashlight. "Alright, but only if we're quick."

Together, they wound their way up the tight spiral stair-case. As they ascended, their initial enthusiasm gave way to fatigue.

Reaching a landing, Emma bent over to catch her breath. "More of a workout than you expected?"

Luke chuckled, pausing to stretch his calf. "If I knew, I would've brought my gym shoes."

Emma playfully nudged him. "Almost there, promise."

When they reached the top, Emma pushed open the door and took Luke's hand, pulling him outside onto the balcony.

"Should we take a picture?" Luke suggested.

Emma grinned as she adjusted her hair. "My hair isn't too crazy, is it?"

Luke shook his head and held up his phone. "You look perfect."

Emma giggled as he snapped a few photos of them.

Luke turned his attention to the view below. "Is that all of Hadley Cove down there?"

Emma's gaze swept across the panoramic view, her face beaming as she nodded. "It looks magical. Don't you think?"

He drew closer to her, wrapping an arm around her shoulder. "It really does. A storybook town, especially with all the places along the water."

She pointed down to the beach, tracing her finger along the coastline. "See how the beach curves? There's The Point, and if you go down a little further, there's my cottage. Beyond that is where the marsh begins." She motioned across the cove. "And of course, there's my old house, or your new one, rather."

Luke followed her finger. "I didn't realize they were so far away. It's amazing that Riley walked all that way back to his old house."

Emma glanced up at him. "That house is special, and Riley knows it."

A smile lit up Luke's face. "You're probably right. But what's even more special than the house is you, Emma."

Her heart fluttered as a warm blush crept onto her cheeks. She was grateful for the darkness that concealed the redness.

"Is that so?" she asked.

Luke turned toward her, his hand reaching out to take hers. "Yes, it is."

The world around them dimmed as Emma turned to face him. The thumping of her heart was the only thing she could hear, each beat echoing with anticipation. Their eyes locked, and time seemed to stretch, each second lingering longer than the last. She could feel the heat rising to her face.

His hand, with a slowness that was almost torturous, came up to cup her cheek. There was a tenderness in his touch that sent shivers down her spine.

She could sense him drawing closer.

The whisper of her name on his lips held so much promise.

Luke tilted her face upward, their breaths mingling, the space between them closing.

Every inch of her body was electrified with desire, and her heart raced as their lips locked together. She wrapped her arms around him, pulling him closer, surrendering to the moment. The kiss deepened, and she felt herself getting lost in it—in him. She felt every nerve come alive. Every sensation magnified: his taste, his touch, the feeling of his fingers threading through her auburn curls.

It felt as if this night was always meant to happen. She'd hold on to this moment forever.

"Wow," Luke murmured, their lips still close.

"Yeah," Emma said, still caught in the moment. "What you said."

They both chuckled as he pulled her in even closer, holding her tight as if he never wanted to let go.

"Should we go back?" he asked. "I don't even know what time it is."

"Yeah, I suppose we should."

Luke's fingers gently traced a path down her arm before releasing her.

To Emma, letting go felt like hearing the close of a favorite song, its final note lingering in the air.

Together, they switched on their phone flashlights and made their way down the lighthouse stairs. A smile stayed plastered on Emma's face during the entire descent. Once outside, they walked through the woods back to the Treehouse Café parking lot. The air was crisp and cool around them, the moon casting a gentle glow on the surroundings.

"Thanks for dinner," Emma said, turning to Luke.

Luke smiled, his eyes meeting hers. "Thanks for the lighthouse tour."

A rush of warmth spread through her body. "Anytime," she said, her voice barely above a whisper.

Luke leaned in and kissed her lips. "I'll see you again soon. Send me a text when you get home, so I know you got there safely."

She stared into his eyes, slowly letting go of his hand. "Promise."

Emma slid into the driver's seat, her heart swelling as the memory of that perfect kiss replayed in her mind like a movie scene.

It was the kind of kiss that made her believe in magic, in the possibility of something greater than herself. Kisses had never been like this with Chad.

With a giddy smile, Emma started the car and left the parking lot, her fingers tapping to the rhythm of her racing heart. The radio played a Taylor Swift tune, and she couldn't resist singing along. Through the windshield, she glanced up at the stars and released a sigh.

She marveled at the way her life had taken an unexpected turn, unfolding like the pages of a fairy tale, penned by the invisible hand of fate.

22

Luke

L<small>UKE'S PULSE QUICKENED EVERY</small> time he thought of Emma. Yet underneath that exhilaration was trepidation. The tattoo of Kate's name on his chest was a constant reminder—not just of love lost, but of the long road ahead to help his son come to terms with his mother's passing.

He'd find himself in quiet contemplation, wondering if embracing this new happiness was okay.

Was it possible to truly love someone from your past, while pursuing someone else in the present?

He grappled with that thought, but deep down, Luke knew he wasn't replacing one love with another. He was simply allowing his heart the grace to expand, to hold space for both grief and happiness, where memories of yester-years coexisted with the hope of tomorrow.

Luke longed for the day he could share the joy Emma had brought into his life and show his son that it was possible to find happiness again, even in the face of tragedy.

In their clandestine relationship, Luke and Emma savored every stolen moment. They took turns planning each outing, carefully avoiding any public places where they might be spotted. Emma had suggested they drive to the neighboring town and catch a movie at the colossal fifteen-screen cinema. For their next date, Luke arranged a dinner cruise on the Savannah River. The sunset views and the coastal air breezing against their skin left them in awe aboard the *Georgia Queen*. Each rendezvous was a mini adventure, and Luke couldn't recall the last time he had enjoyed himself this much.

Together, Luke and Emma found happiness in the simple moments, and it didn't always involve extravagant outings. They cherished the times when they would just unwind and enjoy each other's company, whether it was cooking dinner together at Emma's cozy home or baking dog treats to fulfill orders. Thankfully, Emma's cottage was tucked away, making it difficult for anyone to spot Luke's Range Rover parked there.

One such evening at Emma's cottage, she had pulled him into a spontaneous dance session in the backyard. As the sunset draped the sky in shades of gold, he felt the irresistible urge to capture the moment.

Battling the breeze, they struggled to prop Emma's phone against the Range Rover. Finally, they positioned the phone just right and stepped back into each other's arms. The Bluetooth remote was in Luke's hand as they began to sway to a Taylor Swift tune. Emma's laughter echoed in the air as Luke dipped her. When he pulled her close with one arm around her waist, they pressed the remote, capturing the moment. The camera snapped just as Riley looked back with a playful smile, a scene that felt ripped from a fairy tale—the charming cottage, the brilliant sunset, a rescue dog, and two people unmistakably in love.

It was one of those perfect moments where everything around them fell into place.

Even in such times, the question of when and how to break the news to Jeremiah pressed down on Luke's heart.

Fortunately, he had more time to figure it out. Jeremiah seemed preoccupied with his newfound social life and hardly noticed when Luke was away. Luke was just glad his son was finally getting out of his room and venturing out to the town. He could only hope his son would stay out of trouble.

~elle~

On a Saturday afternoon, while Luke waited outside the rescue for Jeremiah to finish his volunteer shift, Lisa passed by. She smiled as soon as she spotted him and walked over.

"Hey, Luke. Thinking about adopting a pet?"

Luke chuckled and shook his head. "No, not today. I'm waiting for my son to come out. How have you been?"

"Good, except for missing my friend who's been mysteriously busy every time I call her to hang out."

Luke feigned innocence. "I'm not sure I understand what you're getting at."

"Mm-hmm." Lisa gave him a knowing look. "I'm kidding, of course. I'm thrilled that she's finally dating. Especially with her birthday coming up and everything—"

"Birthday?" Luke's eyes widened. "When is it?"

"September twentieth. She didn't tell you?"

"No, she didn't. That's next week!"

"I'm not surprised. She typically doesn't mention it to anyone."

Luke furrowed his brows. "It's her birthday. Why wouldn't she want to celebrate it?"

Lisa sighed. "She used to, but Emma hasn't really celebrated her birthday in years. We still buy gifts and make a cake every year, but that's it. She's never made a big deal of it."

"I don't understand. Is she upset about getting older?"

"No, it's not that. It has to do with her ex."

"He didn't celebrate her birthdays?"

"Well, he'd still get her a little something for the occasion, but it was never thoughtful," Lisa said. "I thought it was strange that we never did anything for her birthday, so I finally told her I was gonna plan a big party. And that's when she told me what Chad had told her."

"Which was?" Luke asked, dreading the answer.

"He somehow convinced her that celebrating her birthday was narcissistic. It was fine to do when you're younger, but not as an adult."

Luke remembered his brief encounter with Chad at The Point and knew he was a scoundrel, but didn't realize he was this cruel. "This guy is really something."

"Oh, I know. It's ironic, really. Chad would always put Emma down about celebrating birthdays, even though he never missed an opportunity to brag about himself. I swear, every dinner with them felt like the Chad Show. I'm so glad he's gone."

Luke couldn't believe what he had heard. Anger rose inside him, but he bit down on his lip to control it. Emma was a sweet and caring person, and the fact that she felt guilty about celebrating her own birthday—he had to do something extraordinary for her.

"Lisa, I want to do something for Emma's birthday, but I'm unsure of what exactly. Can you help me out?" Luke asked.

Lisa's face lit up. "Of course! I'm more than happy to help. Here, take my number. Let me know what you need, and I'll be there."

Luke pulled out his phone and saved her number. "Thanks a ton. I'll brainstorm some ideas and reach out to you soon."

"Perfect! Anything you do for Emma will make her happy, but I know she's always wanted to take one of those coastal helicopter tours. I had one booked for us and some of our girlfriends on her fortieth birthday last year, but Chad told her she couldn't go," Lisa explained.

Luke nodded, a spark of determination ignited within him.

23

Emma

THE FINAL BELL OF the day rang, and students sprang from their seats like a herd of gazelles. The classroom buzzed with chatter as they packed up their books and slung backpacks over their shoulders.

"Don't forget to jot down the homework assignment!" Emma called out, raising her voice over the noise. "See y'all on Monday."

She watched her students heading toward the door, their footsteps echoing through the emptying classroom. Emma sank into her seat, letting out a deep, reflective sigh.

Today was Emma's birthday, yet she had deliberately kept it a secret, even from Luke. She didn't want to make a fuss and certainly didn't want her students to be distracted by it. Instead, she threw herself into her work, trying not to dwell on past birthdays.

With Chad, birthdays had always been a letdown, a reminder of how unimportant she was in the relationship.

Every year, she had hoped he would surprise her with something special, but each time she was left disappointed. Instead of celebrating her special day, he would make her feel guilty for wanting any kind of attention. Until the divorce, Emma hadn't grasped how much he had neglected her.

It was a stark contrast to the joy she experienced now with Luke, who made her feel cherished every day. The mere thought of him made Emma smile from ear to ear. She felt lucky to have someone so wonderful in her life.

After packing her bag, she locked the classroom door behind her and hurried down the hall to the teachers' lounge. Emma's hunger pangs were intense as she eagerly anticipated the delicious flavors of the hummus veggie wrap waiting for her in the fridge.

When she stepped into the teachers' lounge, she noticed several teachers huddled around something, their whispers growing louder with her approach.

Emma leaned forward and tilted her head. "What's going on?"

"Oh, Emma, you sly thing! You didn't tell us you had a secret admirer," one teacher said, playfully nudging her.

What's she talking about?

As Emma approached the table, she saw a stunning bouquet of Gerbera daisies arranged in a vase. A small white envelope with her name on it was nestled amongst the blooms.

"Who's it from, Emma?" one of them asked.

"My husband never buys me flowers," another teacher complained.

With her heart racing, Emma picked up the envelope, feeling its weight in her hands. She tore it open and pulled out the card.

Emma,

Nothing would make me happier than celebrating you on your special day. Happy Birthday! I'll see you tonight.

Luke

A smile spread across Emma's face, and she pressed the card to her chest. She couldn't believe that Luke had sent her flowers on her birthday.

But how did he know?

She leaned toward the bouquet and breathed in, relishing the sweet fragrance of the daisies.

The other teachers looked at her expectantly. "So, who are they from?" one of them pressed.

Emma quickly thought of a harmless lie to avoid further questions. "Oh, they're from my grandpa."

The teachers wore disappointed expressions, but Emma was unfazed. She turned to the flowers again, closing her eyes, and lost herself in their fragrance.

With a contented sigh, she returned to the present and headed for the fridge. As she reached inside for her wrap, Mr. Simmons, the physics teacher, chimed in. "You're just having lunch now? The day's almost over."

"I know, but I didn't have time earlier. I held an impromptu prep session in my classroom during lunch."

Emma's colleague gave a sneer before turning away. She knew some of the other teachers resented her for being an overachiever, but Emma found immense satisfaction in her job. It was more than a means of earning a living; it was an avenue to help others reach their full potential.

As Emma sat at a table, the other teachers left the lounge. She savored her wrap, and admired the stunning vase filled with daisies, which added a touch of radiance to the otherwise mundane space. After a few moments of solitude, she decided to call Luke.

Luke's voice filled Emma's ear as soon as he answered. "Hey, Emma, how are you? How was school today? Is everything alright?"

Emma chuckled softly while listening to Luke's rapid-fire questions. "I'm good, thanks for asking. School was crazy busy, but I survived. And yes, everything's alright. I wanted to call and thank you for the daisies you sent. They're beautiful. No one's ever sent me flowers for my birthday before."

"I'm glad you enjoyed them," Luke said, a hint of relief in his voice. "I was starting to worry they might have gone to the wrong school."

Emma laughed, imagining a bunch of daisies sitting unclaimed in a hallway somewhere. "No, they definitely made it to the right person. And sorry about that, it's been one of those days. I haven't even had a chance to eat until now."

"The flowers are only the beginning," Luke said. "You deserve so much more, Emma. That's why I'm taking you out tonight."

While contemplating Luke's kind gesture, Emma recalled her past birthday when her friends had surprised her with a helicopter ride along the coastline. But before she could even entertain the thought, Chad's voice cut through.

"Why would you want to do something like that? It's just a birthday, Emma. Grow up."

She had looked longingly at the helicopter, imagining the breathtaking views she would miss. She remembered the sting of embarrassment when she reluctantly declined the helicopter ride. Still, Emma could feel the icy touch of Chad's hand as he'd led her away, and the warmth of her friends' concerned glances burning into her back.

Emma hesitated. "That sounds really nice, Luke, but I'm not sure if I can do anything tonight. Riley gets anxious when I leave him alone at night."

"Well, I've got that covered. Lisa will be over at your house at six to stay with him for the evening."

Warmth rose in Emma's chest. She couldn't help but compare Luke's thoughtfulness with Chad's carelessness; Chad had never bothered to think ahead like Luke had.

Emma searched for another excuse to avoid going out, but she realized she couldn't find one. "Alright, Luke. If Riley's good, then sure, I'm in for tonight."

"Awesome! I think you're going to like it."

"Can you give me a hint? I just want to be prepared," Emma asked.

"Nope. It's a surprise. Don't worry—it'll be worth it."

Emma took a deep breath and decided to trust him. "What time should I be ready?"

"Six-thirty. A driver will pick you up at your house," Luke said.

"A driver? Wow, I should grab my stuff then," Emma said,

a bit overwhelmed by the grandeur.

"Okay, Emma. I'll see you tonight."

The flowers were a wonderful surprise. But now a driver? Where was Luke taking her? And more importantly, what was she going to wear? Her mind raced with possibilities.

After hanging up, Emma quickly finished her wrap, gathered her things, grabbed the flowers, and stood up from the table. Glancing at her phone, she realized it was already ten after four. If she didn't hurry, she wouldn't have much time to get ready before the driver arrived.

As Emma made her way to the door, she saw Jeremiah leaving the building.

A knot formed in her stomach, guilt creeping up on her for keeping him in the dark about her relationship with Luke. As much as she wanted to tell Jeremiah, it wasn't her place to do so. Luke would have to be the one to tell him when the time was right, but that time wasn't now.

Emma clutched the bouquet and pushed those thoughts aside, determined not to let them ruin her birthday celebration. Tonight was going to be a night to remember, she thought, feeling a spark of excitement. Neither the lingering guilt nor Chad's hurtful words would spoil it for her. This evening was about her and the man she was falling for, and she was going to enjoy every moment of it.

24

Luke

IN THE DIM GLOW of the bathroom light, a hopeful grin broadened across Luke's face. It was that "Emma" effect again. Every time they were together, he felt like the luckiest man alive. And tonight would be no exception.

Earlier, over the phone, he'd picked up on her reluctance to celebrate her birthday. It pained him, knowing her ex played a role in that, but this evening he was determined to make her feel like the most special woman in the world.

A cold splash of water rejuvenated him as he finished shaving. Stepping into the bedroom, he caught the faint scent of the cologne he'd apply later. A polished suit awaited him, and the tie added the finishing touch. Aware of time ticking away, he dressed in a hurry. Just as he bent to tie his shoes, the distinctive creak of the front door reached his ears.

"Dad? You home?"

Quickened steps brought Luke downstairs. "Jer?" He

paused, watching his son's movements. "How was your day?"

Jeremiah tossed his backpack onto the kitchen table. "Same as usual." He made his way to the fridge and grabbed a carton of orange juice.

Luke leaned over the counter. "How was the rescue?"

"Pretty good," Jeremiah said, filling a glass.

"I'm glad you're enjoying the rescue too, but you know at this point you're going beyond your mandated hours, right?"

Jeremiah took a sip of his juice, shrugging. "Turned out better than I thought."

Luke laughed. "I knew it wouldn't be that bad. Helping animals and working with that girl? Seems it all worked out."

Jeremiah let out a rare laugh and shook his head.

Luke had noticed the subtle shift in his son's demeanor over the past couple of weeks. Perhaps it was that girl at the rescue, he thought, but he decided not to pry.

Luke tapped his fingers on the counter. "Any plans for tonight?"

"Just some homework to catch up on," Jeremiah replied, rinsing his glass.

"But it's your night off. You don't want to go out?"

"Not tonight."

Luke nodded. "Well, I'm off to Savannah with some friends. You'll be good on your own?"

Jeremiah smirked and rolled his eyes. "I'm not twelve, Dad. I'll be fine."

"I know, I know. Sometimes I forget that." Luke smiled

and pulled out his wallet, leaving two twenties on the counter. "For pizza, or there's lasagna in the fridge. I'll be back late."

"I'll figure something out. See ya."

With a casual wave, Luke grabbed his keys and headed toward the front door. He thought it was a little strange that Jeremiah wasn't going out tonight, but he wasn't complaining. If he was at home, that meant he was staying out of trouble.

Luke's heart raced as he drove up I-95 toward Savannah. The heliport they were heading to was just outside the city, and he hoped the traffic wouldn't delay him from arriving before she did. He didn't want her showing up to the airfield lost and confused.

Fortunately, luck was on his side, and he arrived well before the driver.

After parking his Range Rover, he headed to the small building to meet with the pilot. The cool evening air tingled his skin as they ran through every detail, ensuring tonight would be flawless.

When Luke and the pilot finished and made their way to the helipad, a sleek black sedan rolled in. As the driver opened the rear door, Luke's breath caught.

Stepping out, Emma's long black dress hugged her curves in all the right places. A graceful slit gave a glimpse of her elegant stride, and the v-neck captured a hint of her allure.

Her approach was marked by a smile that seemed to borrow the very brilliance of the evening star.

A moment of admiration passed before Luke finally found his voice. "Emma, you look stunning."

Emma put her hands on her hips. "You really think so?" She fidgeted with the edge of her dress, her brow furrowing slightly. "Is it too much?"

"Absolutely not," Luke said, moving closer and brushing a loose curl behind her ear.

Emma let out a sigh. "Okay, good. So, what's the plan for tonight?"

Luke gently turned her to face the waiting helicopter. "That's our ride."

Taking her hands in his, Luke looked deeply into her eyes. "Lisa mentioned last year's ruined birthday with Chad—how you missed that helicopter tour. Tonight, I wanted to change that memory for you."

"Luke, I don't know what to say. This is so—so thoughtful."

Luke noticed the sheen of unshed tears in her eyes. In silent understanding, he pulled her into a comforting hug, feeling her body relax against his. This moment, he hoped, somehow made up for the disappointments of her past, even if she couldn't express it in words.

As they broke apart, he held on to her hand and together they made their way to the waiting helicopter. The pilot opened the door for them as Luke guided Emma into her seat before taking the spot next to her.

Handing her a headset, he smiled reassuringly.

The pilot's voice crackled through. "We're about to lift off, folks. We'll pass through Savannah then up the coast to Hilton Head and down to Hadley Cove. Sit back and enjoy the ride."

Minutes later the helicopter took off. The thrum of the

rotor blades filled the cabin, occasionally drowning out the pilot's voice. Every so often his finger would extend, directing their attention to landmarks that had etched history onto the earth below.

As the helicopter soared higher, Emma's gaze snapped to the window, drawing a sharp breath.

He turned toward her, his own eyes capturing the breathtaking panorama of the coastline: intricate networks of creeks and tributaries winding their way through the lush green marshes, and below, seagulls dancing in midair, their wings catching the light.

For a moment it seemed as if they were suspended in time, in a world that existed only for them.

Emma leaned onto Luke's shoulder and sighed. "This is absolutely gorgeous," she said, the marvel carrying through the static of the headphones.

Feeling the weight of her against him, Luke wrapped an arm around her, drawing her nearer. He winked. "Not as gorgeous as you."

A blush tinted Emma's cheeks, and her lips curved into a half-smile. "Always the charmer, aren't you?" she teased, nudging him with her elbow.

The pilot's voice boomed through the headphones, interrupting their conversation. "Alright folks, brace yourselves for the finale—heading south."

As the helicopter banked gently to the left, revealing more of the landscape below, Emma's gasp echoed through the cabin. Beneath them, Hadley Cove sprawled out, a patchwork of green, brown, and gold intermingling. The beach, with its pristine sands, shimmered invitingly under the sun. And there, like an old sentinel guarding its tales, the Bridwell Lighthouse stood tall, casting a shadow over the waters as it touched the horizon.

For Luke, the sight stirred a potent mix of wonder and nostalgia. Visions of their footprints imprinted side by side on the beach, the feel of her hand gripping his, and their dance at The Point played in his mind. Then, there was the mischievous glint in Emma's eyes as she coaxed him into sneaking into the lighthouse, and how he'd caught a cramp in his leg as they climbed its winding stairs.

He thought about their first kiss and how, in that instant, he knew she was the one for him.

The skies melded into deep shades of indigo as the helicopter veered back toward Savannah. One by one, stars blinked awake, dotting the night sky.

Looking down at her nestled into his shoulder, he smiled, grateful for this moment, for this woman, for *this* love.

25

Emma

As the vibrations from the helicopter's blades faded and the thud of its skids touched solid ground, Emma's pulse began to slow. The reality of the night's unfolding adventure was only just sinking in.

When the world outside the cabin came back into focus, she quickly shrugged off her headset and looped her arms around Luke. "That was amazing!"

Luke drew her close, his hands resting at her waist. "It was. I'm glad you enjoyed yourself."

She gave him a quick kiss on the lips, then pulled back. "So, what's next?"

"You'll find out soon enough," he said, stepping out and offering a hand to assist her.

As Emma's feet touched the ground, a white Rolls Royce awaited them, its chauffeur holding the door open.

Eyes wide, she pressed her palms to her cheeks. "Luke, we could've taken an Uber!"

The corners of his mouth lifted into a sly grin as he guided her over to the car. "We'll splurge tonight."

Sinking into the plush back seat of the car as they left the heliport, Emma's imagination took her somewhere else. Her thoughts floated to a place of uncertainty, pondering how she would fit into Jeremiah and Luke's lives. She barely noticed when he reached over and took her hand, pulling her back to the moment.

"Hey, you alright?"

She offered a hesitant smile. "Yeah, I am. It's nothing."

"You know you can tell me anything," he said, gently squeezing her hand. "It's not nothing."

Her fingers toyed with the edge of her seatbelt as she drew a shaky breath. "What happens when you tell Jeremiah about us? If he's not ready?" Her eyes darted toward the window, then back to Luke. "I'm falling for you. And I don't want to lose you. But if Jeremiah isn't on board—" She swallowed hard. "I don't think I could live with being the reason that your relationship with him never gets fixed."

Understanding seemed to dawn on Luke's face. "Emma, I've already fallen for you. And I don't want to lose you either." He exhaled deeply. "I don't know how he'll react. Nothing worth having is ever easy. But we'll figure it out. Together."

Emma bit her lip. "I'm sorry, I'm not trying to ruin our night."

Pulling her closer, he pressed a soft kiss to her forehead. "Emma, you're not, and never could. Promise."

Emma's vision blurred, tears building behind her eyes, but she blinked them back. Memories of Chad flashed through her mind—those times he'd scoffed at her dreams or belittled her feelings. She squeezed Luke's hand, letting her head fall onto his shoulder, grateful she could open up about her deepest fears and insecurities. Things were different with him.

With every beat of her heart, she knew she was exactly where she was meant to be—in the arms of a man who truly cared for her.

The car's deceleration became more pronounced cruising through the lamplit streets of Savannah. As they neared 37th Street, Luke shot Emma an expectant glance. "So, are you hungry?"

Emma nodded. "I am."

"Well then, you're in for a treat." As the vehicle slowed to a halt, she followed Luke's gaze to the window.

Outside stood one of the swankiest restaurants she had ever seen. The extravagant manor had a timeless grace about it, with stone steps leading up to an entrance flanked by tall white columns on both sides. It looked more like a historical relic than a restaurant.

"It's beautiful! Are we really eating here?" Emma turned back to face him.

Luke chuckled, stepping out and opening the door for her. "Absolutely. We have reservations." He grabbed her hand, leading her up the steps and through the entrance.

Inside, a grand foyer greeted them, dominated by an elegant chandelier above their heads that played with the light in mesmerizing patterns. Emma's eyes wandered, soaking in the sumptuous details of rich colors, vintage furniture, and daring art.

The two eventually made their way to a back terrace that held a picturesque view of the charming square filled with towering trees adorned with Spanish moss.

As they settled into their seats, the scent of fresh bread wafted in the air. Luke ordered a bottle of wine. Meanwhile, Emma's fingers grazed the crisp linen, her attention drawn to the golden play of light from the candlesticks reflecting off the silverware. Every detail spoke of a luxury she had only ever imagined.

"How did you know about this place?" she asked.

With a grin that made his eyes crinkle, Luke confessed, "Just a Google search. The reviews of this place were awesome."

"It's incredible," Emma remarked.

"And," Luke continued, "it's vegan-friendly."

Emma's heart melted. "You thought of everything, didn't you?"

"Just wanted tonight to be perfect for you. For us."

Luke winked at her and opened the menu. She blushed and picked up her own, revealing the elegant script and mouthwatering descriptions of the restaurant's offerings.

Mulling over the options and making their selections, Emma smiled when Luke ordered the portabella steak, mirroring her choice. She'd playfully told him he didn't need to, but his decision spoke volumes. Those tiny, thoughtful gestures reminded her how different he was from her past, and she was still adjusting to the novelty of having someone like Luke in her life.

While they waited for their food to arrive, another waiter approached cradling a bottle of wine. He artfully poured it into their glasses, the ruby liquid capturing the candlelight. She took a sip and savored the complex flavors as warmth radiated throughout her body. Then, in the midst of their conversation, the soft hum of a violin began to fill the air, each note playing in harmony with the magical aura of the night.

It was a moment she knew she would never forget.

Emma took another sip of her wine, then sighed. "You know, tonight still feels unreal. The flowers were a surprise, but this has been beyond my wildest dreams." She paused to breathe in the pleasant scent of the magnolias nearby.

"So, I should've just stuck with the flowers then?" Luke teased, raising an eyebrow.

Her laughter rang out, light and free. "Maybe! But I'm not complaining."

"It's your birthday, Emma. I had to make it unforgettable."

"You've made this night unforgettable. All my birthday wishes, realized in a single evening."

Leaning in, he whispered, "And what about your regular wishes?"

"Meeting you. That was a wish I didn't even know I had." Emma looked down as her cheeks flushed a delicate pink.

"That was a wish we both shared," Luke said, his gaze holding hers intently. "Any other wishes?"

Emma hesitated, then shared, "I've always dreamed of having a brick-and-mortar store for my dog treat business. It's just, I don't even know where to start."

"Well, that's definitely possible." Luke's voice was soft and sincere. "You're capable of so much. I don't see why owning your own shop isn't something you couldn't do."

Emma was filled with a sense of calm as Luke spoke, knowing he *really* believed in her.

Luke raised his wine glass. "To you, Emma. Happy birthday."

She clinked hers with his. "Thank *you*. For everything."

Taking a moment, Luke reached into his pocket, producing a black rectangular velvet box. "Well, there's one more thing," he murmured, setting it before her.

"Luke, what's this?"

"Just a little something for your birthday. Open it."

Emma carefully lifted the lid and found a shiny silver bracelet inside. "It's beautiful! You really didn't have to, but I love it."

"It's a charm bracelet," Luke explained, lifting it and clasping it around her wrist. "One charm is a dog, and the other is a lighthouse."

Her voice quivered as she traced the shape of the dog charm. "It looks just like Riley."

"Yeah, it's our story. The dog is for the day we met, and the lighthouse is for our first kiss."

With teary eyes, she leaned in, pressing her lips against his. "I love it so much, Luke. Thank you."

His thumb caressed her cheek. "I wanted it to be special. Every moment, every detail."

Their intimate bubble was interrupted by the arrival of their meals. After not eating anything today but her veggie wrap, Emma couldn't wait to dig into her portabella steak.

Taking a bite, she turned to Luke, awaiting his reaction. "How is it?"

His eyes widened as he dabbed his mouth with the linen napkin. "It's incredible. I can tell there's a difference from regular steak, but still, I'm impressed."

Emma chuckled. "Plant-based dishes have really evolved. I remember when they were just, blah."

They lost themselves in playful banter, savoring their meals and the wine's mellow buzz, until an unexpected voice intruded.

"Luke?" A figure stepped into the dim glow around their table. "Is that really you?"

26

Luke

THE FIGURE TURNED TOWARD Luke, and they locked eyes in the semi-darkness.

Recognition flickered across Luke's face.

Forcing a business smile, he extended his hand to his former colleague. "Adam! What are you doing all the way down here?"

"Just a brief getaway," Adam replied. "Savannah's always been on the bucket list for Macey and me. Found a free week and just jumped on it. Heard you moved down here?"

"I did." Luke nodded, glancing over at Emma, then back to Adam. "Hadley Cove, about an hour south."

Adam shrugged. "Never heard of it. So, are you liking Georgia? Miss the hustle and bustle of Chicago?"

Luke paused, then shook his head. "There's a certain charm to this place I hadn't anticipated. And Chicago—not really."

Adam chuckled, giving Luke a friendly nudge. "All those

late nights finally got to you, huh?"

"Something like that." Luke kept his tone light. "So how's the old grind in the office?"

Adam playfully slapped Luke's shoulder. "Come on, Luke. Vacation mode. No work talk. But for what it's worth, things are steady."

Catching a quick movement from the corner of his eye, Luke asked, "Is that Macey at the bar?"

"Yeah, that's her. We're actually waiting for a table to open up—didn't realize this place was reservation-only."

Luke gestured to Emma, who had been patiently waiting while they spoke. "Adam, this is Emma."

Extending her hand graciously, Emma smiled. "It's nice to meet you. I haven't met any of Luke's friends from Chicago."

Returning the handshake, Adam grinned. "The pleasure's mine. And hats off to you. Not many can coax Luke into the social scene."

Before the conversation veered into more personal territory, Luke deftly changed the subject. "How are the kids, Adam? Did they come along with you?"

Adam waved the notion away, laughing. "Oh, no, this is strictly 'us' time. Three teenagers back home, believe it or not. It feels like just yesterday they were still in diapers."

A hint of melancholy crossed Luke's face. "Time flies. Jeremiah's heading to college next year. It's all so surreal."

"How's Jeremiah? I hope things have slowed down enough for you two to spend more time together," Adam said. "I know that was always an issue in Chicago."

Luke paused, allowing the silence to stretch just a beat

too long as he sipped his wine. "Jeremiah's doing great, thanks." He bit down on his lip, holding back words he could regret.

"That's great to hear." Adam clapped Luke gently on the back. "I should go; Macey's been waiting. It was fantastic catching up, Luke. And Emma, lovely to meet you."

"It was nice meeting you as well," Emma said in a polite tone, smiling at him as he walked away.

As Adam disappeared inside, the undercurrents of their conversation lingered. Luke, lost in thought, absentmindedly traced the rim of his wine glass. Adam's offhand comment had cut deeper than he would admit. The unsaid implications were clear: his past choices, prioritizing ambition over family, weren't forgotten. The challenge of providing for a family, while also being there for them, was a balance Luke had grappled with for years.

"He seems friendly," Emma said.

Luke gave a single nod, turning back to his portabella steak. They continued eating, mostly in silence, until the waiter returned with a small chocolate cake.

"Luke! When did you order this?"

"Just a little something I arranged beforehand." Luke grinned. "Vegan, just for you. But if you're already full, you can take it home."

Emma patted her stomach, reclining in her chair. "Let's box it up."

Luke flagged down the waiter, then quickly settled the bill. After the cake was boxed, he led Emma out, mindful to avoid crossing paths with Adam once more.

This was *their* evening, after all.

27

Emma

EMMA NOTICED LUKE'S EASY smile had vanished, replaced by a sudden somber and pensive expression.

As they returned to the heliport, Luke's sleek Range Rover stood alone, its polished exterior reflecting the amber lights from nearby streetlamps.

The driver pulled up next to it and hurried to Emma's side, opening the door for her. She stood, the weight of the night settling into her bones. Hours earlier, the dress had seemed elegant, but now it felt cumbersome, and her feet ached from the unfamiliar strain of high heels.

"Are you alright?" Luke asked.

She looked up at him and chuckled. "Ugh, these heels. I love how tall they make me, but they're killing me. They're coming off."

"They look great, but next time, wear whatever's comfy. I'm just happy being with you." He crouched, lifting the hem of her dress and helping remove each of her shoes.

Emma giggled and let out a sigh of relief. "It's like we're acting out Cinderella in reverse."

He grinned, but she saw it didn't quite reach his eyes.

Luke walked over to the passenger-side door and opened it for her. She kissed him on the cheek as she climbed into the seat, placing her high heels on the floorboard.

The drive back to Hadley Cove passed in quiet, the roads now clear from the earlier traffic. It seemed they would reach Emma's house in no time. But as the silence hung between them, Emma glanced at the clock; time was slipping away, and she still hadn't found out what was weighing on Luke.

"Tonight was wonderful, Luke," Emma said.

"It was nothing. You deserved it."

"I'll have to make it up to you on your birthday." Emma turned to study his face, catching the tense set of his jaw and the determined gaze he kept on the winding road. "Luke, what's wrong? Something's bothering you." She took his right hand, giving it a reassuring squeeze.

Luke sighed. "It's nothing, really. It was just something Adam said at dinner when he stopped by the table."

Emma thought back to the conversation. "What did he say?"

"He said he hoped things slowed down enough for me to start spending time with my son since that had always been a problem in Chicago."

Emma realized the remark sounded a bit condescending. "Yeah, that was a little off-handed to bring up."

"But he's not wrong," Luke admitted. "I didn't spend enough time with Jeremiah or Kate. I really messed up in the family department."

"You did the best you knew how to do then, Luke."

A distant look clouded his eyes. "I swore I'd never let my family go through what I went through as a kid. But we saw how that turned out."

Emma's heart ached for him. She gently laid her hand over his, feeling the faint tremor in his fingers.

"But you're here now," Emma whispered, squeezing his hand. "You're making up for lost time, and that's all that matters."

A small smile tugged at the corner of Luke's lips. "You're right. I probably shouldn't let it get to me like this, but it still does."

Emma nodded, feeling a deep sense of love and respect for the man sitting beside her. While she didn't know all the details, it was clear Luke had been through much in his life.

As the miles sped by under the car's tires, they passed a sign that read, *Hadley Cove: 5 miles*. The sight brought Emma back to the reality that their night was drawing to a close.

Luke let out a heavy sigh. "Can I be completely honest with you?" His voice caught in his throat.

"You can tell me anything, Luke."

"Well, sometimes I still dream of Kate," he said. "I think it's because there's so much I should've done differently. At least with Jeremiah, I still have time to fix things."

Emma placed a gentle hand on his arm. "You can't keep blaming yourself."

"I know." Luke hung his head. "I just wish there would've been more time with her."

Emma's grip tightened on his arm.

"I'm sorry for bringing this up. I know it must be strange for you to hear about my late wife." Luke wiped a tear from his eye, each word heavier than the last. "But I think you understand me in a way no one else does. I hope that's okay."

She smiled, reaching down and giving his hand a reassuring squeeze. "It's okay, Luke. Talking about Kate and your past is a part of who you are, and I want to know all about it. I want to know the real you."

He swallowed hard, struggling to keep his voice steady. "Thanks. I can't remember the last time I've had someone to talk to like this."

"I'm here for you, Luke. Always." With empathetic eyes, Emma leaned in closer to him.

He smiled. "You know what's strange? She had always wanted to live on the Georgia coast. It's a big reason why Jeremiah and I moved down here. Then I happened to move into your old house, and Riley showed up and now we're here. Life never turns out the way we think it will. But I'm glad it brought me to you."

A tear slid down Emma's cheek. "Me too."

A heavy pause hung between them.

Then Luke spoke. "I need to tell you something, and it may sound weird. I've been wanting to tell you this the whole night."

At the stoplight, Luke turned to face Emma.

"I love you," he confessed. "It's crazy saying that out loud, but it's the truth. On paper, the timeline doesn't make sense, but everything else about us does."

Emma's heart raced, and a warm flush rose to her neck. Every word from his lips resonated, placing her between the past and the future.

Gathering her thoughts, she looked deeply into his eyes. "It's not weird, Luke. I feel exactly the same way. I love you too."

To Emma, this was the kind of love that made her feel alive again, to take risks and chase dreams—and without a doubt, was worth fighting for.

The hum of the engine faded as they came to a stop in Emma's moonlit driveway. A familiar tune on the radio captured her attention.

Emma turned up the volume, tapping to the melody with a smile. "It's our song, from The Point."

"How could I forget?" Luke turned off the car and extended his hand to her with a playful grin. "Care for another dance?"

The sparkle in her eyes gave away her answer. And there, beneath a canopy of stars, they danced. There were no grand gestures, no audience. Just two souls moving in a way that only they understood. The world around them blurred as the song played on with every step they took, every gentle sway. It was as if the universe had conspired to give them this perfect moment.

As the final notes drifted away, Luke pulled Emma close, their foreheads touching, sealing the memory of the evening with a kiss.

28

Luke

As Luke gazed down at their interlocked fingers, it felt as though the weight of the world had been lifted from his shoulders.

"Thanks again for listening," he said. "I feel like I have a fresh start with you."

Most women, he had believed, might have turned away at the mere mention of his late wife. Emma, however, was different.

"Well, you're already off to a great start," she said. "None of my other boyfriends have ever taken me for a ride in a helicopter."

Luke chuckled, appreciating how she always knew when to throw humor into a conversation.

Together, they moved toward the front door, Emma held her heels in one hand while taking Luke's hand with the other. He thought about how she had grown even more beautiful as the night went on. They reached the porch, where light illuminated the swarm of moths and mayflies circling the bulb. He heard the faint sound of the television from inside.

"I should relieve Lisa of her dog-watching duties," Emma said.

Luke glanced at his watch. "Wow, I hope I haven't kept you out too late. Do you have an early start tomorrow?"

"At six. But I'm used to it. Besides, it'll be Thursday, which means it's almost Friday and the weekend is just around the corner."

"I'm sorry. I should've checked with you about your schedule."

"Don't be sorry. Tonight was incredible. At this point, I wouldn't care if we were coming home at dawn."

Luke wrapped his arms around her waist. "I'm sure Lisa would have something to say about that."

Emma tilted her head up to meet his gaze. "She'd give me an earful for breaking curfew."

"Jeremiah might do the same with me when I get back," he said. "Fingers crossed he's already asleep."

"Well, I suppose I should head inside then," Emma whispered.

Luke nodded, pulling her closer to him. "Yeah, I guess you'd better."

They locked eyes for a few lingering moments, delaying the night's end. He wanted to stay there, with her, forever.

Luke felt the thudding of his heart and her arms tightening around his neck.

He leaned in, pressing his lips against hers.

The door flew open.

Startled, he pulled back. "Oh gosh, I'm so sorry! I didn't mean to interrupt," Lisa said, a blush tinting her cheeks. "I was trying to take Riley out."

Riley bounded through the door and jumped on Luke, then Emma, then back to Luke.

"No worries," Emma said, reaching over to pet Riley. "Was he a good boy tonight?"

"Of course. He loves his Aunt Lisa."

"Well, I'm glad he puts on his best behavior for *you*," Emma said in a playful tone.

"So, how was everything?" Lisa scanned from Emma to Luke, waggling her eyebrows.

"We had an amazing time—Riley! Sit!" Emma said, reaching down to grab his collar to keep him off Luke.

Luke knelt and extended his hand toward Riley, who jumped onto his lap, tail wagging. "It's okay. Riley and I are old buds."

Emma shook her head as she turned back to Lisa. "I'm sorry it's so late. I would've texted you if I had known we'd be gone this long."

Lisa waved off her concern. "Oh, it's alright. I've had a great time tonight. Riley and I went for a long walk up to the marsh and then came back and made dinner."

"Thanks again for watching him." Emma gave a quick nod before diverting her attention to Luke, whose belly rubs had managed to calm Riley down.

Seeing that Emma and Lisa were done talking, Luke stood and brushed the sand off his knees. Emma corralled Riley inside the house and closed the door, then turned back to him.

"Well, I should probably get going," Luke said. He wanted to kiss her again, but thought it might be a little strange in front of Lisa. He'd have to wait until next time. "I'll call you tomorrow, or later today, technically."

"Sounds like a plan. Goodnight, Luke."

"Goodnight, Emma."

Luke stepped off the porch and walked toward his car. "Appreciate everything, Lisa," he called out as he waved goodbye. "You're a lifesaver."

"Anytime," Lisa called back.

As Luke drove home, he gazed out the windshield at the starry sky above. It reminded him that sometimes the best things in life came when you least expected them. He couldn't remember the last time he had felt so alive.

Pulling into his driveway, he smiled at the memory of Emma's laughter ringing in his ears. He couldn't wait to see her again.

Life was good.

He parked the car and entered the house with a slow, deliberate pace, treading lightly to avoid waking Jeremiah. After hanging up his keys, he went up the stairs.

Jeremiah cracked open his bedroom door, peering out as he rubbed his eyes. "You're home late."

Luke put on his poker face. "Had a great time with some old friends. Hope I didn't wake you."

"No, I was just getting ready for bed." Jeremiah let out a deep, prolonged yawn.

"Well, you better get some rest. You have school in the morning. I'll see you then. Goodnight, son."

"Yeah, I know. Goodnight," Jeremiah said, closing the door.

Settling into bed, Luke was consumed by guilt for lying to his son. He knew he needed to tell him about Emma, but he didn't want to disrupt their newfound stability.

He was clueless on how to even start that conversation with Jeremiah, so he reached for his phone and Google-searched for advice, as he had several times before. The articles he found were a mixed bag, yet all underscored the importance of honesty and communication.

Luke made a firm decision to talk to Jeremiah over the weekend. Anxiety knotted his stomach at the idea, but he knew he owed him the truth.

Truth is love.

Reaching over to the nightstand, he plugged his phone into the charger and rolled onto his back.

As he stared at the ceiling, memories of Kate flooded his mind, as they often did. He missed her terribly, and the pain of her loss never seemed to fade.

Luke had never been particularly religious, but after her diagnosis he found himself searching for answers in prayer. Yet every time he tried, he felt they weren't heard.

He'd given up on prayer after she passed away.

Why do bad things happen to good people?

The age-old question haunted him.

Here he was again, in yet another difficult situation with his son. He knew that the conversation with Jeremiah would make or break the future of their relationship and his happiness with Emma.

The weight of his dilemma grew overwhelming, so he did the only thing he knew to do. With a deep breath, he closed his eyes and tried once again, whispering a prayer to God.

"Please, help me with my son."

29

Emma

EMMA'S EYELIDS DROOPED AS she rose from her desk and walked through the classroom, monitoring her students' progress on the practice test she had assigned. After celebrating with Luke last night, she had barely slept. She returned to her desk and took a sip of her coffee.

"Alright, everyone, pencils down," she called out. "Please bring your tests up front. I'll get them back to you tomorrow. Have a great rest of your day!"

The students, Jeremiah included, gathered up their belongings and turned in their practice tests on the way out of the classroom. Though after-school study sessions weren't mandatory, she had hinted that anyone who showed up would receive extra credit in class. She didn't realize how popular the sessions would become; last week she'd only had eight students, but today she had double that number.

Gathering her belongings, she switched off the lights as the classroom emptied. She walked down the hallway and her phone vibrated in her pocket.

Luke: *How was your day?*

Emma: *It was good. Glad it's over though. LOL. Want to come over later? Maybe 6ish?*

Luke: *I'll stop by then. Can't wait.*

Emma: *Me either. :)*

Memories of last night danced in her mind, bringing a gentle smile to her face. She closed her eyes, envisioning tonight, the two of them walking along the beach and dining on her deck with the ocean in view.

A *thud* echoed through the hallway. The stack of papers she held, along with her phone, scattered everywhere as she collided with someone from around the corner.

She looked up and saw Jeremiah. "I'm so sorry! I wasn't paying attention."

"No, my bad. Let me help you with these." Jeremiah bent down to pick up the scattered papers and her phone.

Not wanting him to see Luke's name flash across her phone screen, she stepped over the papers and reached down for the phone. But he beat her to it. "Here ya go," Jeremiah said as he handed them back to her. "Nice bracelet, by the way."

Emma looked down, realizing the bracelet Luke had given her was in full view after she had pushed up her sleeves. "Thank you." She took the papers and moved them over her wrist to hide the bracelet.

"You know, I've never had a teacher who made math so easy to understand. It's always been a problem for me in school, but this year I feel like I might actually do well in this class."

Emma's smile radiated, touched by his unexpected compliment. "It's all you, Jeremiah. The work you've been putting in this semester is really making a difference. I wouldn't be surprised if you're making an A in class by the time the holidays roll around."

"Thanks. Well, I'd better get going. Don't want to be late for my shift at the rescue." Jeremiah's eyes crinkled at the corners as he smiled back.

"I'll pass by the rescue on my way home. Do you need a ride?"

"No thanks, I got my bike. See ya." Jeremiah turned and walked over to the front entrance as Emma went to the side door and out to the parking lot.

After tossing all the papers and her bag in the back seat, she got in her car and started it up as Jeremiah was pulling his bike from the rack. She watched as he got on and pedaled away toward town.

Perhaps now was the time to tell Jeremiah about her relationship with Luke. He was in a better place now, and she believed he would handle the news with maturity. She planned to discuss it with Luke when he came over later.

—ее—

Emma drove into town after leaving the school to grab some essentials for a dog treat order she needed to fulfill. When she arrived home, a nap was tempting, but she knew it would throw off her sleep schedule. Instead, she tackled some overdue bookkeeping, which only exhausted her further.

As Emma worked, Riley slept soundly in his dog bed, his feet sticking straight up in the air.

"Must be nice," she muttered.

After staring at her computer screen for forty minutes, she rubbed her eyes and stood. She headed to the kitchen to make herself a cup of coffee—an unusual choice for her at this time of day, but she needed the caffeine to stay awake. As it brewed, she preheated the oven and gathered the ingredients for the dog treats she needed to bake.

The sun had begun to set when she heard Luke's car pull up outside the cottage. She took off her flour-covered apron and flung it over the back of a chair.

Riley, who had been sleeping, jumped up and ran to the door, barking loudly. Emma tried to hold him back as she opened the door.

"Riley, stop it! That's rude."

Luke's laugh filled the room as he bent down to pet Riley. "I know, I know. I missed you too, boy."

Emma rolled her eyes, amused. It had only been fifteen hours since Riley had last seen him. She motioned for Luke to follow her into the kitchen.

"It smells good in here. What are you making?" he asked, surveying the countertops.

"Dog treats," she said, placing the treats she had pulled from the oven on a cooling rack.

"Well, I guess I won't be taste-testing then."

"Feel free to try one. Technically, they're human friendly." Emma smirked.

"I've got a better idea." Luke walked over to her side, taking the spatula from her hand and turning her to face him.

"Luke, those need to cool," she said. "You're distracting me from my work."

"That's the point," Luke said with a devilish look in his eyes.

In a heartbeat's pause, Luke had pulled her into his arms and kissed her, sending shivers through her skin as her arms clung tighter around his neck.

But their moment was interrupted by a few scratches at the back door, followed by a whine. Emma pulled away from Luke, sighing.

Luke raised an eyebrow. "To be continued?"

"Mm-hmm." Emma nodded.

Luke kissed her once more and turned to the hall. "Where's his leash? I'll take him out so you can finish here."

"Hanging up next to the front door," Emma called out.

She heard Luke grab the leash and attach it to Riley's collar before they bolted out the back door. From the kitchen window, she watched them take off down the beach.

By the time Luke and Riley returned, Emma had started another batch.

"You're baking more?" Luke asked, brushing his feet off on the mat before walking into the kitchen.

"Yeah, I've got a ton of orders to fulfill this upcoming week, so I need to get another batch in before I stop."

A grin formed on Luke's face. "You know what would make this entire process go faster?"

"What?"

He reached over, grabbing an apron. "Not sure how much help I'll be, but tell me what I can do here."

Emma beamed at Luke. "You're amazing. Thank you," she said, touched by his thoughtfulness. "So first you mix the pumpkin puree, and after you're done with that, you can get to work on stirring in the peanut butter and cinnamon."

He chuckled, walking over to the bowl Emma pointed to. "Yes ma'am."

She was delighted by Luke's helpfulness as they worked together. He took directions from her with ease, making sure he was doing things correctly. They continued to find moments of laughter as they bumped into each other in her small kitchen. Soon they had finished enough batches for half of the orders that week, and Emma would be able to deliver them all after school tomorrow.

"You do all this by yourself?" Luke asked as they started cleaning. "Even after working full time?"

"Well, yes, but I've thought about hiring someone to come help me once in a while. I just haven't gotten there yet."

"You've got a great thing going here," Luke said. "And I think you should hire someone. If you had someone doing this, say, eight to ten hours a week, you could put out twice as much product, and reach out to more pet stores in the area with the time you'd save."

Her face lit up. Chad had never shown an interest in her business.

"I should just hire you." She wrapped her arms around his waist and rested her chin on his chest.

"Now that's an idea, but I'd never let you pay me."

"What if I paid you in kisses?"

"Hmm. We might be able to work something out then." Luke dipped his head, taking his first payment.

Emma giggled as she leaned against him, listening to the sound of his heartbeat. "Are you hungry?"

"I am, but I don't know if I'm up for cooking after all that."

"Me either—pizza?"

Luke grinned. "You read my mind. Let's get a veggie one with the Violife cheese. The reviews said it was really good."

"You're so thoughtful."

Luke's consideration took Emma by surprise once again, like at the restaurant last night. She loved that he was willing to try new things and embrace her beliefs, unlike her ex-husband. Chad often ridiculed her choices, mocking her in front of their friends for not eating "real" food, knowing well that it was a deep conviction for her.

Her thoughts drifted to why'd she let him mistreat her for so long. It was probably the fact he had gotten into her head and destroyed her self-worth with his hurtful words. Not all at once, but a slight here and there, and over the years, it had compounded to where she had forgotten her own value.

She was glad those days were over.

After she ordered the pizza, they settled on the couch, deciding to watch a movie. Emma passed the remote to Luke out of habit; it was what she'd always done with Chad.

"You don't want to pick one?" Luke asked.

"I'm okay with whatever you pick."

Luke shot her a side-eye. "So, *Gladiator* is a good choice?"

Emma grabbed the remote from him. "Well, maybe I'll pick one this time. Don't worry, I won't make it too girly."

Luke threw his arm around her. "It's okay if you do. I don't mind chick flicks."

Emma settled on *Crazy, Stupid, Love*, since she enjoyed anything with Steve Carell in it; the fact it also starred Ryan Gosling was a cherry on top.

As the movie began, the doorbell rang with their pizza. Luke got up to answer it, making sure Riley didn't get out and jump all over the delivery guy.

Emma paused the film to grab plates and napkins, as well as a couple of soda cans. Once they had everything they needed, they dug into their dinner and started the movie. When they finished eating, Emma cuddled up to Luke on the couch and got so comfortable that she lost focus on the movie.

I could definitely get used to this, she mused, as her eyelids grew heavy.

She rested her head against his chest, hearing his thudding heartbeat, which drowned out every other sound. Only minutes passed before her consciousness could no longer linger in that place between awake and asleep.

She drifted off, embraced by the man she loved and who loved her.

30

Luke

IN THE DIM ROOM, the TV's dying light played over Emma's features, soft shadows dancing across her skin in a silent ballet. Luke could feel the even rhythm of her breathing against his chest; she had been soundly asleep in his arms for the last hour. The final scenes of the movie had played out, and now, as the credits rolled, he knew it was time to go.

Carefully, he reached for the remote and turned off the TV. He slid his arm beneath Emma's slender frame and with utmost care, he lifted her up and headed toward her bedroom.

When he arrived, he was struck by the beautiful décor: the blue floral bedspread and the serene ocean painting that hung on the wall.

As he laid Emma gently on her bed, Riley jumped up and nestled at her feet. Luke draped a warm blanket over her and as he was about to leave, he heard her sleepy voice.

"Where you going?"

"Heading home so you can get some rest."

"Will you stay with me?" Emma's hand reached out, grasping his.

The request hung heavily in the air as thoughts of Jeremiah flashed in his mind.

How would he explain being out this late to his son?

Luke hesitated. "Of course, I'll stay," he whispered. "Just for another hour."

He took off his shoes, and Emma moved over in the bed so he could lie down next to her. She cuddled up to him as he put his arms around her, falling back asleep only moments later.

The quiet contentment he felt with her in his arms spoke louder than any words ever could.

—ele—

The next morning, Luke rolled over and saw Emma sleeping peacefully next to him. He panicked.

He had only meant to stay another hour. Not overnight. He had to get home now, before Jeremiah woke. Easing himself out of bed, he snatched his shoes and tiptoed out.

He checked his phone; no messages from Jeremiah—a sign that all was well—but he still didn't want to have to explain where he'd been all night.

Finding a pen and a pad of paper in the kitchen, he wrote a quick note to Emma telling her he had to go, and that he'd call her tonight. After making sure he wasn't leaving anything behind, he walked out the front door and headed home.

Muted pastels painted the pre-dawn sky as Luke drove through the slumbering streets of Hadley Cove. The only sign of life was at Phil's Diner, where through the window only one person sat at the counter.

After pulling into the driveway and gently closing the car door, he tiptoed inside, listening for any movement throughout the house.

Silence.

He crept upstairs to his bedroom and closed the door, then walked into the bathroom and started the shower.

As he dunked his head under the hot stream, a knock came on his door.

"Dad, you there?"

Luke hesitated before poking his head out from behind the curtain. Fearing Jeremiah may have heard him come in this morning, his mind raced to find a plausible excuse. "Yeah, what's up?"

"I gotta leave for school and I need lunch money."

"Sure, yeah. My wallet is on the bedside table. Take whatever you need from there."

"Okay. Thanks, Dad."

That was close.

Luke let out a sigh, thinking if he had only arrived five minutes later, Jeremiah would've caught him.

After showering, Luke stepped into his room and got dressed, grabbing his phone from the bedside table. Opening it, he saw Emma had sent him a picture of the bracelet he had given her on her wrist. He replied, complimenting how it looked on her, then set his phone beside his wallet.

Once he finished getting ready for the day, he headed downstairs and made breakfast. He didn't have any meetings today, so he decided he'd tackle a few projects around the house. Since moving in, Luke had been considering repainting the dining room, but wasn't sure which color yet. He wondered if he should ask Emma. This used to be her house, after all.

Browsing through paint colors online, his mind drifted to Emma's dreams of opening her own brick-and-mortar store for her dog treat business. He believed with the right strategy she could truly thrive. Paint color searches shifted to reading articles on small-business startups and taking notes.

A lightbulb moment struck Luke as he remembered the extra bags of dog treats he still had after finding Riley. Driven by love, he immediately set out to find local stores interested in showcasing her handcrafted dog treats.

He first called Cove Corner Crafts. The owner, Susan, seemed excited, especially after learning about the treats' natural ingredients and the charity angle with Second Chance Rescue. Luke insisted his gesture be credited to an anonymous Barking Orders supporter. Encouraged by the positive response from Susan, he phoned two more businesses. Both conversations ended with a resounding yes, prompting him to punch the air.

I'd give anything to see her face when she finds out...

With plans set to drop off the treats later, Luke leaned back in his chair, letting out a contented sigh, reveling in the potential this had for Emma's business. Shortly after, he stood, stretching his limbs to ease the stiffness. He then moved to the living room couch and scrolled through photos of himself and Emma on his phone. He marveled at how they'd met and how quickly he'd fallen for her. That morning, he felt like a teenager sneaking back home past curfew. Exhilarating as it was, he knew he couldn't do this forever, nor did he want to.

He pondered how to break the news to Jeremiah on Sunday. Luke decided he didn't want to leave it to chance and took some time mapping out the conversation. He'd used this approach many times before when pitching to clients, usually with success.

The adage from his Harvard professor rang in his ears: *If you fail to plan, you plan to fail.*

Luke picked up a pen and paper. He meticulously scripted every potential question, objection, and possible scenario. It took hours.

The outcome? He felt his plan would go off without a hitch, but a thought nagged at the back of his mind and reminded him, that on occasion, his over-preparation had made him come off as insincere and rehearsed, like the time it cost him a partnership.

The stakes with Jeremiah were much higher, and he hoped his chosen approach would hit its mark.

31

Emma

EMMA STEPPED OUT FROM behind her desk and began passing out papers to the start of each row. "Alright y'all, here are some worksheets for the chapter we went over. We'll go over the answers once you're finished."

She felt much more alert and refreshed today after getting the best sleep she'd had in months. Sleeping in Luke's arms had become her new favorite thing.

"Pass them back, and you can begin now. This will be on the test in a few weeks and it's a tricky one, so it's important that you take your time on this."

Once everyone received a worksheet, Emma returned to her desk. "Make sure you have your book open to page seventy-six so you can look back to the formulas we went over. And if you're having any trouble, raise your hand and I'll come over and help."

Jeremiah's hand lifted into the air, drawing a soft smile from her. "Yes, Jeremiah?"

"I have a question." He raised his voice. "But not about the assignment. I just want to know how long you've been sleeping with my dad?"

The classroom buzzed with gasps and hushed whispers. Fluorescent lights overhead hummed softly, and the ticking of the large wall clock became pronounced in Emma's ears as she stood frozen in place.

Adrenaline pulsed through her veins. "Jeremiah, that's an inappropriate—"

"But it's true, isn't it?" Jeremiah stood up from his desk as he cut her off. "You're sleeping with my dad."

The entire classroom descended into a frenzy. Some of the students laughed and egged Jeremiah on, others told him to shut up, and a boy by the window shot a video on his phone.

Emma felt a wave of dizziness as her stomach knotted.

Only yesterday he had given her such a nice compliment. Now, she felt trapped in a nightmare, unable to wake up.

"Jeremiah, that's not true."

"Don't play dumb. You're nothing but a..."

Emma's eyes widened and her jaw dropped as a string of expletives spewed from Jeremiah's mouth. Students in the classroom shouted louder and louder as Jeremiah continued, making enough noise that the entire hall could likely hear. She had to do something quick, or the front office would think she couldn't control her classroom.

She felt her face growing hot as she stepped back, bumping against her desk.

"Ms. Wright? What's going on?"

She turned toward the doorway and saw the puzzled

stare on Mr. Simmons' face. The notably lean man bore a crown of graying hair, and his face was etched with deep lines of numerous smiles and frowns—the distinct marks of a seasoned educator.

"Oh, it's nothing. The kids are just getting excited," Emma said, forcing a smile.

"About calculus?"

Emma gave a small, uneasy chuckle. "You know teenagers these days."

The physics teacher looked at her like she was crazy, but Emma couldn't tell him the truth. Jeremiah was already on thin ice at this school and she didn't want him getting kicked out.

"Aren't you divorced, Emma?" Jeremiah asked. "I heard he left you for a hotter woman."

As Jeremiah uttered those words, Emma's hands instinctively flew to her mouth. All the insecurities she had felt during her failed marriage flooded back. Her thoughts spiraled as the pain of her past was dredged up in front of everyone.

Emma was not prepared for this public humiliation. Tears welled up in her eyes.

She turned to face Jeremiah. "Sit down. We'll talk about this later."

"Ooooooh," the class erupted in unison.

Jeremiah grinned, folding his hands across his chest. "Nope. Not in your classroom."

"Don't do this to yourself," Emma said. "You're going to regret it if you keep carrying on."

"Why should I stop? You telling me you don't want everyone to know you've been sleeping with a married man? And how you made him turn his back on his family?"

Emma's face turned a fiery red. He had crossed a line, and there was nothing she could do about it now.

She pointed to the door. "Jeremiah. Principal's office. Get out!"

With a smirk, he sauntered out of the classroom. Emma asked Mr. Simmons, who was still standing there, if he would watch the class for a few minutes. After he nodded, Emma walked out and followed Jeremiah down the hall, wiping away tears. She wished she had a few minutes to compose herself before facing Principal Kennedy, but there was no time.

Jeremiah had to be dealt with immediately.

Reaching the office, she found Jeremiah already seated, looking in every direction but hers.

"I need to see Principal Kennedy right now," she told the secretary.

The secretary took one look at Jeremiah and picked up the phone. "He'll see you now."

Emma walked right into his office and shut the door behind her, leaving Jeremiah outside.

Principal Kennedy took one look at her face and gestured to the seat in front of his desk. "Ms. Wright? What's wrong?"

Emma sat, willing herself not to break down in tears. "I—I have a problem with a student. He just had an outburst and—"

"Who's the student?"

She looked down at the floor and then back up at Principal Kennedy, letting out a sigh. "Jeremiah Grayson."

"Tell me exactly what happened."

Emma paused, collecting her thoughts. "I had just handed out a study guide to the class and Jeremiah raised his hand..." She told him the entire story, not leaving out a single detail.

After listening to her account, the principal picked up the phone and dialed the secretary's extension. "Can you have Jeremiah join us in my office?"

He entered moments later and took a seat next to Emma, inching it away from her.

"Jeremiah, would you like to share what happened in Ms. Wright's classroom?"

The principal's words were met with silence.

"I can't help you if you don't speak. Right now, the only evidence I have of what happened is what Ms. Wright has told me. Are we going to continue on with her word? Or would you like to say something?"

"She slept with my dad, so I called her a..."

Emma looked away, fighting back the tears as she squeezed the armrest on the chair.

"Enough, Jeremiah! You cannot speak to your teacher like that." The principal's voice rose a few decibels. "I thought we weren't going to have any problems with you. But I was wrong. Out. Now."

After Jeremiah left and shut the door, Principal Kennedy phoned his secretary again. "Can you call Jeremiah's father and tell him to come in as soon as possible? Thank you."

When he hung up the line, Emma let out a long breath she'd been holding in. "I'm sorry, Principal Kennedy. I'm mortified this happened in my classroom and I just—"

"No need to explain yourself. Why don't you take the rest of the day off, Ms. Wright, and head on home? You can wait here while I go grab your purse and keys. I'll have someone take over your classes this afternoon."

A tear slid down Emma's cheek as she nodded. "That's probably a good idea."

32

Luke

AFTER DROPPING OFF EMMA's homemade dog treats at the local shops, Luke was looking forward to a quiet drive home. His thoughts meandered, mostly on the smile she'd have whenever she'd find out. As he was passing Hadley Cove High, the unexpected vibration of his phone against the console jolted him from his daydreams.

Frowning at the unfamiliar number that flashed on the screen, he pressed the button on his steering wheel to answer, keeping his eyes fixed on the road.

"Hey, who's this?"

"Mr. Grayson, this is Ms. Jameson, the secretary at Hadley Cove High. I'm sorry to bother you, but we need you to come to the school immediately. It's about Jeremiah."

Luke's grip on the steering wheel tightened. "Is he alright? What happened?"

"Jeremiah's fine, but I'm afraid I can't discuss the details over the phone. It's best if you come in as soon as possible to pick him up."

He nodded, despite knowing she couldn't see him. "I'll be there right away." Ending the call, he swiftly changed his route, driving toward the school.

After pulling into the parking lot, he leaned back and closed his eyes.

Maybe there was some sort of misunderstanding, like at the police station.

Luke reminded himself of what he wished he had done differently in that situation. *Ask questions first. Don't assume it's his fault.*

He turned off the car and walked toward the school entrance.

I wonder if Emma knows what happened.

Stepping into the front office, the scent of freshly waxed floors met Luke's nostrils. The distant bell signaled a class change alongside the muffled conversations of students in the corridors.

He approached the secretary, trying not to notice the curious glances from other staff in the room. "I need to see Principal Kennedy."

"Yes, Mr. Grayson. I'll let him know you're here."

Turning, Luke saw Jeremiah sitting quietly in a corner. "What's going on?"

Jeremiah glared at his father, then looked down at the floor.

"Mr. Grayson, the principal is ready to see you now."

"Come on, Jeremiah," Luke said, waiting for his son.

Jeremiah rolled his eyes and mumbled something under his breath before walking into the principal's office.

"Thank you for coming in so quickly, Mr. Grayson." The principal stood, shaking Luke's hand.

"Of course," Luke said. "Now, can you tell me what happened?"

"Ms. Wright came into my office in tears, and..."

After hearing the principal's account of the incident in Emma's classroom, Luke's veins bulged in his neck.

"Jeremiah will be suspended for the rest of the week. There will be more to follow. I'll ensure you're the first to know, Mr. Grayson."

"I understand. I'm sorry about all of this, Mr. Kennedy. Is Ms. Wright still here?" Luke asked as they got up to leave.

"She's gone home for the day."

He nodded, then left the office with Jeremiah trailing behind. Luke marched out of the building, his steps quick, not speaking a word to Jeremiah until they got into the Range Rover.

"I need you to tell me why, Jeremiah. Why'd you do this to Emma?"

"You lied. When I got the lunch money, your phone went off. I saw the texts and the stupid bracelet you gave her. How could you forget Mom?"

Luke turned toward his son. "I could never forget your mom. That couldn't be farther from the truth—"

"Now it all makes sense. I know why you've been out late all these nights. You never really loved Mom, did you?"

Jeremiah's words knocked the wind out of him. He had to fight to take a deep breath.

With an aching chest, Luke tried to keep his voice calm and steady, eyes fixed on the road. "You've got it all wrong. I loved your mom more than anything. I wish I would've told you earlier about me and Emma, but—"

"Just stop, okay? You know what? When I move out next year, you'll never hear from me again. I hate you."

"Son, I know you're hurting," Luke said. "I promise we can work through this. I never intended for you to find out this way."

"I'm not your son. Just leave me alone. We're done. I don't want to talk to you or have anything to do with you." Jeremiah hopped out, slamming the door.

The abrupt slam of the car door echoed like a thunderclap in Luke's ears as Jeremiah's words replayed in his mind, each syllable cutting through him like shards of glass: *"We're done."*

The finality of those words sent chills down his spine. Luke found himself at the crossroads of disbelief and regret, grappling with the reality that his choices had led them here.

I should've told him earlier.

Luke watched Jeremiah storm into the house and shut the door with a loud thud. He paused for a moment, debating his next move. Memories of past confrontations with his son flooded back. Each time he'd tried to chase after him, it had only escalated, often ending in shouting matches or prolonged silent treatments.

With a pained breath, Luke resisted the urge to follow inside. Now wasn't the time. Jeremiah needed space to cool off, then maybe later they could sit down and talk.

While heartbroken for his son, he couldn't overlook Emma, who was caught in the crossfire of a situation she didn't create and didn't deserve.

Guilt twisted his gut as he recalled Principal Kennedy's account of the events.

Without another moment's hesitation, he reversed the car out of the driveway and sped toward Emma's cottage.

33

Emma

"It's over."

Her relationship with Luke, the man she loved—and who loved her—was truly over. If Jeremiah wasn't ready for Luke to date again, she couldn't in good conscience continue with their relationship.

With that thought, a heaviness fell on Emma's chest as tears poured down her cheeks, blurring her vision. Emma wiped her eyes and pulled over on the side of the road. The sight of the shoreline spread out before her brought back a flood of memories with Luke, amplifying her sense of impending loss.

She took a moment to collect herself then turned the key in the ignition, and merged back onto the road. The journey home felt longer than usual, with every streetlight and landmark reminding her of Luke.

Arriving home, Emma shut the door behind her. Riley wagged his tail and bounded over to greet her, offering the type of comfort only an animal could provide.

Emma set her keys and purse on the table, then headed to her bedroom. The clothes she had worn that day, a pencil skirt and blouse, felt suffocating. She changed into a comfortable, oversized t-shirt and sweatpants and pulled her long hair up into a messy bun.

She sank to the floor, leaned against her bed, and closed her eyes. Riley sat by her side, placing his paws on her lap, and licked her face.

She reached up with both hands and rubbed behind his ears as she rested her head on him. "Thanks, boy. I love you too."

This wasn't the first time Riley had been there for her. He was a constant for Emma and had a charming way about him that always brought her reassurance.

Her mind raced as her thoughts tumbled over one another.

Jeremiah's discovery of her relationship with Luke confirmed Emma's deepest fears. As if that weren't enough, it would only be a matter of time before the entire town was aware of the events that transpired in her classroom today.

Knock. Knock. Knock.

Riley barked and sprinted to the door. Emma stood and followed behind him.

Knock. Knock. Knock.

Emma stepped over to one of the front windows and pulled back the curtain only enough to peek outside.

It was Luke—of course, it was Luke.

He'd probably already gone up to the school and heard about everything that had happened.

"Emma, I'm so sorry about what happened," he said through the door. "Can we talk?"

Emma retreated to the couch, curling her feet beneath her. Although it broke her heart to leave him standing there on the porch, she couldn't face him right now.

Knock. Knock. Knock.

She continued to ignore his knocks and Luke eventually got back in his car and drove away. She told herself she just needed time—and ice cream.

Emma made her way to the kitchen and grabbed an entire carton and a spoon. She took it back out to the living room, sat down, and turned on the TV. Between running her dog treat business and dates with Luke, her Netflix queue had been sorely neglected. After peeling off the top of the ice cream, she turned on a housewives' reality show.

It was time to take it easy.

Emma stayed on the couch all afternoon, binging episodes of rich women in pretty dresses yelling at each other. As the evening rolled around, she had already made it through two full seasons. Although she didn't care much for the show, it took her mind off things. The entire time, Riley stuck close to her side, as if he knew something wasn't right with her.

—*ele*—

The next morning, Emma woke up with a stomachache from eating too much ice cream. She wasn't ready to return to work. Though she'd never called out from a job a single day in her life, she wasn't ready to face everyone yet, especially if they all thought what Jeremiah had said was true. And she didn't want to break down in front of her students again, which she knew would one hundred percent happen.

Grabbing her phone, she ignored the texts, missed call notifications, and went straight for the stored number for Hadley Cove High.

"Hey, can I speak to Principal Kennedy please? It's Emma Wright."

"Oh, of course, Ms. Wright, you poor thing. I'll patch you through," the secretary said.

Emma took a deep breath as she waited to be transferred.

"Ms. Wright," Principal Kennedy answered. "How are you doing?"

"I've been better," she said. "That's why I'm calling. I don't think I'm ready to come back yet."

"I understand. Why don't you take a couple more days to yourself? I'll check in at the end of the week. How does that sound?"

"That would be wonderful."

"Okay let's do that then. And if you would just email me your lesson plans for this week, I'll see that the sub gets them."

"I'll do it right now. Thanks so much."

"You're welcome. Get some rest and don't worry. This all will blow over soon."

Emma sighed. "I hope so."

After hanging up, a weight lifted off her shoulders knowing she wouldn't have to plaster on a brave face and go on as if everything were okay.

Days blurred into one another as Emma stayed cooped up with Riley, only leaving to take him out for walks. Her phone was bombarded by texts from Lisa, Kara, and Luke.

Lisa: *Emma, are you okay? Want me to bring dinner later?*

Kara: *Let me know if you need anything. I can swing by your place anytime.*

Luke: *Emma, please talk to me. I'm worried about you.*

She ignored them all.

Though Riley was the only company she wanted to keep for now, every unread message from Luke weighed heavily on her heart, reminding her of the looming conversation she wasn't ready to have.

She couldn't come between Luke and his son's relationship, even if she was the happiest she'd ever been with anyone. Time and again, she'd stepped aside for the happiness of others, especially with Chad. For Emma, such sacrifices were second nature, and she saw this situation no differently.

Tears streamed down her face at the thought of letting Luke go. Although they'd only been together a short while, it felt like they'd shared a thousand moments.

Emma had fallen deeply in love with him, but now, she had to fall out of it.

How can one even do that—fall out of love?

To ask her heart to deny the very thing that had awakened her soul was like asking the sun not to rise, or the tides not to ebb and flow. Love is a force of nature that cannot be contained or controlled. It was the spark that had ignited a fire within her, and once lit, was not easily extinguished. Denying the pull of her heartstrings was to deny her very nature, and to do so was a feat she knew few had been able to accomplish.

34

Luke

LUKE PACED IN HIS office after sending what felt like his hundredth text to Emma. A week had passed since the incident at the school, and she still hadn't replied to any of his messages. He had even stopped by the rescue, hoping to catch her, but she wasn't there. The Barking Orders treats also hadn't been restocked, which only added to his concern.

If she wasn't leaving the house and she wasn't answering her phone, what was she doing? Was she okay?

The silence from her end was unnerving.

Looking down at his phone, Luke realized he couldn't wait around any longer. Enough was enough. The gnawing uncertainty became too much; he needed to know she was alright, so he grabbed his keys and headed to the Range Rover.

During his ten-minute drive across town to Emma's cottage, he passed Phil's Diner. Luke thought about how they'd first met there and how they'd found love again.

Everything had seemed surreal, but now he couldn't shake the unsettling feeling that something was terribly wrong. It wasn't like her to ignore his messages.

When he turned onto Emma's street and drove up to her cottage, a weight lifted from his chest.

She was outside playing catch with Riley.

Everything's okay.

Releasing a sigh, he parked and practically jumped out.

"Emma!" he called, waving and jogging over, as Riley sprinted toward him. As he drew closer, he noticed her stiff shoulders and her distant gaze.

"What are you doing here?" Her voice wavered, eyes darting to Riley. "Down, stop that."

Luke squatted to give Riley a head scratch while keeping his eyes on Emma. "I was worried. I called and texted and stopped by after everything happened. I haven't heard from you in a week."

She hesitated, biting her lower lip, then threw a tennis ball across the yard. "I know you did. You don't have to worry about me, though. I've just been thinking, that's all—about us."

Luke slowly rose, a knot of dread forming in his stomach. "I've been thinking about us too. Maybe we can talk about this inside?"

"No, I'd rather stay out here."

He took a step closer. "Okay, let's stay out here then. What have you been thinking about?"

With a deep breath, her gaze found his. "You and me, it's not going to work."

Luke's pulse quickened. "End it? What are you talking

about? Emma, I'm crazy about you—"

She held up a hand, silencing him. "We should've been upfront with Jeremiah from the beginning. Relationships can't be built on lies. You and I can't work. I won't be the reason you can't fix things between you and your son."

Luke hung his head. "Maybe we should've told him sooner. But Jeremiah misread our situation, and I'm so sorry he said those terrible things to you. I know they're not true, and so does everyone else. We just need to give it time—"

"Don't make this harder than it needs to be." She called Riley over and walked toward the porch.

"Emma, we can work this out—"

She turned back to him and folded her arms. "Good seeing you. But you need to go and please, don't come back."

"Emma, please don't do this."

"I'm sorry. Goodbye, Luke."

35

Emma

ENDING HER RELATIONSHIP WITH Luke had been as heartbreaking as she had imagined. Although her words had been cold and blunt, she sobbed for weeks behind closed doors. She missed him with every ounce of her soul but took comfort in knowing she was doing the best thing for Luke and Jeremiah. Or at least, that's what she kept telling herself.

Emma eventually reached out to her friends, sharing she had ended things with Luke and asking them not to bring it up again. Lisa and Kara respected her wishes, though she could sense Lisa's angst for more details.

Returning to work was easier than the stories she had told herself. Initial snickers among students faded fast, replaced by newer gossip. And with Mrs. Anderson's return from maternity leave, Emma was back to part-time subbing.

During one of her tutoring sessions, she took note of the empty seat Jeremiah usually occupied. Although what

Jeremiah had done was inexcusable, she wondered if his month-long suspension had been too harsh. She hoped his time at home would give him and Luke the space they needed to rebuild their relationship.

Now with extra time on her hands, Emma distracted herself, as best she could, from thinking of Luke. She focused on growing Barking Orders and even picked up two new stores that wanted to sell her dog treats. She also threw herself into other activities, like tennis at the rec center and joining her favorite author's online book club.

Still, Emma found herself scrolling through her phone's photo album she titled, "Since the Day We Danced." In it, all the memories made with Luke. Those photos held so much love, joy, and possibility. Many times, her finger hovered over the delete button, but she just couldn't bring herself to do it—to let go once and for all.

Some days were harder than others, as everything reminded her of him: the memories at Phil's Diner, the sound of the crashing waves on the beach, and even Riley.

In the quiet of the night, she'd lose herself in old texts from Luke. Emma thought about him and how he was doing, and wondered if he missed her as deeply as she missed him. If he didn't, she couldn't blame him, considering the way she had ended things. A thousand times Emma had typed out a text to him, deleted it, and retyped it, but never hit the send button.

It was a complicated situation and there was no winning for anyone.

One Month Later

After a long walk with Riley, she called her grandfather to catch up.

"Hello, Em."

"Hey, Grandpa. How are you?"

"Oh, I'm fine," Liam said. "Although my knee's acting up, so that means it'll probably rain later."

"Are you busy?"

"Me? Busy? Not at all. I was just getting ready to eat."

"How about I come over and whip up some lunch for you?"

"Sounds like a real treat. I hope to see Riley too."

"He'll be there. We'll see you soon."

Emma stepped into her kitchen and scanned the pantry and fridge. She gathered all the ingredients for lunch, then put them in a canvas bag. After grabbing Riley's leash and some treats, she loaded her car and drove across town to her grandfather's house. It was even smaller than her place, but it was all Liam needed. After her grandmother's passing several years ago, Liam had adapted to a quiet, simple life, filled with volunteering at the animal rescue and soaking up ocean views from his dock.

She pulled up in front of his house and let Riley out of the car. He ran up to the door and started scratching and whining. Liam opened it and welcomed Riley with some pats on his head. Emma grabbed her bag from the car and walked over to join them.

"Hey, pumpkin." Liam kissed her on the cheek.

Emma leaned in, giving him a hug. "Good to see you."

"Well, come on in." He held the door open for her and Riley.

"How do you feel about soup and sandwiches?" Emma asked, holding up her bag. "Since it's getting chilly, I thought it might be a good day for something warm."

"Sounds perfect, Em."

She walked into his kitchen and set her bags on the counter, then got to work. Emma chopped everything up for tomato basil soup and threw it into a pot to simmer. Once it was finished, she made a few vegan grilled cheese sandwiches and poured the soup into a bowl. After setting the table, she found Liam playing tug of war with Riley on a piece of rope.

"Lunch is ready, Grandpa."

Liam stood up, clasping his hands together. "It smells delicious, Em."

As they sat down at the kitchen table and ate, Liam looked up at her. "So, how are things with you and Luke?"

Emma released a heavy sigh, resigning herself to the fact that she couldn't avoid the topic any longer. It wasn't that she was unwilling to confide in her grandpa: she didn't want to burden him with her emotional baggage. He had been her rock since her mother's passing and had an un-canny ability to make her feel safe. Emma knew she could always count on him to be there for her. She dreaded the thought of breaking down in front of him again, especially over something she couldn't change.

Drawing in a deep breath, she lifted her gaze to meet his kind eyes. "We've ended things, Grandpa. It's for the best."

Liam frowned. "The best for who, Emma? I thought he made you happy."

"He did, but that's not the point. I had to break up with him."

Liam reached over and placed his hand over hers, giving it a gentle squeeze. "And how did you come to that decision, sweetheart?"

Tears welled up in Emma's eyes. "Because I don't want to come between Luke and his son."

Liam scooted his chair closer to Emma and pulled her into a hug. "Hey, I've got an idea. I think the rain might hold off for a while. Why don't we take the boat out and ride around the cove?"

Emma nodded, leaning back to give him a watery smile. "That sounds nice."

After lunch, they approached the small motorboat, its hull gently rocking by the dock. Riley, always excited for a new adventure, was the first to leap in, with Emma and Liam following suit. She was thankful he hadn't pushed her to talk more about Luke, or tried to convince her she was overreacting.

The boat roared to life, and they cruised along the coast, weaving through the marshes and past Hadley Cove. The salty sea breeze ruffled Emma's hair, reminding her of the simpler times when her grandfather would steer through these very waters and she, a little girl, would watch the way the light played on the water. Every trip ended with her grandmother on the dock, draping a soft, cozy blanket around her shoulders.

Gazing out, Emma noticed the water's transformation as

the sun began to lower. The once-vibrant blue sky turned into deep shades of orange and crimson, painting a stunning mosaic on the horizon. As they neared Bridwell Bay, another boat glided by them, its passengers waving in friendly greeting. The fleeting interaction, alongside the boat ride down memory lane, deepened Emma's appreciation for today's escape.

Dark clouds gathered as the day wore on, mirroring the storm brewing in Emma's heart. They raced back. Raindrops started splattering just as they reached the dock. The droplets quickly turned into a downpour, causing them to scramble out of the boat. They ran across the yard, shoes squelching in the mud, up to the porch, and then inside.

"Since you made lunch, how about I make dinner?" Liam asked.

Emma grabbed the throw off the back of his couch and wrapped herself in it as her teeth chattered. "That sounds good."

Entering the kitchen, she caught a whiff of something delicious cooking on the griddle. It was the familiar scent that used to fill the house when her grandmother was alive—he had made blueberry pancakes.

Emma smiled, touched by the simple joy he brought her.

"Have a seat," Liam said. "I know these aren't as good as the ones your grandmother made, but I think they'll do for now."

"They look great, Grandpa. I don't think anyone makes them as good as she did."

"And no one ever will." Liam gave her a wink and fixed each of them a plate before walking over to the table.

As they ate, he tore off a piece of his pancake and fed it to Riley. "Don't tell your momma," he whispered behind his hand.

Emma chuckled as she wiped syrup from the edge of her lip.

"How's your dog treat business doing?" Liam asked.

"Really great," Emma said. "My orders have doubled over the last month."

"That's incredible, dear. If you need any help, I could come and help you bake, Em. I am retired, you know."

"That's nice of you to offer, but you've done enough for me throughout the years. I'll think about it though."

"Well, I'd do anything for you, sweetheart. You know you're my favorite granddaughter, right?"

Emma burst into laughter, shooting her hand up to cover her mouth. "I'm your only granddaughter. But I guess that does have its perks."

After dinner was finished and they cleaned up, Emma decided it was time for her and Riley to hit the road.

As they neared the door, Liam pulled her aside. "If you love Luke, you should be with him. You deserve to be happy. You know, Emma, when I was younger, after I met your grandmother, circumstances pulled us apart. For a while, it felt like the world had ended. Then we found each other again and everything changed."

A lump formed in her throat as she looked back at him. "I don't know, Grandpa. I do still love him, but it just feels impossible."

Liam placed a comforting hand on her shoulder. "And often it feels that way. Sometimes, what seems impossible is just one chapter of life. Life isn't about rushing through the pages but experiencing every word, every moment. If Luke is meant to be in your story, he will be, in one way or another."

Emma paused, letting his words sink in. "Thanks, Grandpa. You always know exactly what to say."

She hugged him and kissed him on the cheek, promising to visit again soon.

36

Luke

AFTER THE BREAKUP, LUKE focused on putting the pieces of his life back together. As much as he missed Emma, he had to push those thoughts aside and find a way to fix things with Jeremiah.

Luke and his son had hardly spoken since the incident at the school. Although Luke tried several times, he was shut out. Jeremiah didn't make it any easier by keeping himself locked in his bedroom, only going downstairs to eat, then right back up.

At a loss for what else to do, Luke made Jeremiah's favorite meal: French onion soup with sourdough rolls. Jeremiah came downstairs as Luke was ladling the soup into two bowls.

"Hungry?" Luke asked, gesturing to the soup. "I accidentally made enough to feed a small army."

Jeremiah took a seat on one of the counter stools. "Yeah."

Luke pushed a bowl and a plate with two rolls toward

him before grabbing a stool and sitting down across from his son. This was the moment Luke had waited for over the past month.

They ate in silence for a few minutes while Luke chose his words carefully. "Jer, can we talk and have a rational conversation, like two adults?"

"Fine. Let's talk."

"Thank you," Luke said. "I appreciate your openness."

"Now that we've had some time to ourselves, I want to tell you the truth about me and Emma."

Jeremiah frowned. "But—"

"With no interruptions," Luke said, taking a sip of his water. He inhaled deeply, then released it. "I love your mother more than anything. Even after she was gone, I couldn't imagine the thought of loving anyone else."

Jeremiah looked downward, stirring his soup aimlessly.

"But then Emma came along, and I learned that it's possible to love more than one person in a lifetime. We wanted to tell you sooner, but I didn't know how. I'm so sorry that you had to find out from a text. I hope you can forgive me someday for keeping that from you. But you don't have to worry about that anymore."

Luke cleared his throat, trying to tamp down the bubble of emotion rising in his chest. "We broke up. I went to her place to see if she was alright after the incident, and that's when she ended things."

Jeremiah's eyes met his father's. "You guys broke up?"

Luke gave a slow, deliberate nod. "Yes, it's over. But tomorrow, I'd like us to take a trip back to Chicago. It'll only be a day. I want to take you somewhere."

Jeremiah scrunched his eyebrows. "Where?"

"You'll see."

———

The next morning, they headed to the Savannah airport and flew back to Chicago. Instead of staying in their former, posh neighborhood, Luke checked them into a hotel close to Fuller Park. Its streets were lined with aged buildings, small convenience stores, and graffiti—a world apart from the life Jeremiah knew.

"Why are we staying here?" Jeremiah asked as they got to their room. "This place sucks."

Luke shrugged. "It does. But you'll see why soon enough."

Later that day, Luke steered the car slowly down the streets of his childhood neighborhood.

"That's where I went to high school," he said to his son, pointing to an old, brick building, its windows now boarded up. He paused for a moment, remembering the sound of the school bell, the rush of students in the hallway, and the hours he spent on the basketball court, trying to master a perfect jump shot.

Luke's voice grew softer as they approached a convenience store with chipped paint and a broken neon light. "I earned my first paycheck here. Used to stock shelves and sweep the floors every evening after school." He laughed, recalling the owner, Mr. Peterson, who always slipped him an extra candy bar on Fridays.

Further down the road, he gestured to a corner shop

with a faded sign. "And that's where I first met your mom." Luke's eyes twinkled with the memory. "I was trying to act all cool, buying a soda. Dropped my change everywhere when she looked my way. She helped me pick it up."

But the memories took a somber turn when they reached the end of the street. An old, crumbling apartment building stood there, its windows broken, graffiti marring its walls. "That's where I lived with my father," Luke murmured. "It wasn't much, but it was home."

Jeremiah's eyes widened. "You lived there?"

Luke looked toward the second floor. "Up there, apartment twenty-six. My mother left me and my dad when I was a kid, and he struggled to pay our bills. I remember the time our power got cut off, and we had to sleep in the car to have heat." Luke paused, pushing down the lump in his throat. "I told myself this wouldn't be my future. So, I worked as hard as I could to get into Harvard. After your mom and I got married, and when you came along, I found a high-paying job. It demanded a lot of me, but I stuck with it because I thought it would give both of you the best life possible. Or what I thought would be, back then."

Jeremiah nodded and stared at the building without saying a word.

⸎

When they arrived home the next day, Jeremiah and Luke had lunch together.

"Dad?"

"Mm-hmm?" Luke swallowed a bite of his sandwich and

reached for his water.

Jeremiah let out a sigh. "I shouldn't have said what I said to Ms. Wright. She didn't deserve that, and I'm sorry I embarrassed her in front of the entire class."

Luke put down his sandwich and wiped his face. "I know you are. I think deep down she knows that too. But it's not me who deserves the apology."

Jeremiah rubbed the back of his neck as his eyes darted downward. "I don't want to go back to Hadley Cove High."

"I thought you liked it there?"

"I do," Jeremiah said, "but I can't face Ms. Wright after what I did to her. Maybe I can transfer to another school? Bridwell High? It's not too far from here."

"You know, it'd show a lot of maturity if you owned up to what you did and went back," Luke said. "I'm sure she would forgive you if you apologized to her."

"I just can't, Dad."

Luke paused, giving Jeremiah a long look. "You can. You'll see." He hesitated, searching for a change of topic to lighten the mood. "How about you mow the lawn while I finish up some things around here? Might help clear your head a bit."

"Yeah, sure," Jeremiah said, standing and bringing his plate to the sink.

The sun was setting by the time Jeremiah came inside from mowing. Luke, who had been compiling a stack of freshly printed papers into a neat folder, looked up and passed it to his son. "Your assignments for the week. I've been in touch with your teachers."

Jeremiah took the folder and flipped through the pages with a furrowed brow. "I can't do this."

"What do you mean?"

"I need a graphing calculator."

"Don't you have one?" Luke asked.

Jeremiah shook his head. "Yeah, but I lost it."

"Alright. Give me the model you need, and I'll check the store."

Jeremiah jotted down the model number and ripped off a slip of notebook paper, handing it to Luke.

He folded it and stuffed it into his pocket, then grabbed his car keys from the counter. "Be back in a bit."

37

Emma

"OKAY, I'LL MAKE IT happen." Emma hung up the phone and glanced over at Riley, who was looking up at her expectantly. "I'm sorry, I haven't fed you yet, have I?"

Riley responded with a resounding bark. Emma chuckled as she grabbed the bag of dog food from the pantry and filled Riley's dish. Kara had just called and told her about an upcoming fundraiser at Second Chance Rescue. She needed to double her usual order of Riley's Recipe for the event.

Emma sealed the dog food bag and took inventory of her current dog treat supplies. She realized she needed to run to the store and grab more pumpkin puree and a few jars of all-natural peanut butter. After double-checking the back door, ensuring it was locked, she reached down and gave Riley a head scratch.

"I'll be home soon. Momma's gonna miss you. Be a good boy, okay?"

Riley whined and plopped himself down by the door.

Emma grabbed her keys, locked the front door behind her, and walked out to the car.

After setting her purse down in the passenger seat, she paused to admire the simple beauty of the cottage. This wasn't how she'd envisioned her life: single, in her forties, and living paycheck to paycheck. But nothing good would come from dwelling on the "should'ves" or "could'ves" of life, she told herself.

Things will work themselves out.

Her attention shot over to the window where Riley was peeking through the sage curtains. A wisp of a smile touched her face as she blew him a kiss and waved before pulling out of the driveway onto the main road.

After Emma pulled into the parking lot, she parked and quick-stepped inside. The faint hum of conversations filled the supermarket, underscored by the occasional clatter of a dropped can, the beep of the checkout scanners, and the soft rustling of plastic bags being stuffed. Making her way to the baking aisle, the inviting scent of freshly baked bread teased her senses.

On trips like this in the past, she'd end up coming home with two armfuls of bags stuffed with things that weren't on the list. But since the divorce, finances were tight, making her more budget conscious and only buying what was needed for now. She had even followed the supermarket's Facebook page to receive coupons and updates about their newest sales. Years ago, she never would've imagined herself being so thrifty, but was proud of how quickly she had adjusted.

As she headed for the checkout line, she was relieved to

see all the lines were open, pushing the droves of people through. The store manager paced between the registers, using his approval card here and there, clearing out the lines.

One cashier waved Emma down. "Ma'am, I'm open over here."

She walked over, setting her items on the checkout counter, and dug through her purse for her store rewards card. Just then, a familiar voice called out from behind her, "Emma? Is that you?"

Emma froze. A chill ran down her spine. The voice belonged to the one person she thought, or rather had hoped, she would never see again, and yet—

She sucked in a breath and turned to face him.

"I thought that was you, Em."

Emma felt as if she'd seen a ghost. It had been almost thirty years since she had seen him and time had not been kind to him. His hair was now gray, and his belly had grown round, showing through his Hadley Cove Police Department uniform.

"That'll be fourteen fifty-three, ma'am."

Emma blinked, her thoughts snapping back to the present. She turned to the checkout counter. "Oh, of course." Her fingers, though trembling, managed a semblance of speed as she pulled a twenty from her wallet and extended it to the cashier. "Just...just please take it. I've got to go."

Despite the years that had passed, Emma struggled to hold back tears as she confronted the man who had caused her so much pain. She wondered if he saw the hurt in her eyes, the anger and disappointment still simmering beneath the surface.

Paul's eyes darted away, then back to hers. "Emma, I'm sorry about the way I left," he said. "It took me a few years to get my life back together."

A few years? Try almost three decades.

She clenched her shopping bags tighter, feeling the edges dig into her palm, and forced a smile. "Good for you, Paul. I'll see you around, or actually, I'd rather not."

She spun on her heel and moved quickly, her feet carrying her toward the exit with purpose. Paul trailed behind. "Wait, Emma! Can we talk?" He pointed to his badge. "I just got my old job back on the force and I'm here to stay this time. I can see you're in a hurry right now, but maybe I can get your number and we could meet for coffee? Things have changed. I've changed. I promise."

Emma stopped and turned to face him with a scorching glare. "You promise? Oh, I've heard that line before. And you want to meet for coffee? Really, just like that? Like nothing ever happened. You really don't get it, do you? You've been dead to me for years now."

Paul winced. "I know I hurt you, sweetheart. But I'm here now to make up for it—"

"Don't call me sweetheart!" she yelled, then stormed out of the store and over to her car.

Paul was close on her heels. "Please give me another chance, Em. I messed up at being your dad, but I want to make it right. I did and said a lot of things I shouldn't have, and for that, I'll always be sorry."

She popped her trunk, placing the bags inside. "Well, thanks for your 'apology,'" Emma said, her hands making air quotes, "but I don't need to hear it. I don't want it. You can keep it for all I care."

Paul let out a deflated sigh, putting his hands in his pockets. He looked down, then back up to her. "Are you sure I can't just have your number? Maybe we can talk when you've had time to think about it—"

"No, Paul. I don't want to give you my number and I don't want to talk. Ever."

She fought back tears as her dad persisted. She truly thought she'd never see him again, and now here he was, trying to weasel his way back into her life.

"Alright, Emma. I hope you change your mind, and I'll give you all the time you need. When you're ready, I'll be here."

She waited until she heard him walk away to turn around. Emma let out a frustrated sigh and leaned against her trunk as a rush of memories flooded her mind. At her mother's funeral, she remembered her dad hugging her tightly and telling her he'd always be there for her.

When his day drinking started, she thought she'd be a good enough reason for him to stop, but that didn't happen. After everything he'd put her through, she couldn't forgive him; not easily, anyway.

Once sure he'd reentered the store, she slid into her car. As she put the key in the ignition and turned it, nothing happened. She tried again. Nothing. She took the key out and tried it once more. Still, nothing.

"Not again!" she shouted, smacking the steering wheel.

Emma leaned her head on the headrest and closed her eyes, counting backward from ten, and expelled a deep, drawn-out breath. As she gathered herself, she remembered Gary's Garage had a new tow truck. She'd just call them and have them tow it to the shop, where, hopefully, they would find out what was wrong. She could still get home in no time to start baking for the upcoming event. Things were going to be okay.

She rifled through her purse for her phone. Turning it upside down, lint and wrappers tumbled out, but no phone. She checked her pockets and looked under the seat.

It must be at home.

Emma closed her eyes again and let out an even louder scream.

Could today get any worse?

38

Luke

LUKE FIRED UP THE car and eased out of the driveway. He reached for the console, turning on the radio and cranking the volume. An oldies tune faded out as he took the turn from Muscadine Drive onto the main road.

As the next song began, Luke's heart jolted like a needle skipping on vinyl. It was the song he and Emma had danced to at The Point.

Drifting back to that moment, he remembered it being a time when he had been genuinely happy. But now, that was all it remained—a memory. Luke knew the sting of losing Emma would eventually fade, but it was still too raw.

Should he start dating again?

The thought lingered, but was unsettling.

The idea of being with anyone other than Emma, kissing anyone other than her, didn't sit right with him. He doubted it ever would.

Pulling into the supermarket, he parked, and his pulse

began to pound like a drum. Directly ahead, Emma was leaning against her car. He caught his breath, unbuckled, then stepped out.

He halted a few steps away, raising his hand in a tentative wave. "Hey, Emma."

Emma's eyes widened, a fleeting moment of surprise crossing her face. She hesitated for a second, then looked up at him, biting her lower lip. Her eyes were puffy and bloodshot, and her nose was red.

Luke hurried over to her. "What happened? Are you okay?"

She shook her head. "Just one of those days."

Before he could say anything else, Emma crumpled into him, her tears soaking his shirt. He held her close, gently stroking her back. With vivid clarity, his thoughts drifted to when he'd held her as they danced at The Point. Once again, he felt the ocean breeze against his skin, the sound of her beautiful laugh, her perfume's fragrance, and the way she had gazed at him with those kind brown eyes.

Even after telling himself a thousand times it was over, in his heart, it was far from over.

39

Emma

EMMA BURIED HER FACE in Luke's chest, causing a flood of emotions to run through her body. The aroma of his laundry detergent, so unmistakably him, brought back a rush of cherished memories. She felt at home in his arms as she dreamed for a moment they were still together.

"Emma, don't cry," he said, reaching down and taking her hand. "Can you tell me what's wrong? I want to help if I can."

Through tear-filled eyes, she looked up at him and realized if she stayed in his arms for one second longer, she might not have the strength to walk away again.

"It's my father," she said, tears blurring her vision. "I ran into him."

"Your father?" Luke tilted his head to the side. "But I thought you hadn't seen him since you were a kid?"

Emma nodded, wiping her eyes. "I haven't. For him to come up to me out of nowhere like we can just pick up where we left off, is just—I don't have the word."

"Jarring." Luke finished her sentence, wrapping his arms around her.

She felt his heart beating against the side of her head. "Exactly. And now he's back in town, and he's back at his old job on the police force, and he wants to make amends, but I don't think I can. Not yet."

Luke rubbed her back up and down. "You don't have to make amends if you don't want to, Emma. If you're not ready, then that's fine too. You can take as long as you need."

Emma stepped back and looked up at him. "He asked me to get coffee so we could talk. Was I too harsh by saying no?"

Luke shook his head. "Definitely not. And I'm not saying he deserves it, but it might help you if you let him explain himself."

She paused and considered his advice. It reminded her of a recent discussion with the other ladies in the online book club she had joined after their breakup. In this month's reading of *Braving the Wilderness* by Brené Brown, a particular excerpt had stood out to her so much that she underlined it twice: *People are hard to hate up close. Move in.*

Easier said than done, Brené.

Maybe she should let him explain. Even if not for him, for her own peace.

"You might be right," Emma said.

Luke reached up and wiped her tears away with his thumb. As she looked up at him, she felt her knees go weak.

"I think I ruined your shirt."

Luke looked down and laughed at the large stain of tears and smudged makeup. "Don't worry. I have others."

"I can buy you a new one," she blurted before mentally facepalming. The man drove a Range Rover and had taken her on a date in a helicopter. He didn't need her money.

He reached up, tucking a loose curl behind her ear. "No need for that."

"Alright, if you say so." Emma's lips formed a smile, her heart fluttering as she swayed back toward him.

"I love your smile," Luke whispered. "I was wondering when it was going to show up."

As they gazed into each other's eyes, Luke reached down and grabbed Emma's hand, squeezing it. Her mind wandered to the time he had looked into her eyes before kissing her on top of the Bridwell Lighthouse. She could still recall every intricate detail, as vividly as if it happened yesterday. The woody and spicy notes of his cologne, which blended seamlessly with the scent of the crisp night air and the starlit sky, with its twinkling constellations, had cast a magical glow around them—and the way his lips felt pressed against hers. She had replayed that memory countless times in her mind before.

Luke's phone rang, breaking the spell between them. "Sorry, it's Jeremiah. Hold on one second."

He hit the talk button and took a step back.

"Hey bud...Dinner? Sure, I can grab something...Subs it is. I'm just heading into the store. Be home soon...Bye."

Luke hung up and put the phone back in his pocket.

"How is he doing with the suspension?" Emma asked.

"Good. Great, actually."

Emma wanted to ask more about Jeremiah and how they were getting along, but knew it was none of her business anymore.

"So, how about you?" he asked. "Heading home?"

Emma threw her hands in the air. "I can't. My car won't start. It was fine when I drove here, but now it won't turn on."

"Can I do anything? Need a ride?"

Emma was torn, her heart longing to be alone with him again but her head telling her it would only make things harder. She sighed. "No, that's okay. But can I use your phone? I was going to call for a tow, but I left mine at home."

"Of course." Luke fished in his pocket and pulled out his phone, punched in the unlock code, and handed it to her.

"Thanks." Emma dialed Lisa's number. "Hey, Lisa. It's Emma."

"What? Why are you calling from Luke's phone?" Lisa asked. "Are y'all back together?"

Hoping Luke hadn't heard, she replied, "No, my car's dead. Can you come and pick me up? I'm at the supermarket."

"Be there soon."

"Thanks Lisa, you're the best."

After hanging up, Emma sighed and handed the phone back to Luke. "Thank you."

Luke nodded. "Well, I should probably—"

"Yeah, you should probably do your shopping. I'm going to wait here until Lisa shows up."

"You don't need anything from inside?" Luke asked.

Emma chuckled. "I already grabbed everything I needed. Good to see you, Luke. Thanks for your help."

"Anytime. It was the least I could do," he said, giving her

a knowing wink before walking away.

Emma retreated to her car, sinking into her seat with a deep breath. Her eyes traveled up to the rearview mirror, and she watched Luke walk across the parking lot and into the store. His shoulders were slumped, and his hands were stuffed into the pockets of his jeans.

She felt a tear and wiped it away. This was for the best, for everyone.

40

Luke

THE SCENT OF EMMA'S hair—a delicate blend of vanilla and jasmine—took Luke back to their parting moment as he entered the supermarket. The warmth of her touch still radiated on his skin, a heat that seeped deep into his bones. Closing his eyes, he could feel her fingers tracing paths along his back, making him wish they were still together.

Moving with intention, he darted through the aisles, searching for the calculator.

When Luke reached the office supplies, he stood still for a moment, his thoughts drifting back to Emma. The weight of their encounter pressed on his mind, making the task more difficult than it should have been. He reached into his right pocket, searching for the slip of paper, but found only the cool emptiness. He tried the left pocket next, chastising himself for being so distracted. When his fingers finally grazed the crumpled paper, a small sigh of relief escaped his lips. He unfolded it, trying to focus on the written model number, but Emma's face persistently appeared over the faint pen markings.

Shaking his head, he pushed away the thoughts and began scanning the calculators. After what felt like an eternity, his eyes landed on the calculator he needed. Holding it in his hand felt oddly grounding, bringing him back to the present.

Luke headed toward the front of the store. As he stood in the checkout line, his eyes drifted toward the window. His heart sank as he watched Lisa's car pull up, and Emma climbed in. Luke sighed, wishing it was him behind the wheel, taking her home.

The faint murmur of a question entered his ears. He frowned, then turned to see the cashier looking at him. "Pardon?"

"Cash or card?" she repeated, with a hint of annoyance.

"Card," Luke replied quickly, hoping he hadn't held up the line. He paid, grabbed the bag, and left.

The pale yellow light of the sun brushed Luke's face as he turned out of the supermarket parking lot. Pulling up to the next stoplight, his grip tightened on the steering wheel.

Shoot, I forgot.

He was supposed to pick up subs for dinner.

Luke made a U-turn and drove a few blocks over to the deli across the street from the courthouse. When he walked inside, an older man, who seemed to be the only staff in the building, greeted him with a welcoming smile.

"Let me know when you're ready," the man said, washing his hands and then putting on a pair of gloves.

Luke placed his order, then walked a few steps over to the

register. As he waited, he pulled out his phone and texted Jeremiah.

Be home soon. Just ordered the subs.

After pressing the send button, Luke spotted an un-opened notification from around the time he and Emma had their first kiss. It was a photo album she had shared with him titled, *Since the Day We Danced*. Scrolling through the images, his heart was filled with bittersweet memories of their time together. One particular photo caught his eye—a snapshot of the two of them dancing in Emma's yard as Riley looked back at the camera. Luke remembered how difficult it was to prop her phone up against the Range Rover to get the shot because of the wind.

Together, they had clasped their hands tightly around the Bluetooth remote, and as he dipped her, with one arm around her waist, they squeezed their fingers together and captured a perfect moment—the golden colors of a setting sun that illuminated Emma's charming cottage and Riley's infectious smile. More than anything, it captured what it felt like to be in love again.

Studying the photo, Luke contemplated whether he should remove the album from his phone, knowing it would only keep him stuck in the past.

Perhaps it was time to move on.

When he moved his finger to the top right corner of his phone to delete the album, a warning message popped up:

Deleting this album will permanently erase all of its contents. Are you sure you want to proceed?

His chest tightened as he let out a deep breath. These weren't just photos to him. They were evidence that happiness could be found again, even after the most devastating losses. He wasn't willing to part with that hope. Not today, at least.

He snapped out of his daze as his order was completed.

"It's gonna be sixteen thirty-five, sir."

Luke closed out the photo album and held his phone to the card reader to pay. The man behind the counter handed over the bag of subs.

"Hope you have a good day, sir."

Luke gave a single nod, taking the bag. "You too."

———

Arriving home, Luke closed the front door and walked into the kitchen. "Jer! I've got dinner," he called out, looking toward the stairs.

Jeremiah came running down. "I'm starving."

Luke set the subs on the table before filling two glasses with water, handing one to Jeremiah. "So, how's the studying going?" Luke asked, pulling a chair out to join him at the table.

"It's been going pretty well," Jeremiah said, smiling. "I skipped the math part since I didn't have the calculator, and I've already done English and science. Next is history."

"Well, you'll probably breeze through that section," Luke said, unwrapping his sub. "I saw the videos your mom took at your history tournaments. You're a natural at that stuff, Jer. Much better than me. I think you get that from her. She was always a whiz at trivia nights."

"Trivia nights?" Jeremiah asked, stuffing his mouth.

Luke's face broke into a wide smile. "When we were first married, we used to go to trivia night at this bar down the street from our first apartment. We won a couple of times, all thanks to your mom."

"She never told me that."

"That's surprising. She *never* would let me forget we won because of her."

"I didn't know you used to do stuff like that together."

"Back when I wasn't working so much, I actually had time to have a life. We used to have a blast, me and her," Luke said, his voice tinged with nostalgia. "But then you came along and ruined all the fun, of course." Luke leaned over and ruffled his son's hair.

Jeremiah laughed and swatted his hand away. "You got grease in it. Seriously?"

"I hear that's good for it."

Jeremiah rolled his eyes. "Right."

After dinner, Jeremiah settled back into his study guide in the living room as Luke made his way to the office. Finding an email from Mark Whitaker, his boss at the firm, was a surprise.

Hey Luke,

Guess what? I put your name forward for this wild opportunity over in NYC. It's with the biggest client our firm has ever snagged. They're looking forward to working with you. Since you've wrapped up your other contracts, this would be your main gig.

I've got a good feeling about this one. Apart from the obvious opportunity of the role, I made sure they understood the importance of a decent schedule for you: Monday through Friday and off by five. No overnight trips. A fresh start for you and your boy in the Big Apple. And speaking of Jeremiah, the relocation package they're offering? Top-tier. They've even got this great school lined up that'll make sure he graduates without a hitch.

Hope that sparks some excitement in you. Let's chat more about it when you're free.

Catch you soon,
Mark

He leaned back in his chair and reread Mark's email for the third time. The prospect of having everything taken care of—for him and Jeremiah—was tempting, to say the least. With him and Emma broken up, there was nothing keeping him here in Hadley Cove.

After he turned off his computer, he stood, stretched, and then walked into the living room.

"Hey, Jer, can you take a break for a minute?"

Jeremiah put his pen down. "Sure, what's up?"

Luke took a seat on the sofa and told Jeremiah about the email he'd received with all the details of the job offer. Once he finished, he looked over at his son. "So, what do you think, Jer?"

Jeremiah waited a few moments before replying. "It sounds like it could be good, and I do kinda miss the big city. It would be nice to have a fresh start again, but Hadley Cove is growing on me."

"So, is that a yes from you?" Luke asked. "I promise things

will be different this time."

Jeremiah sighed as he stood, picking up his study guide. "I don't know. You've made promises like that before."

Luke nodded. "You've got me there. I want to show you things have changed. We still have some time to think about it. Didn't mean to interrupt. Goodnight, son."

"Goodnight."

Lying in bed with heavy eyes, he mentally tallied the pros and cons of the offer, weighing each carefully. Although his thoughts were focused on mending the relationship with his son, he couldn't help but think about the eight hundred miles that would separate him from the woman he still loved.

41

Emma

I CAN DO THIS.

Today was the day Emma would do it.

It had been a week since she'd last seen him at the supermarket.

Pacing in the kitchen, she picked up her phone, her fingers trembling as she dialed the Hadley Cove Police Department.

"Hey, I'm looking for Paul Wright. I think he's just newly rejoined the force, and I—"

"Yes, I can connect you. May I ask who's calling?"

"This is Emma."

"Alright, Emma. I'll patch you over to him."

"Thank you." As the line clicked, she sat and started drumming her nails on the table.

"Emma?"

"Uh, hey, Paul. I changed my mind. Are you free this afternoon?"

"My shift is ending in fifteen minutes, so I can meet you—"

"Great," Emma said, her tone direct. "I'll meet you at Phil's in a few."

Emma stood up from the table and hung up the phone. It was only coffee, she reminded herself. Paul would do all the talking. She only had to show up.

———

Emma spotted Paul in a back booth as soon as she entered Phil's Diner. She waved at Phil, then joined Paul, taking the seat opposite him.

"What can I get you, darlin'?" Margie came over, her pen and pad ready.

"Just coffee," Emma said. "I won't be eating."

"Same for me," Paul said, smiling up at her.

"Easy enough. I'll be right back."

Emma leaned back in the booth, looking over at Paul. "So, you wanted to talk?"

Paul nodded, his fingers fumbling with the hem of his shirt. "Emma, I don't expect you to forgive me or anything like that, but after your mom died, I lost it." He took a shuddering breath and his eyes became glossy. "You were probably too young to remember, but I went on a month-long bender. I missed her so much, but you needed a parent, and I wasn't there for you. I can't ever take that back, but I can do everything in my power now to make things right."

The moment was interrupted as Margie brought over their coffees. Emma looked down at it and took a sip. It was hot, and she burned her tongue, but she didn't care. All she thought about was that scared little girl who saw her father passed out on the floor, surrounded by beer bottles.

Still, she knew what heartache could do to a person. What she didn't understand then, she could try to understand now. Her heart told her it was time to let the past go. If Paul wanted to reconcile with her, she would let him—on her terms.

A tear ran down Emma's cheek as she looked up at him, feeling some of the anger melt away.

"Been sober going on two years, even got my old job back, and an apartment in town too. I'm putting my life back together, Em, or trying to. Look, I know what you must think of me, and I just want to say sorry. I'm sorry. I'm sorry for the life you had because of me. I'm sorry for—"

He looked away for a moment, then returned his gaze to her. "I...God, I never expected you to...forgive me, or...or anything like that." He swallowed hard, a brief flash of pain crossing his eyes—eyes that held decades of heartache and missed opportunities. Eyes that looked so much like hers.

Emma's fingers wrapped tightly around the mug, its warmth seeping into her palm, contrasting the chill she felt inside. As she stared into the dark liquid, swirling patterns of steam danced above. The surface of the coffee was like a murky mirror, and for a split second, she thought she caught glimpses of the past: a little girl with braided hair waiting at the window, an empty chair at dinner, birthdays with one less cheer.

She took a hesitant sip, while the muted sounds around her—the clink of spoons, the distant chatter of conversations—faded away, leaving only the heavy weight of Paul's confession and her thoughts.

Emma finally lifted her eyes to meet his, finding them filled with a desperate hope. Her voice was soft but firm when she spoke. "I'm not saying I forgive you, but I guess I'm open to getting to know you again, a little at first. It's going to take some time."

Her phone vibrated in her pocket. Pulling it out, she read the message and gasped.

The words of the text echoed through her mind, and she let her thoughts trace back over them one syllable at a time.

Emma, I really messed up and I'm sorry for what I put you through. I'll do anything I can to get you back. Please don't give up on us.

"Everything okay?" Paul asked.

Emma looked up from her phone, putting it face-down on the table. "Uh, no. It's my ex."

"I'm sorry to hear," Paul said.

Emma nodded. "Yeah, he's no good. I mean, we had some good years, I think, but he turned out to be a creep in the end." She paused furrowing her brows. "Now that I think about it, I don't think we had any good years. He was terrible to me. Left me for another woman."

She picked her phone back up and typed out a text.

We're never getting back together. Don't ever contact me ever again.

She smirked, hearing one of her favorite Taylor Swift tunes playing in her head.

After pressing send, she blocked his number and dropped her phone into her purse, letting out a long, satisfying exhale. Ashley must have dumped him and now he was all alone. Emma shook her head, not caring one bit.

"This might be something you don't want to share with me, but has Chad ever threatened you before, or hurt you?" Paul asked.

Emma stirred her coffee. "Not exactly. He's grabbed me really hard a few times and punched a wall after an argument. Made him sleep on the sofa that night. Now that I think of it, he did send me a few crazy texts while we were separated."

Paul frowned. "Do you have a security system installed in your house? I've seen situations like this before, and they haven't played out well."

"I got one of those doorbell cameras if that's what you mean. Granted, it hasn't worked in weeks. I've been meaning to get it looked at but haven't gotten around to it yet."

"I could come and check it out for you if that would help," Paul offered.

"That would be nice," Emma said.

One less thing to worry about.

Margie brought over their check and two to-go coffee cups.

"We can go right now if you want to," Paul said, laying a few bills on the table.

Emma shrugged. "Sure. If you insist."

They got up from the table and headed outside. Emma walked toward her car, while Paul got in his police cruiser. Her phone vibrated again, but she ignored it.

Gathering her thoughts, Emma's gaze drifted to the window of Cove Corner Crafts next door. The storefront was filled with a colorful display of handcrafted items, yet a small, distinct section captured her attention, stopping her in her tracks.

Her steps involuntarily drew her closer to the window, and there it was—a small, carefully arranged section showcasing little bone-shaped biscuits, distinctly labeled *Riley's Recipe.*

A part of her wanted to step inside to ask Susan, the store owner, how she got them, but she refrained. She knew the answer.

As Emma turned away from the window of Cove Corner Crafts, her phone buzzed in her pocket. Pulling it out, she saw Lisa's name flash across the screen.

"Hey, Lisa. What's up?"

"Hey, Em! Guess what I just saw."

"What?"

Lisa's words came rushing out. "I just saw Riley's Recipe in the window at the Bark & Brew. Congrats! You should've told me."

As Emma listened to Lisa's bubbling excitement over the phone, her mind struggled to process the information. Her treats in the Bark & Brew, on the other side of town—a fact as startling as it was unexpected.

"Lisa, I...I didn't know they were there. I have to go."

"Everything okay, Em?"

"Yeah, just something I need to handle. I'll text you later," Emma said, ending the call.

Standing motionless, Emma's thoughts instantly darted to Luke. Only he could have thought to do something like this. He had always believed in her, even when she doubted herself.

Luke had remembered her dream. He still cared.

Releasing a soft sigh, Emma forced herself to turn away from the window and continue toward her car. Every step felt heavy. With an aching heart, she wished they were still together.

—*elec*—

After the short drive to her cottage, she let Paul inside. Riley immediately took to him, wagging his tail and attempting to give him a faceful of licks as he knelt to inspect the doorbell camera.

"Riley, get down!" Emma said, grabbing his collar. "Sorry, he has terrible manners."

Paul chuckled, scratching behind Riley's ears. "That's okay. Riley's a nice guy, aren't ya?"

Riley let out a bark, then ran into the front yard, sniffing at the tall beach grass.

"Is the camera synced to an app on your phone?" Paul asked.

Emma pulled it out. "Yeah, it's on here somewhere."

"I'm going to look at the settings," he told her, swiping through her phone. "Ah, here's the problem."

Emma leaned over and looked down. "What is it?"

"You have two wireless networks here," Paul explained. "The camera and the app were on separate ones. I've synced them, so the video should work now."

He handed the phone back to Emma and showed her a crystal-clear view of Riley nosing through the tall beach grass.

"Thanks. Had no idea it was that simple."

Paul chuckled, stepping out onto the porch. "Glad to help. Let me get out of your hair. Call me if you have any trouble at all, okay?"

Emma smiled. "I will." She cupped her hands over her mouth and called out, "Riley, come on. Let's go."

<hr />

The following morning, Emma was packaging a case of dog treats to take to a store in Bridwell Bay when there was a knock at the door. She opened her camera app, and her breath caught when she saw who was standing on the front steps.

Why is he here?

She approached and opened the door slightly, making sure Riley didn't escape. Emma exhaled. "Hey, I'm swamped right now. This isn't the best time—"

"Wait." Jeremiah held up his hands. "Please, I need to talk to you."

Emma opened the door a little more and leaned against it. "Okay. What is it? I've got some deliveries to make, so you need to be quick."

"I'm sorry about what I did. I thought my dad was choosing you over me and my mom. But I was wrong." Jeremiah's voice wavered. "And I was wrong to call you those names. I don't think you are—what I said you were. I'm really sorry."

She reached over and put her hand on his arm. "Jeremiah, it was very sweet of you to come all this way and apologize, but I forgave you ages ago. The last thing I want is to come between y'all."

"But that's the thing," Jeremiah said. "My dad needs you. He's miserable without you. When you were dating him, he was the happiest I've seen him—ever. And he's about to take some job in New York City because he thinks that it's over between you two and there's nothing left for him here."

Emma's chest tightened at the mention of Luke taking a job an entire world away.

"Thanks for the apology." She grabbed the box of treats that she'd left by the door. "But I really have to get these deliveries out, so if you don't mind."

Riley wiggled his way through the door and ran outside, leaving the front yard and heading for the road. "Riley! Get back here!" she called out.

Jeremiah grabbed a bag of treats sticking out from the box and took off after Riley. "Riley! Hey boy! Lookey what I have here! Come on, come back!"

Jeremiah opened the bag of treats and pulled a few out, holding them in his hand. Riley turned toward him, and Jeremiah, bending down, fed him the treats and grabbed his collar.

Emma breathed a sigh of relief as Jeremiah walked Riley back over to the porch. "Jeremiah, thank you. Got my hands full. Can you put him in the house and lock the door?"

As Emma walked over to her car to put the box of treats in her trunk, she paused and looked out toward the water, taking in a deep breath of salty sea air. The light breeze and gentle warmth of the sun kissed her face.

When Emma closed her trunk, an obnoxiously loud sports car came tearing down the road, kicking up dust and stopping in front of her house. The engine still rumbled as an all-too-familiar figure emerged from the driver's seat. Emma froze as he approached her.

"Why haven't you been answering my texts?"

The boom in his voice deafened the thump in her chest. She glanced toward the house and wished Jeremiah had left already. He didn't need to see this.

"Look at me when I'm talking to you!"

Although she was afraid, she turned away and walked toward her car. In the past, he had never taken no for an answer. But she wasn't going to let him control her anymore.

Not today. Not ever again. She was just going to get in her car and leave.

"You're not going anywhere." Chad walked over and yanked her arm, sending the box of treats falling to the ground.

Jeremiah yelled from the porch as he tried to wrangle Riley inside. "Hey! Don't touch her."

Emma spun around to see Jeremiah sprinting in their direction. Riley following close behind, letting out a fury of barks through the air like crackling thunder.

The collision of bodies caused a shockwave as Jeremiah's shoulder drove into Chad, hurling him away from Emma.

Chad retaliated, shoving Jeremiah, and sending him flying over the box she had dropped.

A heavy thud sounded as Jeremiah hit the ground, sending a primal fear through her body.

"What are you doing?" Emma cried out. "Get out of here,

Chad!"

A disoriented Jeremiah let out a groan as he sat up. Emma tried to go over to him, but Chad lunged, grabbing her again and squeezing even tighter.

"Let go!" Emma shrieked as her fight-or-flight response kicked in. "You're hurting me, Chad!"

Tail raised and teeth bared, Riley let out a murderous snarl Emma had never heard before. He pounced on Chad's leg, clamping down with an ironclad grip, biting through his pants as Chad tried to shake him off.

"Get off me, you stupid dog!"

As he fought to shake Riley off, Emma reached for the little can of pepper spray she kept on her keychain and sprayed a thick cloud of fumes right into Chad's face. He screamed, releasing her arm, and staggered back as Riley continued to tear away at his leg.

Chad choked and sputtered, rubbing at his temporarily blinded eyes. "You fat, worthless, dumb..."

Emma stood tall and exploded, screaming the most un-Emma-like words she'd ever said to anyone. Her use of expletives even shocked herself.

As Chad recoiled, pain contorting his face, Riley's teeth sank even deeper. Adrenaline pulsed through Emma's veins as she pulled out her phone and dialed 911.

"Stupid mutt!" Chad kicked Riley, making him howl.

Riley took off, running toward the street as Chad hobbled to his car and peeled off.

Jeremiah, finally on his feet, came over to Emma. "You okay?"

"I'm fine," she told him. "We need to get Riley—"

Suddenly, a deafening tire screech came from the road, sending Emma's heart plunging. She raced to the scene, dropping her phone in the grass. Jeremiah was at her heels when they both stopped dead in their tracks.

A middle-aged woman leaped out of the car, panic clear in her eyes.

"I'm so sorry! I didn't see him. I'm getting help now." The woman fell into tears, scrambling to grab her phone.

Emma collapsed to the ground. Tears poured down her face as she whispered to him, "I'm so sorry Riley, Momma's here. Stay with me. Don't leave. Please don't leave me."

Flashbacks of the day she first met Riley at Second Chance Rescue filled her mind: his trusting eyes meeting hers for the first time, his wagging tail. She had promised to always be there for him, to protect him from harm.

Now, her fingers traced a slow path over his fur, each stroke an attempt to hold on to the spark in his dimming eyes. Cradling his head, the subtle rise and fall of his chest became more pronounced. She listened to his strained breathing, each one more fragile than the last. With every shallow breath he took, she felt him slipping away, pulling him nearer as her tears and heart-wrenching sobs echoed throughout the empty street.

A part of her soul crumbled at the thought of facing a world without him.

"We have to go now!" Jeremiah sprang into action. He bent down and carefully grabbed Riley, placing him in the back seat of Emma's car. "Give me the keys, I'm driving," he said. "We got to get him to the animal hospital."

42

Luke

"Dad, you've got to get over here!"

Panic rose in Luke's throat. "Jeremiah, where are you?"

"All Creatures Animal Hospital, with Emma. Riley's hurt."

"On my way." Luke hung up and grabbed his keys.

Peeling out of the driveway, he sped down the street.

Upon pulling up to the hospital, he barely remembered parking. The faint smell of antiseptics hit him as he pushed through the main entrance, mingled with the distinct scent of animals. Soft whimpers and the occasional bark echoed in the background. His eyes darted, searching, until they landed on the sign marked *Emergency*. As if propelled, he sprinted down the hall, passing a cat in a carrier, and a child clutching a bird cage.

There they are.

His heart hammered in his chest as he rushed toward them.

"Luke!" Emma leaped up from the chair.

"I'm here," he breathed, scanning her face for signs of how bad the situation might be, then stepping close.

She wrapped her arms around him, her fingers digging into his back as if clinging to life itself. Her breath, ragged and broken, puffed against his neck, each exhale heavy.

He pulled her close, trying to shield her and absorb her pain. They clung to each other for a long moment. Luke could feel the tremors running through her body.

He buried his face into her hair, taking a deep breath, the familiar scent grounding him. "It's okay," he whispered, rubbing circles on her back. "I've got you."

As they stood, the initial panic slowly subsided, replaced by the sterile lights and the faint hum of the air conditioning. People moved around them, their faces blurred in Luke's peripheral vision, and he caught snippets of conversations from other worried pet owners.

He felt a weight in his chest, a heavy realization that they weren't out of the woods yet. A need for understanding bubbled up. "Emma..." He gently pulled back, his thumb brushing a tear from her cheek, and looked deeply into her eyes. "What happened?"

She swallowed, struggling with the words. "He was..." Her voice faltered, but before she could finish, Jeremiah interjected, "A car hit him."

Luke's face paled. "Did the vet give an update?"

Jeremiah shook his head. "Not yet."

Luke glanced down at Emma, seeing her distress mirrored in her eyes. With gentle care, he guided her to a nearby chair and made sure she was seated, his hands lingering on her shoulders. "We'll wait here as long as it takes," he whispered to her.

Turning his attention back to Jeremiah, he took a seat beside him. "Jer, why were you with Riley?"

Before Jeremiah could respond, Emma turned and met Luke's gaze. "Your son's a hero, and so is Riley."

She began to cry all over again as Jeremiah passed her a box of tissues, his own eyes filled with tears.

"Thank you," she said, reaching for a tissue.

Luke leaned forward, grabbing Emma's hand. He looked into her eyes, then glanced at Jeremiah. "I'm having trouble following all of this. What happened?"

Emma steadied herself and wiped away her tears. "I was about to leave to make some deliveries when Jeremiah came over to apologize for everything, and that's when Chad showed up..."

Luke's grip on Emma's hand tightened, an unconscious reaction as he pictured Chad approaching her. His jaw clenched at the thought. Anger, sadness, and disbelief all competed for space in his heart. His other hand balled into a fist at his side.

His mind raced.

Visions of his son as a young boy flashed before him. He remembered a sunny afternoon at the park, Jeremiah, no older than seven, running with the red kite trailing behind him, looking back with wide eyes, waiting for Luke to catch up. The memory of his tiny sneakers pounding the grass, his carefree innocence, and his absolute trust that his father would always be there to guide him and protect him, made a lump form in Luke's throat.

The contrast of that memory with the present hit him hard. Jeremiah was no longer that little boy but somewhere in between a child and man. Bittersweet emotions washed over Luke: all at once, guilt for not being there to protect his son, and surging pride that Jeremiah had thrown himself in the face of danger to defend the woman that Luke loved.

With watery eyes, he turned to Jeremiah. "I'm so proud of you, son. Are you okay?"

"Yeah, I'm fine," Jeremiah said with a smile.

Without a word, Luke pulled him close, burying his face in the crook of his neck, just as he used to during thunderstorms when Jeremiah was a toddler. Jeremiah's hands, though larger now, grasped the back of Luke's shirt with a familiar intensity, transporting Luke back to days long past.

This was a moment Luke would hold on to forever.

Luke then turned his attention to Emma. "I wish I had been there. If I knew, I would've—"

"I know you would've," Emma said.

Luke nodded and looked at his son. "Jer, you can head home if you want. I can sit with Emma."

"I want to be here—for both of you."

The three of them sat down and settled into the floral-patterned wooden-armed chairs from another era. The room buzzed with soft conversations, the rustling of old magazines, and the occasional low whimper from a nearby pet. An overhead fluorescent light flickered intermittently. Time seemed to hang heavy, every second accentuated by the relentless ticking of the clock above and the distant footsteps of medical staff. Jeremiah scrolled through his phone while Luke wrapped his arm around Emma as she fell asleep on his shoulder. They remained like that for what felt like an eternity, but in reality was only another hour.

"Emma Wright?"

"Yes, that's me," Emma said, shooting up from her chair. Luke stood with her, squeezing her hand.

"I'm Dr. Evans. After reviewing the x-rays, it looks as if Riley ran into the car, instead of the other way around. He's in stable condition now, thankfully, but he has sustained some bruising and is understandably shaken up by the trauma. We've made him as comfortable as possible, and given his strong vitals, I believe he can go home today. However, you'll need to keep a close eye on him, ensure he rests, and bring him back immediately if you notice anything concerning. We're here if you need us, day or night."

Emma let out a long exhale. "So, he's going to be okay?"

"Absolutely. I'm going to prescribe him some anti-anxiety pills and pain medication to take over the next week. I'll be right back."

After Dr. Evans walked away, Emma collapsed into Luke's arms. "He's going to be okay. He's really going to be okay."

"Of course he is," Luke said, hugging her. "He's a tough guy."

Emma chuckled and reached out for Jeremiah, bringing him into the hug. "I don't know how I can thank you enough. The both of you."

Jeremiah grinned. "Maybe you can bring Riley over once in a while. He's a pretty cool dog."

"You got it," Emma said, wiping a tear from her eye.

Dr. Evans returned to the waiting room as they broke

apart. "Someone's eager to see you."

The sound of paws clicking against the vinyl floor filled the room. A vet tech struggled to keep up with Riley, who pulled eagerly on his leash, dragging the tech behind him. Spotting Emma, Riley let out a series of joyful whines and his tail wagged wildly.

"Never scare me like that again!" Emma bent down and hugged Riley around his neck. She pulled back to look at him, her hands cradling his face. "You saved your momma today. I love you, I love you, I love you," she repeated, kissing his head with each declaration before resting her forehead against his.

Luke looked on and smiled down at them.

Jeremiah's stomach let out a low growl, drawing a half-smile from him. "I'm starving. Think I'll grab something to eat," he said, stretching his arms over his head.

"Take my car?" Luke suggested. "I'll drive Emma's car. I'll text you to come get me after I get her and Riley home."

Jeremiah took the keys from Luke and bent down to pet Riley before leaving.

Luke looked to Emma. "Ready to go?"

"Yeah, that sounds good."

In his heart of hearts, Luke knew his love for her was as strong as ever, and now the universe had brought them together again, even if just for a drive home.

The car ride back to Emma's house was quiet. Riley had dozed off in the backseat on Emma's lap, while Luke stole glances of her in the rearview. When they pulled up to her cottage, those dark-brown eyes of hers caught him.

A rush of emotions overwhelmed Luke as their eyes

locked, hoping beyond hope she'd understand what he really wanted to say. He wanted to tell her how he'd thought about her every day since they met at Phil's. How he missed seeing her name pop up on his phone. How he couldn't imagine a life without her.

Although his lips were still, his heart sang.

Could he really accept that job in New York, while the woman he loved sat mere feet away from him, here in Hadley Cove?

Luke took a deep breath and grasped her hand. "Emma, I want to tell you that—"

43

Emma

"Riley, down!" She burst into a fit of laughter as he leaped from the back seat and licked her face.

"He seems better already." Luke smiled as he reached over, petting Riley's head.

Taking a moment to wipe her face, she turned to Luke. The intensity of his gaze caught her off guard, sending her heart aflutter. Unspoken words seemed to drift like a mist between them as she felt every bit of what his eyes were saying—that he still loved her.

"I guess he's ready to get out," Emma said, reaching for the door handle.

As they exited the car, the sun had begun to set. The warm, salty breeze gently tousled Emma's hair as she surveyed the scene.

There's the smashed box of treats I was supposed to deliver. I'll need to bake more tomorrow.

Her phone still lay in the grass near the driveway, its sleek surface glistening in the fading light. After picking it up, she walked toward the porch, noticing a piece of fabric from Chad's torn pant leg. There was also a note tucked under the door.

I'm so sorry I hit your dog. I swear I didn't see him.
Please call or text me when you get a chance.
912-555-555
Katie

Emma decided she'd call her later to let her know Riley was okay.

Folding the note, she looked back toward Luke and Riley. Her breath hitched as she caught sight of the tire marks from Chad's car in the driveway. The memory of the day's events left an unnerving stillness in its wake.

Emma turned to Luke. "Would you mind staying? Just...the thought of him still out there creeps me out."

Luke nodded. "Of course. I'll stay for as long as you need me."

The fear melted away at those words.

...for as long as you need me.

Stepping inside, Riley came between them, sitting down in front of Luke's legs. He laughed and bent down to scratch behind his ears.

"How's it feel to be a hero, bud?"

Riley let out a little whine, then rolled over on his back for belly rubs.

Emma's heart warmed, watching the exchange between them. "How about we get you some treats, boy?"

Riley barked and followed Emma to the kitchen.

Setting the note aside, she checked her phone. She scrolled through several missed calls and stopped at a voicemail from her father. Emma pressed the phone against her ear.

"Hey, Emma, it's Paul. We got a call about an incident at your house and the caller mentioned someone matching your ex-husband's description fleeing the scene. We're trying to track him down. Call me back when you get this and let me know you're okay. Also, let me know if you were able to catch any of the incident on your security footage. Thanks."

Emma hung up the phone and shot him a quick text:

It was him and I'm fine, now. I'll send the video later. I'm exhausted. Let me know if you find him. Call you tomorrow.

She put her phone back in her pocket and gave Riley a treat.

"Need anything?" Luke asked, peeking around the corner. "Water? Ice? A large strawberry margarita?"

A smile tugged at the corners of Emma's mouth. "A drink sounds tempting, but right now, I just need to sit."

Emma walked out to the living room and sank into the couch, letting out a long sigh. Luke settled beside her, and Riley hopped onto his lap.

"Well, I missed you too, boy," Luke said, patting him gently.

"Riley, get down," Emma said with a sharpness in her tone. "Sometimes he forgets how big he is." Riley looked up at her and whined, then did as he was told. A second later, he lay across Luke's feet.

Emma and Luke laughed. "He really does like you," Emma said. "Maybe even more than me."

Luke arched an eyebrow and let out a small chuckle. "I doubt that."

Emma's eyes held Luke's a moment longer, her lip caught gently between her teeth. Leaning forward, she rested her elbows on her knees, drawing slightly closer. "I want to thank you. I know it was you who got my treats into those stores."

A soft knowing smile spread across Luke's face. "It was me. I believe in you and your dreams. I had to help, somehow."

"That means everything to me." She felt an urge to reach out and touch his hand, but she didn't. Her heart was full, yet a part of her remained cautious.

A silence fell as Emma absorbed the depth of his actions and words. She exhaled a deep breath, clasping her hands. "So, tell me about this job offer in New York. You going to take it?"

"I thought I would," Luke said, his gaze never leaving hers. "Until I saw you again today."

He leaned in, bridging the gap between them. "After we broke up, there was really nothing left for me here. But the thought of being so far away from you doesn't sit well with me. And Jeremiah's not too excited about it. I think this place has grown on him."

As he spoke, the distance between them closed inch by inch. The subtle scent of his cologne reached Emma, a smell she remembered all too well. Her fingers tingled and heart thrummed as she anticipated his next words.

Luke paused and the room fell silent, with only the faint sounds of their breathing filling the air.

He took Emma's hand, lacing his fingers with hers. "I'm still in love with you. I haven't stopped thinking of you since the day we met. You've brought a joy to me I never thought I'd have again."

Emma's eyes welled and her breath caught in her throat. "Jeremiah mentioned the job. It sounds great and all..." She squeezed his hand and glanced away for a moment. "But I don't want you to move there. I know that sounds selfish, but that's how I feel. You said there was nothing left for you here, and that's not true."

"It's not?"

She shook her head. "I shouldn't have pushed you away. You've made me so happy. I love you, Luke. I don't want to lose you."

"Emma, I never wanted it to end. In some ways, it never did. I love you with everything I am. And always will."

His words lingered between them, seeping into her skin, where she could feel every syllable in her bones.

They said it, confessed it, and she wanted to hear it again. "Luke, I love you."

He reached out, tucking a stray strand of hair behind her ear. "I love you too, Emma."

There was a moment of stillness, where the world seemed to hold its breath. And then, driven by passion long held back, Luke leaned in, sealing his lips to hers in a collision that felt like a thousand unspoken words. Her fingers clenched his upper arms as her breath quickened, their heartbeats dancing together in a way only they could understand.

It felt as if every heartache had led her to this singular moment where she discovered the kind of love she'd always dreamed of.

The kind of love that feels like coming home.

Epilogue

Six Months Later

EMMA UNLOCKED THE SHOP door, soaking in the moment.

Who would have thought she'd ever make enough money to open a store in Hadley Cove?

She remembered how nervous she'd been, presenting in front of the town's council. But Mayor Williams, with her kind demeanor, had eased her anxiety with a reassuring nod and a soft-spoken, "We believe in you, Emma."

With the success of Riley's Recipe dog treats, Emma had hired two part-time bakers and left her job at Hadley Cove High, though she still tutored from time to time when extra help was needed. Riley even became a local celebrity as the smiling "face" of Barking Orders.

Emma no longer felt threatened by her domineering ex-husband. He had been caught and arrested by her father, with the help of her doorbell security footage. She'd even gotten a restraining order against him for good measure, making sure he'd never bother her again. He hadn't said a single word to her since the incident, and sometimes, she wondered if Ashley ever took him back. For Ashley's sake, she sincerely hoped not.

And then there was Luke.

After turning down the job offer in New York, Luke completely left the financial world to pursue something he was more passionate about—her. He used his experience to help Emma expand her dog treat business and had even assisted with closing the deal on the shop. They made a wonderful team.

As Emma meandered through the aisles, she surveyed the branded products: rows lined with Riley's Recipe treats waiting to be sold. She paused in awe. Her heart swelled with pride, realizing her faith in herself had paid off in ways she never could have imagined.

Before the ceremony, she did one final walkthrough.

"Ready?" Luke emerged from the back, wrapping his arms around Emma and kissed her on the cheek.

"I think so. Are there a lot of people out there?"

Luke's lips curved playfully. "Oh, not really. Just the whole town."

Emma's eyes widened.

"They're here for *you*," Luke said, taking her hand. "So, let's get out there and give them what they want."

The sounds of clapping and whistling filled the air as they stepped through the front door. Luke squeezed her hand as Emma looked out into the crowd and grinned. Her grandfather and Lisa were at the front, along with Kara and Charlotte next to them. And there, in the very center, was

Riley, held on a leash by Jeremiah. She even spotted Phil and her father off to the side.

"Thank y'all so much for being here today for the grand opening of Barking Orders!" Emma said. "I want to remind everyone that with every bag of Riley's Recipe sold, a portion of the proceeds will go to Second Chance Rescue!"

As she prepared for the ribbon cutting, a familiar, friendly face approached. Mayor Williams, always involved in town events, stepped forward with her signature warm smile and handed Emma the giant scissors. "Congratulations, friend. The honor is all yours."

When she cut the ribbon, Riley barked; out of the corner of her eye, she saw him slip from Jeremiah's grip.

Emma felt a jolt of panic and yelled, "Riley! Can someone grab him, please?"

She darted in the direction she last saw him, the crowd parting as they tried to help. She could hear shouts of, "He went that way!" and, "I almost got him!" but Riley seemed to be eluding everyone.

Her heart pounded with each step. "Riley, where are you?" she called out.

She spotted a wagging tail behind the funnel cake stand and raced toward it.

But it wasn't him.

Releasing a sigh, she turned in the other direction.

The distant chatter of the crowd faded as Emma's gaze fixated on a familiar figure. Then, as if drawn by an unseen force, a clearing came into view among the sea of people.

There he is.

Emma's heart raced. Without realizing, her pace quickened, feet almost gliding over the ground. As she neared, she instinctively reached out to grab Riley's leash.

But as her fingers slid down it, they brushed against the velvety texture of a crimson ribbon. Tied intricately around the leash, it held a small box, more precious than anything she could have imagined. There was a weight to it, making her heart skip yet another beat.

The murmurs grew louder, turning into excited shouts. "Look behind you!" a voice echoed, followed by several others.

She whirled around. And there he was.

Luke, with a nervous yet genuine smile, was on one knee. Gently, he took the ribbon from her hand, his fingers deftly untying the knot and opening the box. He held it up as it glimmered in the sun like a tiny star, casting its own light across everything nearby.

The world seemed to pause.

Whispers of the crowd, the faint strumming of an acoustic guitar from the gazebo, and the distant laughter of playing children—everything faded into the background.

All that remained was Luke's voice. "You've made me the happiest man in the world, Emma. Will you marry me?"

She nodded quicker than she could speak. "Yes! Yes, Luke—I will."

Tears filled her eyes as Luke slipped the ring on her slender finger. Emma threw herself into his arms, laughing and crying all at once. Riley jumped into their hug too as the cheers swept through the crowd, growing louder with each passing second.

Looking into Luke's eyes, she whispered, "I can't believe

this is all happening."

Luke brought his hand up to her face, his fingers gently grazing her cheeks before resting at the small of her back, pulling her closer. "It is, though," he said as he wiped under her eyes with his thumb. "I promise to make you feel loved every day of your life." A sob caught in her throat, a mix of past pains and present joys. "You already do. I love you, Luke."

He cupped her face, his eyes searching hers. "I love you too, Emma. Forever and always."

Then Luke gently tilted her chin up, closing the distance between them.

Emma's heart soared when their lips met.

This was the moment she had been waiting for.

She let herself fall into him, her fingertips tracing the profile of his cheekbones, feeling the stubble and the warmth of his skin. Their beating hearts collided, like the cosmic miracle that created the stars and galaxies.

It was a kiss that felt like the beginning of time itself.

With Luke by her side, anything was possible. And in this moment, their wandering souls had finally found home.

—ееее—

I hope you enjoyed the story, but your stay in Hadley Cove doesn't have to end here.

You're officially invited to Emma and Luke's wedding!

Read the free bonus scene:

kerkmurray.com/products/bonusscene-sincethedayw
edanced

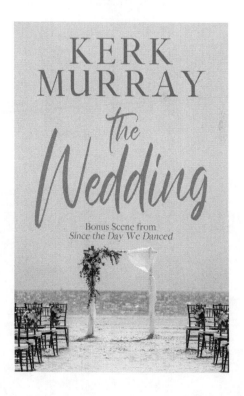

Binge the rest of the series for up to 60% off!

Bundle & Save at kerkmurray.com.
Apply this coupon at checkout for an additional 10% off:
GET10

Read Lisa's story next!

Lisa never saw it coming—a failing bed-and-breakfast, a rescue dog, and a second chance at love.

At forty-two, Lisa Miller's life takes an unexpected turn when she inherits her late mother's struggling beachside bed-and-breakfast and a rescue dog named Daisy. Just as she's finding her footing, in walks Noah Jacobs—a famous author plagued by writer's block, looking for a change of scenery in Hadley Cove. A charming mishap with Daisy sets the stage for a creative collaboration that could save both Noah's novel and Lisa's business.

But when past secrets and ex-lovers come knocking, their newfound love is put to the test.

Can Lisa and Noah weather the storm and find their happily ever after, or will their final chapter end in heartbreak?

Love this book? Don't forget to leave a review!

Help others discover the *Hadley Cove Sweet Romance* series. Every review matters and it matters a lot. It can be as short as one phrase to a few sentences. Wherever you bought this book, you can use this link to leave an honest review on Amazon, Goodreads, Bookbub, or your favorite retailer:

kerkmurray.com/products/review-sincethedaywedanced

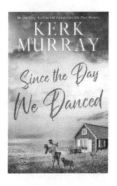

Hadley Cove Recipes

All recipes are vegan-friendly

<u>Amelia's Blueberry Pancakes</u>

To awaken the soul

Ingredients:

- -1 cup of unsweetened vanilla almond milk
- -1 teaspoon of vanilla extract
- -1 tablespoon of apple cider vinegar
- -1 cup of flour
- -2 tablespoons of granulated sugar
- -1 tablespoon of baking powder
- -1/2 teaspoon of salt
- -1 cup of washed blueberries

Optional Toppings:

-Syrup of choice
-Plant-based butter

Directions:

In a medium mixing bowl, combine all dry ingredients. In a separate mixing bowl, combine all wet ingredients. You will then pour the liquid mixture into the dry ingredients and whisk until smooth. Let the batter rest for 5 minutes, and then pour about a 1/2 cup of batter onto a nonstick pan on medium heat. Once the top of the batter begins to bubble, flip the pancake and cook until golden brown.

Ada's Banana Muffins

To connect with others

Ingredients:

-2 cups of all-purpose flour
-1 cup of granulated sugar
-1/4 teaspoon of salt
-3/4 teaspoon of baking powder
-1 cup of chopped walnuts (optional)
-3 medium bananas puréed
-1 teaspoon of apple cider vinegar
-1 teaspoon of vanilla extract
-1 teaspoon of banana extract
-1/4 cup of unsweetened vanilla almond milk
-1/2 cup of melted coconut oil
-1/2 cup of brown sugar

Directions:

Preheat oven to 350 degrees. In a medium mixing bowl,

begin puréeing the bananas with a fork until smooth. In the same bowl, add the apple cider vinegar, vanilla extract, banana extract, almond milk, and coconut oil and mix until ingredients are combined. In a separate medium mixing bowl, combine the flour, sugar, salt, and baking powder. Next you will add the liquid mixture to the dry mixture and whisk until ingredients are combined. Add walnuts to mixture if desired. Scoop mixture into baking cups, filling no more than 3/4 of the way. Sprinkle brown sugar on top of mixture. Place pan in heated oven and bake for 20-25 minutes.

Emma's Tomato Basil Soup & Grilled Cheese

To reminisce on fond memories

Soup Ingredients:

-6-8 Roma tomatoes
-1/4 cup diced onion
-8 fresh basil leaves or 2 tablespoons of dried basil
-2 tablespoons of oregano
-2 tablespoons of minced garlic
-8 oz. of vegetable broth
-4 oz. of vegan heavy cream, can also substitute with plant-based milk
-1/2 teaspoon of salt, or to taste
-1/2 of teaspoon of pepper, or to taste

Soup Directions:
Start by prepping the onion and garlic. Then, cut the

tomatoes into quarters or cut into 1-inch pieces if using larger tomatoes. Bring the chunky soup to a boil, cover, reduce heat and simmer for 15 minutes. Once the soup is done, let it cool for 10 minutes. Using an immersion blender or cup blender, puree the soup until desired consistency. Taste for flavor, adding more salt as needed.

Sandwich Ingredients:
-Sliced wheat bread, or other preferred bread
-Sliced vegan cheese, Chao is a recommended brand
-Plant-based butter, Country Crock is a recommended brand

Sandwich Directions:
Lightly butter one side of each slice of bread and place a slice of vegan cheese in between the two slices. Toast the sandwich in a nonstick skillet on medium heat with buttered side facing outward until bread is golden brown, and then flip to toast the other side.

Riley's Recipe Peanut Butter Pumpkin Treats

To bribe your fur babies

Please consult with your veterinarian before making any changes to your pet's diet or feeding routine

Ingredients:

-1 can of 100% pumpkin purée
-1/2 cup of natural peanut butter
-2 tablespoons of ground cinnamon
-1 cup of coconut flour

Directions:

Preheat oven to 350 degrees. Combine all ingredients until well mixed. Roll dough mixture into quarter-sized balls. Place on a baking sheet lined with parchment paper and press the rolled dough with a fork. Bake for 10-12 minutes. Let it cool for 10 minutes before serving.

Book Club Questions

If you're interested in facilitating or joining an in-person or virtual book club for Kerk's books, please contact info@kerkmurray.com.

1. Reflect on how Emma and Luke's shared experiences with lost love shaped their relationship. What positive and negative impacts did it have on their dynamic?

2. How does the theme of valuing time manifest throughout the novel, particularly in the context of Emma and Luke's attitudes toward it?

3. Identify the character you related to most and explain why.

4. Discuss the ways in which Emma and Luke's past traumas influenced their relationship. By the end of the novel, do you believe they found closure?

5. What role does Riley play in the symbolic landscape of the novel, in your view?

6. Why do you think the author set the story in Hadley Cove? How does this location contribute to the narrative?

7. Evaluate Luke's struggle to balance work and family. Do you think he achieved this balance by the end of the story?

8. If Luke had chosen to leave Hadley Cove, do you believe Emma would have pursued him?

9. Discuss the parallels between Emma's reconciliation with her father and Jeremiah's reconciliation with Luke.

10. Consider the potential impact if Luke had revealed his relationship with Emma to Jeremiah sooner. How might the narrative have shifted?

11. How do you think Emma and Luke's individual coping mechanisms for their past losses influenced their approach to their relationship?

12. What role do you think the setting of Hadley Cove played in Luke and Emma's healing process?

13. Which secondary character do you believe had the most significant impact on the story and why?

14. Explore the role of forgiveness in the novel. How did it influence the relationships among the characters?

15. How did the novel explore the concept of starting over? Discuss with specific reference to Luke and Emma.

16. How did the author use symbolism and motifs in the novel to deepen your understanding of the characters and their experiences?

17. Luke and Emma both express a desire to not take time for granted. How do you interpret this sentiment in the context of their personal growth throughout the story?

18. If you could give advice to any character in the book, who would it be and what advice would you give?

19. If you were to write an epilogue for the book, how would you envision the characters' lives after the story ends?

20. How did your feelings about the characters change throughout the story, and what specific events or moments sparked these changes?

21. In what ways does the author highlight resilience in the face of adversity through the characters of

Emma and Luke?

22. What are some moments in the story where you believe the characters demonstrated significant personal growth?

23. How did the author use the character of Riley to bring out the vulnerabilities of the main characters?

24. In the story, how do Luke and Emma's experiences of loss shape their perspectives on life and love?

25. How does the narrative handle the concept of healing? Are there any particular scenes that stood out to you in this context?

26. What are your thoughts on the portrayal of familial relationships in the novel?

27. How does the author develop tension in the story, particularly around Emma and Luke's relationship?

28. Do you believe the characters' reactions to the various conflicts and challenges in the novel were realistic? Why or why not?

29. If the story were from a different character's perspective, how might the narrative change?

30. Do you believe the author successfully resolved all

the main conflicts by the end of the story? If not, what do you think was left unresolved?

Giving Back

"Never underestimate the power of a small group of committed people to change the world. In fact, it is the only thing that ever has."

—Margaret Mead

"Together redeeming the lives of animals and ending their suffering through our compassion."

THE LEXI'S LEGACY
FOUNDATION INC

Kerk Murray's readers make a difference. Since the release of his memoir, *Pawprints On Our Hearts*, his generous readers have raised over $20,000 toward the care of abused animals through book proceeds as well as donations to the nonprofit he founded, *The Lexi's Legacy Foundation*. If you feel compelled to donate, you can do so right here:

donorbox.org/everydollarmatters

Here's a list of the animal rescue organizations that readers are supporting monthly through each Kerk Murray book sale:

1. 2nd Street Hooligans Rescue – California

2. Cuddly – California

3. Little Hill Sanctuary – California

4. Love Always Sanctuary – California

5. Sale Ranch Animal Sanctuary – California

6. The Shore Sanctuary – California

7. Viva Global Rescue – California

8. Road To Refuge Animal Sanctuary – Connecticut

9. The Riley Farm Sanctuary – Connecticut

10. Love Life Animal Rescue & Sanctuary – Florida

11. Live Freely Sanctuary – Florida

12. Operation Liberation – Florida

13. SAGE Sanctuary and Gardens for Education – Florida

14. Farm of the Free – Georgia

15. Humane Society Greater Savannah – Georgia

16. Society of Humane Friends of Georgia – Georgia

17. Ruby Slipper Goat Rescue – Kansas

18. Shy 38 Inc. – Kansas

19. Sowa Goat Sanctuary – Massachusetts

20. Angela's Ark – North Carolina

21. Billie's Buddies Animal Rescue – North Carolina

22. Fairytale Farm Animal Sanctuary – North Carolina

23. Blackbird Animal Refuge – New Jersey

24. Broncs and Buns Rescue and Rehab – New Jersey

25. Fawn's Fortress – New Jersey

26. Happily Ever After Farm – New Jersey

27. Goats of Anarchy – New Jersey

28. Maddie & Sven's Rescue Sanctuary – New Jersey

29. Marley Meadows Animal Sanctuary – New Jersey

30. Old Fogey Farm – New Jersey

31. Rancho Relaxo – New Jersey

32. Runaway Farm – New Jersey

33. Troll House Animal Sanctuary – New Jersey

34. Wild Lands Wild Horse Fund – New Jersey

35. Happy Compromise Farm – New York

36. Sleepy Pig Farm Animal Sanctuary – New York

37. Woodstock Farm Sanctuary – New York

38. Enchanted Farm Sanctuary – Oregon

39. Harmony Farm Sanctuary – Oregon

40. Morningside Farm Sanctuary – Oregon

41. Charlie's Army Animal Rescue – Pennsylvania

42. Happy Heart Happy Home Farm & Rescue – Pennsylvania

About the Author

Kerk Murray is the international bestselling and award-winning author of *Pawprints On Our Hearts* and the *Hadley Cove Sweet Romance* series. He's a romantic at heart, with a passion for celebrating life, love, and the beautiful connections between humans and animals. His soulful stories capture the essence of opening oneself up to the possibilities that love can bring, and the magic that can unfold when we do.

If you're a fan of sweet, clean and wholesome, swoon-worthy romance stories that will leave you feeling uplifted and inspired, then his novels are a must-read.

Kerk is also the founder of *The Lexi's Legacy Foundation*, a coastal Georgia 501(c)(3) nonprofit organization committed to ending animal suffering. A portion of his books' proceeds are donated to the nonprofit and together with the support of his readers, the lives of hundreds of abused animals have been changed forever.

Join him on his mission in creating a more compassionate world for all living beings, one heartwarming story at a time.

Follow Kerk on social media and sign up for his mailing list at **kerkmurray.com** to stay updated on his latest releases and sneak peeks into his upcoming works.

amazon.com/stores/Kerk-Murray/author/B09C39NLYT

goodreads.com/author/show/21719388.Kerk_Murray

bookbub.com/profile/kerk-murray

instagram.com/kerkmurray

facebook.com/kerkwrites

tiktok.com/@kerkmurray

Made in the USA
Middletown, DE
18 May 2024

54265337R00205